# The Road Home

The Road Home
Copyright © 2011 by Wanda Pothier-Hill. All rights reserved.

This book is a work of fiction. Names, characters, places and events are the result of the authors' imagination. Any resemblance to actual persons, living or dead, is strictly coincidental. Some places may be real but used in a fictitious manner.

Published by Muse Publishing USA, Ashburnham, MA.
ISBN: 978-0-9835164-0-8
Library of Congress Control Number: 2011937209
Manufactured in the United States of America

Book design by Brion Sausser of BOOKCREATIVES.COM
Concept art by Jill Moninger

# The Road Home

## WANDA POTHIER-HILL

MUSE PUBLISHING USA, ASHBURNHAM, MA.

# ACKNOWLEDGEMENTS

This novel would not have been possible without the love and support of my fabulous family and friends.

To my husband, Tim, thank you for believing in me and supporting my dream. I love you so much! To my children, Rachel, Chris, and Sam, thank you for being the light in my life. You are the best kids in the world! To my dad, Gerry, thank you for teaching me patience. To my sister, Carol—the stress queen—thanks for lighting a match and helping me through this first novel. I am so lucky to have you in my corner, always believing in me and never once giving up on me. You're the best! To my brothers, Timmy and Billy, thanks for being in my cheering section. To my dear, sweet mother, Anita (1930-2007), none of this would be possible without you. When I was just a little girl, you never said no to me whenever I asked for a book, thus fostering my love for reading and writing. I will never, ever forget you. To my wonderful friends Jill, AJ, and Chrissy, thanks for always being there for me. You're the best friends a girl could have! To my editor, Rachel Pollack, thank you for your keen observations and insight. I couldn't have asked for a better editor. To those of you (you know who you are) that have cheered me on and followed my journey down this crazy road, I thank you all.

# DEDICATION
......................

This novel is dedicated to my mother, Anita Marie (Gallant) Pothier. You taught me how to believe in myself and chase my dreams. This one is for you!

# CHAPTER ONE

. . . . . . . . . . . . . . . . . . . . . . .

## *Leaving Montana*

The 1985 Ford pickup coughed and sputtered its way onto Interstate Ninety, spilling black smoke out its tailpipe into the cool blue, April sky. Karen coaxed the rusted out half-ton up to a conservative fifty miles per hour, all the while praying to make it out of Montana. Sobriety made the obvious appear so much more clearly. Karen tightened her grip on the steering wheel and pressed her foot down on the accelerator as she watched the small town fade in the rearview mirror.

She shook her head. Never again would she let Jimmy lay a hand on her. He's right where he belongs, she thought. Her escape from hell had been a long time coming. She had spent too much time forgiving and trying to forget his violence. But it had been easy for her to fall for him, she admitted. He was free spirited, charming, and ruggedly handsome—but more importantly, he welcomed her with open arms when the people she had been closest to had given up on her. He didn't care that she was three months pregnant when they met; he had been more than eager to fill the gap in her life. In fact, he liked the idea of having his own little family, and though they never exchanged weddings rings, everybody in town knew that Karen belonged to him.

Once Karen had seen the childhood scars on his back, it became easy for her to excuse his actions—a shove here and there, a bruising hold on her arm, a slap. But his pain, his revenge, eventually became too much for him to contain, and she bore the brunt of his anger. He was a bottle, a boot, and a fist followed by flowers and apologies. Fuck his tears, flowers, and empty apologies! She absently traced her finger along the scar that ran through her lip. No more, Karen thought. No more.

Although the road home was long and urged her on, she knew there would be no welcome wagon waiting for her. Shame, too many bad decisions, and a history of running away from the truth had driven Karen across the country, away from the people she loved, and into the hands of Jimmy, a man who didn't really know what love was.

Karen glanced over at Robbie as he slept with his teddy wedged between his head and the truck's doorframe. He deserved better. The more she looked at him, the more convinced she was that he was Steve's child, not some complete stranger's. He had his father's sandy blonde hair, but her hazel eyes. He rubbed his knuckles against his forehead whenever troubled or deep in thought, just like Steve always did. She didn't need some blood test to convince her. He was Steve's boy; he had to be.

∽

Though it happened over five years ago, her memories still left her feeling bruised. She remembered that warm sunny day in early October. She was standing in her kitchen, listening to music on her stereo and sipping from a glass of merlot when Steve stopped by. He walked through her door, with a smile on his face, a notebook in his hand and backpack slung over his shoulder. Seeing the glass in her hand, his smile faded a little. Karen set the glass on the counter and turned up the music. A Shakira song came on, and something took hold of her—was it the rhythm? Was it the thumping beat that pulsed through her body? It didn't matter what it was. The only thing that mattered was here and now with Steve. She pulled the notebook from his hand and threw it on the kitchen table, then tossed his backpack on a chair. Karen took hold of his hand and began swinging her hips back and forth it time with the beat.

"Dance with me," she said, picking up her glass from the counter and taking another sip.

Steve cocked an eyebrow, but couldn't help but smile as she danced around him. Karen placed a hand on his hip, coaxing them into rhythm with her own. Steve took the glass from her hand and set it back down on the counter. Karen circled around him again, sliding her hand up his chest and grasping the buttons of his shirt. Steve's grin grew wider.

"What if Carol comes home?" Steve asked, catching her hand and kissing her knuckles.

"She's working," Karen whispered, brushing her lips across his. The next song came on and the music slowed. Karen slid his shirt off his shoulders. Steve leaned forward and kissed her lips, her cheek, and her neck. He wrapped his arms around her and they danced in rhythm, slowly making their way towards her bedroom.

"You know," he said glancing at the clock, "you're going to miss the game. The Red Sox come on in five minutes." His lips brushed the nape of her neck.

"Well, I thought that maybe I could at least make it to second base with you," Karen said kissing his chest.

"Second base? How about a homerun?" Steve scooped her up in his arms and kicked the bedroom door shut behind them.

Karen remembered the way he held her after they made love, and later how they curled up together on the couch and watched the Red Sox come back from a three game deficit to clinch the American League Championship. She remembered the tenderness in his voice, the way he looked at her, and how he made her lose herself in his brown eyes. It was the last time they were truly together.

Karen tried to shake the memory from her head, knowing that Steve probably had someone in his life by now, maybe even a "Mrs. McKenzie." But the more miles she drove, the more he overtook her thoughts. As she made her way east across Montana, she remembered how the days that followed their last time together had begun tearing them apart. They had been arguing again. It was always about the same things—the wedding, her stepmother, her spending sprees, but most of all, her drinking.

"Baby, come on. Can't you just let loose this once?" Karen slipped her thumbs through the belt loops of Steve's faded blue jeans and pulled him closer. Steve scuffed the toe of his sneaker against the sidewalk and stared at the ground. Karen gave a tug on his belt loops and waited for an answer.

"Karen, I've got midterms this week. Don't you have one for lit tomorrow?" He hiked his backpack up over his shoulder and glanced at his watch.

"No, Classics. And I've got Pliny, Pompeii, and Vesuvius down to a science." She snapped her fingers and cocked her eyebrow, but her humor only seemed to irritate him. "Come on. You never used to turn down dancing with me at Salza's." Karen smiled and swung her hips side to side. Steve let out a biting laugh.

"Yah, I used to like dancing with you when you were still sober enough to hold yourself up on the dance floor."

"What? All right, I admit it. I got a little carried away last week," Karen said with a little laugh. Steve didn't even crack a smile. "So what? It isn't as if you haven't ever done that." Karen folded her arms across her chest and looked away. Steve, she thought, was beginning to sound more and more like her stepmother, Lillian, every day. God, she wished her father was still alive. At least she would have someone to talk to, someone that wasn't so bent on directing every moment of her life. Lillian, on the other hand, made it her life's work to nag the hell out of everyone. "Too much lemon meringue pie and red meat," Lillian had said to her late one night, shortly after he died. Lillian nagged him about his health all the time, but Robert Black was more stubborn than any other man she had met, she often said to Karen. Yes, she admitted, Lillian was right about that. Despite having a heart condition, he often neglected to keep to his diet and take his medications regularly, leaving her these last four months without a father. Karen shook her head. Her dad, though, knew how to make the most out of every moment of life. Life was too short to bother with taking everything so seriously. She looked at Steve, his face tight, serious, his backpack overloaded with books and notes. She shook her head. There was more to life than college.

"Can't we just go out and have some fun for one night? Come on, Steve. You never want to do anything lately. Let's go to Salza's and then we'll go back to your place and do a little dirty dancing of our own." Karen pressed up against him, wrapped her arms around his neck, and brushed her lips against his. Steve grinned as he bent forward to kiss her, but then pulled away, his expression a mixture of anger and surprise.

"Really?" He stared at Karen, waiting for an explanation.

"What?"

"I'm worried about you." Steve brushed his hand against her face. Karen closed her eyes for a moment. Another lecture was coming on; Karen could feel it.

"Why?" She let out a huff of air and kicked a small stone across the walkway.

"You really need to cool it with the drinking."

"Shit! You're going to start this again?" Karen held his gaze for a moment before turning away. "I had a glass of wine. What's the big deal?" Some days she didn't know who was a bigger nag, Steve or Lillian. "I'm really getting tired of her games," Karen said, quickly changing subjects.

"What are you talking about?" Steve asked.

"Lillian. Can you believe that just last week she finally signed over the twelve thousand dollars worth of stock my dad left for me? She kept going on and on about how my dad wanted me to let it mature, so I'll have more savings for the future, and how she's afraid I'll cash in the stock and spend it recklessly. She thinks I can't handle anything."

"Look, she just wants what's best for you."

"You know, I'm really getting tired of her trying to control my life, and now you're taking her side. That's just frickin' wonderful!"

"No one's trying to control your life. We just don't want you to wreck it by drowning yourself in this shit."

"You know, I think Lillian has sucked you right into her little web of lies. She doesn't like me, and she never has."

"Wait, Lillian's the liar? You know, maybe it's time you took a good look at yourself."

"What the hell is that supposed to mean?"

"It means that you've got a problem, but don't have the guts to admit it. It means that I know you stop at the bar on your way home, and it's not just to play pool! And I know that you've been buying bottles of 'cooking' wine, but that you can't cook worth shit!"

"And who's the hypocrite that sucked down a six pack just last night?" Karen thrust out her chin. Steve could drink and it was okay, but she couldn't? "You're acting a little pious, don't you think?"

"Hey, I may have had a six pack last night—but unlike you, I didn't suck it all down at once."

"I had a couple of margaritas, so did Carol and Paul. You, Rick, and Celine were all sucking down beers—everyone was drinking, not just me! Why don't you go preach to them?" Karen stood with her arms folded across her chest and Steve raked his fingers through his hair. She couldn't look at him, take the way he stared at her like she was broken and in need of serious repair.

"Listen, I didn't mean," Steve began, but the sound of a car pulling into the parking lot cut him short. Carol pulled into the spot next to Karen's Mustang, Pink blasting on her radio.

Carol hip checked her car door shut. "What's going on?" She glanced from one to the other.

It was pointless to stand here and explain anything to her roommate; after all, when it came down to it, she was more likely to take sides with her twin brother than her best friend. Karen yanked the keys from her purse, and stopping half in—half out of her car, nodded in Steve's direction. "Ask Saint Steve." She slammed the door shut, turned the key, and threw her Mustang into reverse, squealing the tires as she pulled out of the parking lot. Glancing in her rearview mirror, she could still see Carol standing there with a perplexed look on her face.

Heading south on Route 16, grinding the gears and picking up speed, Karen headed out of town. If it wasn't one thing, it was another. First Lillian's interrogation and mothering, and now here was Steve throwing more crap at her: She was spoiled, didn't take college seriously enough, and she partied too much—and all of this, he told her, he said out of love. Bullshit! To hell with them! Karen jerked the wheel hard to the left and headed down Route 9 towards Northampton.

Ten minutes later, Karen brought her car to a stop in front of Pete's Tavern. It was around four in the afternoon, and although the bar was nearly empty, she quickly found her target. He sat at the bar making ridiculous passes at the well-endowed female bartender, despite the wedding ring on his finger. Karen shook her head and pulled up a stool next to him, then ordered a rum and Coke. He turned and gave her an appraising smile. Karen gulped down the rest of her drink, ordered another, and then began walking around the pool table. She ran her hand along edge of the table, staring at it wistfully. From the corner of her eye, she saw him watching her.

"You want to shoot some?" Karen heard him call over to her from his seat at the bar.

"Oh, well I'd love to, but I'm not very good at it," Karen said, and the first of many games began. A couple of guys she had played against before stifled a laugh and leaned back against the bar, waiting for the show to begin. Karen leaned over the pool table, holding her cue stick clumsily in her hand, and balanced daintily on one leg as she positioned her stick. Karen made her shot. The solids seemed to have a mind of their own. One, then another was quickly lost.

"Don't get discouraged, honey. Pool takes some time to learn," he said to her. "Here, let me give you some pointers." He moved closer to Karen and placed his hand over hers.

"Like this?" Karen thrust her stick forward and drove the ball into the corner pocket, then walked around the other side of the pool table to take another shot. He looked at her with a dumbfounded grin.

"You've taught me so much that I think I'd like to play another game," Karen said with a sweet smile.

"Okay, showoff. That was a lucky shot. Let's play."

"What do you say that we put a little wager on this game? I'll put up ten bucks that says I'll kick your ass," Karen said with a wink and a flip of her long, black hair. He looked her up and down, and with a scratch of his stubbly chin, accepted.

Karen lost that game, and the one after that. She gave a little pout and smiled; it was time to turn the tables.

"Double or nothing." Karen chalked her cue.

"You really wanna place that bet? My grandmother can play better than you, and she's half blind!"

Karen leaned over the pool table and waved a twenty under his nose. He snatched it away from her, let his gaze fall to her breasts, and then placed the money on the bar in front of the bartender.

"Hey sweetie, would you be so kind as to hold this little lady's money?"

Karen rolled her eyes at his back and continued chalking her cue. She looked over at the bartender and smiled. The game began miserably like the others. Karen watched her opponent's grin grow more and more confident. Now it was time. She lined up her shot. Solid, center pocket—sunk. Solid, corner—sunk. One solid after the next—sunk. Last, eight ball—sunk.

Karen's opponent stared at the pool table and scratched his head. For once, Karen thought, he was staring at something other than her breasts. When she laughed out loud, he abruptly turned back to her.

"Beginner's luck." He flipped open his wallet and slapped another twenty on the bar before racking up the balls again. Karen cocked her eyebrow, let out a little laugh, and placed another twenty alongside his. It was like fishing in a bucket. The bartender slid another rum and Coke across the bar for Karen and a Miller for him. Karen took a swallow and began another game. The bar was beginning to fill with five o'clockers stopping by for a couple drinks before heading home. Many of them swung their stools around to watch the show. This time Karen didn't show any mercy. Solid, right corner—sunk. Solid, off the side, to the corner—sunk. And so it went until her companion's smile completely faded into a scowl. He tossed his cue onto the table and walked back over to the bar.

"Oh, don't look so sad. I bet you can play Granny sometime and win your money back," Karen said, clasping her stick in her hands. When the crowd roared with laughter, Karen turned to them and offered an exaggerated curtsy. She toasted them with her rum and Coke in one hand, while in the other she thrust her cue in the air like a trophy. Music erupted from the jukebox. Happy, laughing faces surrounded Karen. Nobody was judging or lecturing—everyone was just having fun. Karen circled the pool table, keeping time with the beat, fueled by the music, cheers, and laughter. She took another swallow from her glass.

"Come on. Any takers? Come on, boys. You're not afraid of being beat by a girl, are ya?" Karen was answered by laughter and more cheers. A man dressed in blue jeans and donning a white cowboy hat stepped through the crowd. Karen let out a laugh. Perfect! He looked as though he had just stepped out of a western movie. The man tilted his head, removed his hat briefly, and smiled at Karen.

"Well sweetness, I reckon I'll take that bet. In fact, I'll even buy you another drink."

"Wow, a real cowboy and a gentleman." Karen swallowed the last of her rum and Coke. She looked him over. He was a tall man—six foot one, she guessed. Locks of white blonde hair fell just past the tip of his shoulders. He had a mustache that drooped down the sides of his mouth. His cool blue eyes wandered the length of her body. Karen smirked. Another womanizer, another target.

"Let the games begin," Karen said, and placed another twenty on the bar. The cowboy set down another drink in front of her, and racked up the balls. He took his shot. The white ball hit dead center on a solid and thrust it into two stripes, right corner, left—both sunk. Karen bit down on her bottom lip, unable to hide her dismay as he continued to out play her.

"Okay, big shot," she said with a smirk. "Two can play this game."

"Play is always more fun with two," he answered, while stroking his mustache.

"Just keep your eyes on the game big guy."

"Sweetness, I always got my eye on the game."

Karen raised her eyebrows at him, shook her head, and holding up her left hand, showed off her engagement ring. Despite the smile on her face, she wondered for a moment if Steve was still mad and if he had gone out to look for her. She hated the fights they were having lately. Every day, it was always one thing or another—he didn't want to go to the parties anymore or even want to share a couple beers while watching the ball game. Everything she did just irritated him. With a shake of her head and another swallow of her drink, she tried to wipe those thoughts from her brain. Squatting down next to the table, Karen looked over a possible play: Solid, corner pocket. Standing back up, she took another deep swallow before making her shot. Leaning across the table, she knocked it in.

"Luck, sweetness. That's all that was," the cowboy said, winking at her. His gaze stayed on her, moving slowly down her body. Karen felt her face flush, but she couldn't tell if it was because his eyes were on her or if it was just the rum and Coke. She stood back up, the room swaying slightly, and looked around the bar. The faces that laughed and voices that cheered were anonymous. Where was Steve? She was half-hoping he would walk through the door and take her home.

The cowboy moved around the table and considered his next move. He was so close; she could practically feel the heat from his body. Using the edge of the pool table for balance, she made her way to the other side. With one quick thrust of his cue stick, he knocked his ball in the pocket directly in front of Karen. Soon Karen found that her opponent was not only good; he was merciless. He had one game, then another under his belt. With each victory he bought her a consolation drink. Her feet felt unsteady beneath her. Maybe there were too many people in the bar stomping across the floor. Maybe it was all the vibration from the stereo that seemed to be louder than usual. Where was Steve?

The cowboy handed her another drink. Karen stumbled against the pool table, spilling the rum and Coke on the front of her white blouse.

"Awww shit. Wha' a waste of a perfely good drink," Karen whined.

"Don't you worry, sweetness. I'll buy you another."

Karen chewed on her bottom lip, trying to concentrate on the solids, but the room was moving faster. Her cue stick skidded across the table and clattered to the floor.

"Damn. Somethin's wrong with that stick. I's too slippery," she said, staring at the pool table. "Oh well. Tha's your game too." Karen brought her wrist close to her face and squinted at the numbers that seemed to dance about her watch.

"Shit, I gotta find Steve. I gotta go home."

"Don't you worry. I'll see to it that you get home safely, sweetness."

# CHAPTER TWO

· · · · · · · · · · · · · · · · · · · · · · · ·

## *The Morning After*

Karen dug her fingernails into the steering wheel, wishing that she could turn the wheel hard enough to turn back time. Try as she might, she could not remember in any great detail what happened from the time she left the bar to the time she woke up the next morning. Her memories came in shattered pieces. She remembered playing pool. She remembered wanting to go home. She remembered riding in a car—and then—remembered his shadow, his weight, his hands wrapped around her wrists—the ache in her crotch the next morning. She couldn't remember if she said yes, couldn't remember if she said no. But she remembered waking up with nothing but a sheet thrown over her in that filthy, empty motel room.

The bed sheets, twisted and yellowed, hung off the sunken mattress. The stink of her own vomit and his cologne enveloped the air, overpowering any trace of autumn's decaying leaves. On the top of a nightstand made of pressed wood, an empty bottle of Jack Daniels lay on its side, the last few sticky drops seeping into the cracked veneer. At the foot of the bed, Karen's blue jeans sat tangled, her underwear still caught within the leggings. Lit by dull yellow vanity lights, her white blouse laid in a crumpled ball against the bathroom door. Her bra was on the opposite side of the room on the high traffic carpet and laid below a shaded window that fought to keep out the bright morning sun. Next to the bra was a discarded black high-heeled boot, its match kicked under the bed, keeping dust and bad memories in hiding.

Karen brought her hands to her head, trying to stop the incessant pounding. Fighting back a wave of nausea, Karen quickly pulled on her panties and picked up her bra. "Oh God," she whispered, while fumbling with the buttons on her blouse. She couldn't have anyone see her here. She pulled on her jeans, slid her feet into her boots, and grabbed her jacket and purse. Flipping open her wallet, she saw that her credit card and cash were still there. Opening the motel door, the light from outside flooded into her eyes, making her head pound even harder. Pausing for a moment, she tried to orient herself. She was on Northampton Road in town. Quickly she darted out the door, not stopping long enough to shut the door behind her. Even under the cover of the bold orange and red leaves that were still clinging to the trees, the brilliant October sky blast piercing rays of sunlight that seemed to go straight through her eyes and into her brain. She put on her sunglasses, but found no reprieve from the bright light. Despite the pounding in her head and heaviness in her heart, Karen sprinted away from the motel known as the "drive in" by the locals. She kept running, her high-heeled boots smacking loudly against the pavement, and didn't stop until she reached the bus stop at the corner of routes nine and one-sixteen.

It seemed as though the sun could have risen and set a dozen times before the PVTA bus finally lumbered down the road. When the brakes hissed and the door opened, Karen quickly climbed the steps and took a seat in the very back of the bus. The bus roared, jerking back to life, and rolled down South Pleasant Street, past Mama Rosa's Pizza, Tell Tales Book Emporium, and the Amherst Golf Club, maneuvering easily through the noontime traffic. Karen kept her head down, never looking up whenever the bus stopped to let passengers on or off. When the bus approached the corner of route one-sixteen and Mill Lane, Karen hopped off and headed down the road to her father's house. She walked slowly past the stark colonials—all dressed with shutters and painted in historic colors—and dragged her purse along the tar.

No matter how hard she tried, she couldn't pinpoint the moment when everything went wrong. She had hustled pool dozens of times before, but nothing like this had ever happened. The word "no" may have never escaped her lips, but she was sure that "yes" didn't either. This man had no name, no history, no business buying drinks for a woman who was clearly engaged, Karen argued with herself while twisting her ring about her finger. Why hadn't Steve or Carol been there for her? They had always been there for her, but last night she was left alone and without the protection of her friends.

When her father's white colonial came into view, Karen began to run. The driveway was empty when she reached it, and she stopped just long enough to see whether or not Lillian's Mercedes was in the garage. Quietly, Karen tiptoed inside the house and closed the door behind her. She didn't want to deal with this woman, who was barely fifteen years older than her.

Karen dropped her purse on the floor and slowly padded up the stairs. At the top, she turned to the left and went into the bathroom, closing the door softly behind her. Karen leaned against the door and closed her eyes. After some minutes passed, Karen turned to face the mirror. Long locks of her dark brown hair fell in front of her eyes, partially covering up her smudged mascara. One by one, she began unbuttoning her blouse that was stained with rum and Coke, and reeked of an anonymous man's aftershave. Her fingers paused halfway down her shirt; a button hung by a single thread. Tears collected in the corner of her hazel eyes and her lips began to tremble.

"You stupid, stupid fool," she said to her reflection. She pulled off the rest of her clothes, then crammed her shirt, panties, bra, and jeans into the wicker wastebasket near the sink. "What the hell did you just do?" She screamed at her reflection. She pressed her fingertips against her eyes and felt her tears roll across the back of her hand. "Shit!" Karen screamed out and kicked at the wicker basket again and again. It splintered, scratching the top of her foot and drawing blood. She kicked it again with more force. It bounced against the wall, tumbled on to its side, and rolled across the floor.

She turned on the shower, pulled back the curtain, and stepped in the stinging water. "Oh God, why?" Karen cried. She scrubbed furiously with a cloth, creating red streaks on the insides of her thighs, across her breasts, and along her belly. Beneath her streaked skin, she could still smell his cheap cologne. She scrubbed harder and harder. When she couldn't get the stink of him off, she threw her face cloth against the shower faucet with force. Her sobs grew louder. Heavily, she fell against the shower wall and the slid down to the floor. Her head tipped forward into the palms of her hands, and hot tears slipped between her fingers, mixing freely with the warm shower water. "Shit! Shit! Shit!" She pounded the shower wall with her fist.

"Karen? Karen? What are you doing home?" Lillian's voice called from the other side of the door. Karen bit down on her knuckle to keep from crying. Her breath caught in her throat.

"You nearly scared me half to death. I went to unlock the front door, but it was already open." Her stepmother's voice drew closer. There was a knock at the door. A muffled cry escaped. Karen pressed her hands over her mouth. "Karen? Honey? What's going on?" The doorknob jiggled. Karen looked up for a moment, and then let her head fall back into her hands. The doorknob jiggled again. "Karen? Karen, open the door." Karen didn't move, just sat on the shower floor staring at the small trickle of blood leaking out of the top of her foot. A minute later, Karen heard the doorknob jiggle back and forth, followed by the pop of the lock. Lillian stepped into the bathroom and waited.

"Karen, what's going on?"

Karen could see Lillian's silhouette through the shower curtain. She placed her hands over her mouth again and tried to suffocate the cries that kept breaking free.

"Go away. Please just go away."

"Not until you tell me what is going on."

Lillian stood outside the shower and waited, but except for her staggering intakes of breath, Karen remained silent. After a few minutes, Lillian pulled the shower curtain open slightly and looked in. Her face bore an expression of confusion. Reaching for the knob, Lillian shut off the water and grabbed a bath towel.

"My God, Karen. What's wrong?" Lillian asked, while wrapping the towel around Karen's shoulders.

"What do you care?" Karen stared at the little trickle of blood on her foot. A thirty-five year old hadn't the right to marry her fifty-year old dad, she reasoned. The only women she knew who went after older men were either gold diggers or desperately shy and plain. Lillian was far from shy and plain.

"Damn it, Karen! If I didn't care, would I be standing here?" Lillian said, letting out a sigh. Karen couldn't meet her eyes. What could she possibly tell her? She would never understand.

"Please, Karen. Tell me what is going on."

"Nothing!"

"You're home instead of in class, crying in the shower, and Steve and Carol have been calling here since last night, so don't tell me nothing's wrong." Lillian waited for a response, but none came. "Steve said you two had an argument." Lillian knelt down beside her, but Karen didn't answer her. "Come on. Get up before you freeze." Lillian slid her arm around Karen and started to help her to her feet.

"I don't need your help," Karen said, pulling away from Lillian.

"What did you do this time?"

Karen looked up, then looked away. Another lecture was coming on. Lillian wouldn't understand a thing, much less care. She got what she wanted—the house, the business, and her father's affection...everything. But most of all, she was the one who had driven her parents apart.

"Your path is so predictable. Let me guess. You drank too much again and made a fool out of yourself once more, and as usual, you come running home crying. Dear God, these last few months..." Lillian waved her hands in the air and shook her head. "What did you do this time? Run naked through campus, waving a pool stick and praising Jose Cuervo?"

Karen looked at her stepmother...if it was only that simple. Her heart was pounding so loudly and her mind was racing so much that she almost didn't hear herself answer Lillian.

"Steve and I had an argument yesterday, so I left. I went to shoot pool." Karen turned away from Lillian's inquiring gaze. She could still feel her eyes boring into her. "I just needed to get away from his preaching and all the bullshit."

"So you were drinking? Karen, he's not preaching. He loves you."

"Yah, well it seems like you've infected his head with your crap. It's like you're trying to destroy my life entirely."

"Jesus, Karen! Do you have any idea how ridiculous you sound?" Lillian shook her head and picked the wastebasket up off the floor, regarding the splintered wicker for a moment before letting out a sigh and setting it on the counter. "Carol said you never came home last night."

"I told you. I went to shoot pool."

"All night? Alone? You're saying that you spent the entire night shooting pool? I'm not buying it."

Karen looked at Lillian, then looked away. The truth? What exactly was the truth? She didn't know. All she knew is that she could feel the bile rising in her throat every time she thought about last night. "Maybe Steve and I just weren't meant to be."

"Oh my God." Lillian clasped hands together in front of her face. "You're not saying what I think you are? Are you? Did you cheat on him?"

"I'm saying that Steve and I had a fight, and I'm through with everyone trying to run my life! And my life most definitely isn't any of your business!"

"So what? Are you going to just run away whenever someone says something you don't want to hear?"

"I don't want to talk about this anymore!" Karen stood up and pulled the towel tight around her body. She could still smell his stink on her. A faint wave of nausea came over her. Karen covered her mouth with one hand and pressed the palm of her other hand against her stomach.

"What the hell has gotten into you? You're staying out all night, running around with God knows who. You're sabotaging your own future!" Lillian slapped her hand down on the counter. Karen looked at her for a moment. Lillian wouldn't understand—nobody would. Karen couldn't hold her gaze, couldn't stand the way Lillian scrutinized her. She couldn't look at her, much less tell her. If only Dad was still alive…

"What in God's name is going on in that head of yours?" Lillian waited for an answer, but Karen remained silent. "Karen?"

"Just leave me alone!" Karen yanked her father's old bathrobe from the hook on the bathroom door and slid into it before storming past Lillian.

"You can't keep running away from the obvious. You need help. You need to talk to him." Lillian's voice trailed close behind her.

"I don't need anyone's help, especially yours! This is between me and Steve, not you! Now would you just drop it?" Karen paced the floor in the hallway and chewed on her bottom lip. Everything seemed to be collapsing in her life, just like a house of cards in the breeze. Everywhere she turned, there seemed to be someone waiting to interrogate her or dictate her next move.

"You've got to be honest with him. You can't build a relationship on a tower of lies. You're deluding yourself if you think you can just pretend everything is okay." Lillian caught Karen by the arm, their eyes meeting. "Promise Steve that you'll check yourself into a program. I'll take you to one. I know of this great place…"

Karen's eyes blazed as she cut Lillian's words short and shook her hand off. "I don't have a problem! I am not some fucking alcoholic! I got drunk, okay. Steve drinks. Carol drinks. You drink. Everybody fucking drinks, yet all you ever do is act like a damned hypocrite and tell me how much I drink! Like you're some kind of fucking saint!"

"Open your eyes! Not everybody gets drunk every day of the week!"

"Maybe I wanted to get drunk! Anything, something, just to make all of you shut up! I'm so damned tired of you and Carol and now even Steve trying to run my life!" Karen took a deep breath. "Look, I made a mistake. Okay, I admit it. I drank a little too much last night—but so do lots of people. Listen, I don't drink from morning to night, and I don't reach for a drink first thing in the morning, and I certainly don't sit around on some street corner drinking from a paper bag."

Lillian looked at Karen and shook her head. "Honey, you need help. When are you going to admit that and just let us help you?"

She didn't need any help. She kept up with her college studies. She was passing all her classes with "B+"s or higher. She didn't wake up and reach for a drink first thing in the morning. "If I really had a problem, do you think I would be doing so well in school and holding down a part-time job," Karen said, growing tired of defending herself. "Explain that." Karen leaned in close to Lillian, her jawed clenched tight. "Right. You can't," she said as she whipped around towards her room.

"You're a functioning alcoholic." Lillian's voice was calm, somber.

*Shit, when was she going to stop with the labels? When is she going to mind her own business and stop diagnosing everyone with some fucking problem?*

"I can take you to this place a friend of mine recommended. She said you'd be with plenty of people your own age."

"Holy shit!" Karen whirled around to face Lillian. "You've been blabbing to your little socialites about me? Why don't you stop worrying about me? I'm not the one with the problem."

"Don't you think it might be a bit of a problem when you wake up in some stranger's bed? You're an alcoholic! Don't stand there and make excuses. Do something about it!" Lillian dropped her hands to her sides. "God, your poor father. What would he say?"

"Don't you bring him into this! You got what you wanted from him!" Karen stared at Lillian long enough to register the anger in her face. "Yah, you know what I mean. You hustled your way into his bed long before my mother's body was even cold!" Karen watched her stepmother's face redden, and then turned away.

"How dare you! You have got to be the most disrespectful, self-centered, spoiled brat I have ever met. I loved your father more than you'll ever know—and that's a lot more than I can say about your mother's feelings for him! There was no love there...not after what she did to him."

"Mami loved him! And he loved her!" Karen stormed down the hallway.

"Yes, at one time I believe she really did. But she ruined it. We tried to help her. She threw everything away, Karen! Don't you see that? She threw his love away. She threw yours away, all for a damned drink!"

Karen's face reddened. She stopped in her tracks and spun around to face Lillian. "Just shut up about my mother!"

"No! It's time for you to stop deluding yourself with all these fantasies of your mother! Night after night, when she didn't come home, and your father was pacing the floor and worried sick, I was the one that tucked you in at night, not her!"

"You drove them apart!"

"There was nothing left to drive apart!" Lillian quieted and put a hand on Karen's shoulder. "Your mother, she loved you…and your father, but she had problems. The drinking, the 3a.m. phone calls, it was just too much for your father. And you were so young, just twelve, that he couldn't, wouldn't tell you that she was leaving, that she was drunk when she crashed the car."

"You bitch! That's a lie! She wasn't leaving us!" Karen said, whirling around to face Lillian.

"Jesus, Karen, wake up! If it weren't for your father," Lillian said, holding her hand in front of her like a stop sign, "I would never have put up with all of your crap!"

"Well, you won't have to put up with it anymore." Karen stormed down the hallway and into her old room. She stopped suddenly in the doorway and looked around. The lacy pink and white sheets on her canopy bed were just as neatly made up as the day she moved out to share an apartment with Carol. Two stuffed bears and a heart-shaped pillow rested against two other pillows near the headboard. Karen ran her hand along the silky sheets and stopped to stroke the tattered bears that Mami had bought for her during one of their many family vacations spent in Puerto

Rico, in Mami's homeland. Sensing Lillian watching her, she moved over to the bureau and pulled open the top drawer, forgetting for a moment that it was empty. All she could do was stare into the drawer and fight back the sting of tears. Lillian leaned against the doorframe and sighed.

"You can wear something of mine if you'd like." Lillian turned towards her own room and dug through her drawers, pulling out a pair of brown crepe trousers, a burgundy cashmere sweater, and some undergarments. "These should fit you," she said as she handed them to Karen.

Karen opened her mouth to speak, but the words wouldn't come out. She took the clothes, nodded, and began to dress. Lillian left the room for a moment, and returned with a pair of brown suede pumps. "These might fit you. If they don't, you can check my closet for something else," she said as she set the shoes on the floor. Their eyes met. Lillian's piercing blue eyes held hers for a moment. Stifling the crazy urge to run into her arms, Karen shook her head and wiped a tear from her cheek. The room seemed to close in around her. "I've got to get out of here," she said, barely above a whisper.

"Where are you going?"

Karen looked around her room once more. Except for her bed sheets and a couple raggedy teddy bears, her room was empty. There was nothing left here for her anymore. "I don't know. I can't even breathe in here," she said and walked out of the room.

"Karen, please, I'm worried about you. Please tell me where you're going."

"Anywhere but here." Karen ran down the stairs, snatched her purse off the floor, and went out the front door, letting it slam behind her.

Karen walked back down Mill Lane, past the bus stop, and kept on walking down route one-sixteen. The chilly October wind raised goose bumps on her arms, but she kept walking. *What if Lillian wasn't lying?*

*What if all those awful things she said about Mami were true?* No, Karen shook her head. *Mami loved me. She would never have left me and Dad. She wouldn't have just abandoned us.*

Karen was only twelve when it happened. She remembers her father's somber footsteps on the stairs, his warm tears falling onto her pillow, and his voice cracking when he told her the news—that Mami had been killed in a car crash. He never said anything about her being drunk, never said anything about the suitcases in her trunk, or about her leaving with another man. Mami would never do that. *Lillian's a liar.* Karen hugged her arms to herself, giving in to the autumn chill, and sat down on the bench at the bus stop.

She rode the bus back to Northampton and found her Mustang still parked where she had left it in the lot behind Pete's Tavern. Climbing in, she started the engine and slowly made her way back to her apartment in Amherst. When she pulled into the lot, Carol's car was nowhere to be seen, causing Karen to let out a sigh of relief. She unlocked the apartment and welcomed the silence—no accusations, no interrogations, just solitude. But within the silence her shame grew louder. *Sweetness, I always got my eye on the game.* She could still feel his eyes roaming over her body, but his stink—that was what got to her the most. She pulled open the top drawer of her bureau, tossing her socks and undergarments onto her bed until she found what she wanted. She pulled a nip of rum from within a pair of rolled up socks, then shut the drawer.

Pausing by the window, she saw Carol's parking space still empty. It was nearly two-thirty. She was probably working at the book store until five. After twisting the cap off the nip, she tipped her head back and swallowed the rum. Looking about the apartment, she took in all the happy faces in picture frames that stared back at her. There was one of Steve piggybacking her, another of the two of them kissing at the top of Mount

Monadnock, and one of her, Steve, and Carol standing side-by-side with their arms draped over each other's shoulders. She twisted the cap off the nip bottle once again, tossed the rum back, letting its sweet sting slide down her throat, and threw the bottle in the small wastebasket that sat in the corner of her room. Plopping down on her bed, she hugged her pillow to herself. *Maybe Lillian wasn't lying about Mami. Maybe I'm just like Mami.*

The ringing of the phone jolted her from her thoughts. She placed her hand over the receiver, but hesitated when she saw the caller ID. It was Steve's cell number. After a few minutes, she checked her voicemail: "Karen, pick up. What the hell's going on? I've tried your cell, Lillian's...I'm getting pretty sick of these games." A moment later, his voice softened. "Hon, I hate worrying about you like this. Look, I know these last four months have been pretty rough without your dad...call me, okay? I just want you to know that I'm here for you. I love you and I hate seeing you like this."

Karen clicked off the phone and held it to her chest. *What the hell have I done?* She set the phone back in the charger and went to the kitchen. Before pulling a bottle of Luna Pinot Grigio from the counter, she glanced once more out the window. As she was pulling the cork from the bottle, she remembered Carol's comments about her drinking the 'cooking' wine. She pushed the cork back in with the palm of her hand, and set the bottle down on the counter with a thud. After pacing the floor and casting cautious glances out the window, she grabbed her purse and ran out the door. P & T's Corner Mart was only a half block away.

Ten minutes later, Karen returned with a fifth of rum. She twisted off the cap and took one swallow, then another and another, savoring its sweet sting. She repeated the process again and again until the cowboy's stink faded away and the nagging voices in her head silenced. Karen lay face down on her bed. The nearly empty bottle dropped from her hand and bounced onto the carpet, as she slipped into oblivion.

Karen didn't hear the door open two hours later. Light flooded into her darkened room from the kitchen. She could feel someone's hand pushing her hair from her face.

"Karen, Karen..." A hand gently shook her by the shoulder. "Karen, wake up." Her eyes opened. The room was spinning. Carol's faced seemed to dance in a circle in front of her. Her stomach began to well up, and she started to dry heave. "Oh no you don't. Not on the carpet," she heard Carol say. Carol slid her arms around her and sat her up. "Stand up," she said as she pulled her to her feet. Karen's legs wobbled beneath her. Carol placed Karen's arm over her shoulder and grabbed her firmly by the waist. Karen stumbled towards the bathroom and dropped down to her knees with a thud in front of the toilet. Everything in her stomach found a route out, burning her throat and nose on its way through.

"Shit!" Carol pulled out her own hair-tie and used it to keep Karen's hair out of the way. After a few minutes, Karen struggled to her feet.

"Gross bile shit," she stumbled forward. "Want a drink of water."

"No. Water will just make you puke again. Sit down," Carol said, grabbing her around the waist. Pushing away, Karen turned on the faucet and bent forward to drink, but smacked her bottom lip on it instead. Still, she tried again, this time succeeding. After gulping down a few mouthfuls, she brought her hand to her mouth again.

"See? I told you." Carol steadied her as she sank in front of the toilet bowl again. Karen vomited once more, and then rested her head against the porcelain bowl. After a few minutes, she tried to get to her feet again.

"No, no, no. Stay right where you are. Your lip is already bleeding," Carol said, throwing a rolled up towel on the floor and guiding Karen's head to it.

"No. I gotta wash the stink off..."

"Just frickin' lay down, will you?"

Karen muttered about the stink again before passing out on the bathroom floor. Sometime later, Karen heard voices coming from the kitchen: "Yah, she's in there—out cold on the floor."

"Did she get drunk again?"

"What do you think?"

"She's got to stop with the partying."

"Steve, partying is what you do with your friends. She's drowning herself in her room all alone. She's got a problem and she's not going to slow down until she realizes it."

"I think maybe she's just having a hard time dealing with her dad's death."

"You know, maybe if you weren't so ambivalent about her having a problem she'd realize that she does."

"What are you talking about?"

"By getting mad at her one minute and feeling sorry for her the next, you're just enabling her."

"What are you, some kind of psychologist now?"

Karen groaned and the voices fell silent. Footsteps came slowly towards her. She tried to open her eyes, but the light set off tiny explosions in her head. She felt Steve's hand brush against her face. He leaned over her and then scooped her up in his arms. Once he set her down on her bed, he began to remove her soiled clothing. Carol pulled her shoes off her feet and tossed a nightshirt to Steve. He slipped it over her head and then rolled her onto her side. Carol set a bucket on the floor next to the bed.

"I didn't mean to…" Karen groaned.

"Shhh…we'll talk later. Just sleep it off," Steve said as he ran his fingers through her hair.

# CHAPTER THREE

......................................

## *Long Way To Go*

The truck rattled and sputtered, slowly making the bend southeast. Craggy hills and tall stands of trees lined both sides of the highway, reminding Karen of just how far from home she really was. Only the blacktop of route ninety separated her from Jimmy and the endless forest that surrounded her. The long, lonely highway with its vast world covered with greens and browns, dappled with April's melting snow, seemed so far removed from civilization.

After reaching Billings, Karen pulled off the highway and rolled up to Kirby's Service Station. A stocky, middle-aged man dressed in brown coveralls, smelling of diesel fuel and Old Spice, leaned towards the window of the truck.

"Good morning, Ma'am. What can I get you?"

"Fill it with the cheapest, please," Karen said. The attendant nodded and began filling the tank. Robbie sat up rubbing his eyes and looked around questioningly.

"Where are we, Mommy?"

"We're in Billings."

"Is that near Massachusetts?" His eyebrows arched and he craned his neck to look out the window. Karen smiled and shook her head.

"No sweetie. We have a long way to go."

As they continued down the highway, Karen searched for a radio station. The radio crackled and buzzed until the cry of WMTN's country station came through. One oldie after another played, singing out songs of broken down trucks, cheating hearts, and rye whiskey. When an old number of Reba McEntire's *Whoever's in New England* played, Karen's eyes began to fill up as she thought back to her last few days in Massachusetts.

∽

When Karen awoke the next morning with a splitting headache, she found a glass of water and two Tylenol on the nightstand beside her. She sat up and popped the Tylenol in her mouth. Carol leaned in the doorway and stared at her for a moment, then sat down on the edge of the bed.

"Steve just left a little while ago," Carol said. "I had to kick him out—he's got midterms today."

Karen looked at the clock; it was ten-thirty, and her midterm had ended a half-hour ago. None of that seemed to matter, though.

"Karen, you can't keep doing this to him—or yourself."

"I'm really sorry about last night. Thanks for taking care of me."

"I'm not just talking about last night."

Karen looked up and then stared out the window. She shrugged her shoulders.

"Don't ignore me. I know what you did the other night."

Karen swung around to face Carol. Sometimes, she wondered if she and Carol were somehow related in another life. No matter how hard she tried, she could never pass a lie by Carol without her knowing something wasn't right. Karen turned back to gaze out the window and swallowed hard. *Oh, God.*

"What are you talking about?" Karen kept staring out the window.

"Please, Karen. Don't act like you don't know what I'm talking about. I know you got wasted again."

"Who told you that?" Karen turned back around to face her, her eyes wide.

"Nobody had to tell me that. I just know you," she said with a laugh. "Sometimes I think I know you better than you know yourself." Carol nudged her shoulder with her own. "Hey, you can talk to me. Remember me? Your best friend?"

Karen looked over at Carol and offered a little smile, and then began to cry. Carol put her arms around her, and Karen leaned against her. She wanted to tell her everything, tell her what Lillian said about Mami, about how she said Mami was leaving them…and about *that* night—but she couldn't. She couldn't tell her how dirty she felt. Just even thinking about the other night, let alone talking about it, made her feel unwashed and rotten. Karen bit down on her lip. The truth would destroy everything. But she couldn't do this to Steve, to Carol. They deserved better. She was like Midas, except everything she touched turned to poison. She loved Mami and now she was gone. She loved Dad and he was gone too. She could feel her poison filling the room. Maybe Lillian was telling the truth. Fuck them all! Maybe she was just like her…

"I'm here for you," Carol said, pulling Karen from her thoughts. "Maybe you ought to at least talk to Lillian's friend." Karen stiffened and then sat up.

"What the hell? Just how many people did she talk to? God, that woman hates me." Karen folded her arms across her chest.

"Oh stop it. You know she doesn't hate you—she just doesn't like you very much," Carol said with a laugh and nudged Karen again. "Seriously, you've got to stop drinking like a fish."

"What the hell is it with you guys? Everybody is on my back. First Steve, then Lillian, and now you."

"Jesus, Karen. You really can't stop drinking, can you?"

"I drink because I want to…not because I can't stop."

"Really? Okay, how about now?" Carol folded her arms across her chest, mimicking Karen.

Karen rolled her eyes and muttered under her breath. Carol leaned towards her, waiting for a reply, and then tilted her head and smiled.

"Okay, let's make it interesting. You're a betting woman. Fifty bucks says you can't go three days without a drink."

"Oh please. Three days?" Karen forced a smile.

"Three days, or you'll be buying me a nice, fat juicy steak at Mariano's."

"Ah, no. You'll be the one buying *me* a filet mignon, baby." Three days, Karen thought smiling. *I can do three days.*

# CHAPTER FOUR

····························

## *Three Days*

As the truck rumbled down the interstate, Karen recalled just how long three days really were. Minutes had stretched into hours, hours into days. The first day had gone uneventful. She didn't have one drink all day, and the one time she had gotten the urge, she plunged herself into a rowdy game of Rummy with Steve, Carol, and some friends. One of Steve's friends had popped off the tops of Coronas and started sliding them across the table. Karen picked up the bottle, smiled, and slid it back. "No thanks. I'm saving my appetite. Carol's taking me out for steak this weekend." When Steve looked up at her, Karen turned to Carol and smirked.

The next night, though, wasn't so easy. Without a soothing shot of rum, Karen found it impossible to drown the loss and shame that kept surfacing. Rum, wine, beer, it didn't matter. She just wanted to forget about what Lillian said, and especially forget that night, but in everything she did, everywhere she went, shame followed her like a late afternoon shadow. She couldn't get his smell out of her mind, his cheap cologne, the aftershave that he wore, his breath. It seemed as though it was on every item of clothing that she owned. Even the potpourri that Karen had placed in her drawers couldn't rid her clothes of his smell, so she threw everything into a bag and brought them to the Laundromat. When Carol cocked an eye at her, Karen simply told her that the potpourri smell was too strong. But even after Karen had washed all her clothes, she could still smell him. So in the name of charity, she gathered up all the clothes—with the exception of the ones on her back—and dropped them off at the local Salvation Army. But still, his stink was everywhere. Twice that day, she showered and tried to get the smell off. She tried lotions, perfumes, and powders; none of it could cover the stink that seemed to be engrained in her pores.

Later that night, when Steve asked Karen to spend the night at his place, she told him she wasn't feeling well. Steve stared at her for a moment, then nodded and agreed that she looked pale. Her stomach had been bothering her for the last couple of days, and little waves of nausea kept coming and going every morning. Steve kissed her and offered to stay that night, but Karen didn't want to be alone with him; he'd see her shame and smell another man's scent on her skin. Karen shook her head and told him that she just needed to get some sleep. Carol assured Steve that she would take care of her, but all Karen really wanted was to lose herself beneath an amber sea of rum and Coke. She wished that she could just be alone.

On the third morning, Karen was agitated. Carol and her boyfriend, Paul, invited Karen and Steve to Gabby's Place for breakfast. Worrying that Steve would offer to stay with her if she refused to go, Karen got up, showered and dressed, and headed out the door with them. The waitress poured a round of coffee for everyone and took their orders. Karen picked up her cup, and as she sipped it, her hands started to tremble. The hot liquid rocked back and forth against the sides of the cup. Karen tried to steady her hand, but coffee spilled over the lip of the mug and onto the back of her hand. She jerked her hand, spilling more coffee onto the table. Steve gathered up napkins and sopped up the spill.

"Are you okay?" Steve reached for her hand.

"I'm fine."

"You didn't burn yourself, did you?" He turned her hand over and looked at the back of it.

"I said I'm fine." Karen pulled her hand away and reached for her cup of coffee once more. Her hands began to shake again, so she set the cup down with a thud. Everybody looked at her, but nobody spoke. Breakfast came and went in relative silence. As soon as the waitress brought the bill, Karen opened her wallet and passed thirty dollars to her.

"I've got to go," she said, gathering up her purse and coat.

"Hey, wait a minute. I thought we were all going out together," Steve said, setting his knife and fork down abruptly.

"Uh…yah, I'll meet you later. I've got to run a couple of errands first." Karen was turning to go when she saw Steve stand up and grab his coat. "I don't need a damned babysitter," she said as she held up a hand to him.

"What the hell is your problem today?"

"I'm sorry. It's not you. I've just got a lot on my mind. I missed my final for lit, didn't do so hot on my art history exam, and I've got that art project due this week. I didn't mean to bite your head off. Look, I'm going to run over to the Rainbow Palette and pick up some acrylic paints, and I'll meet you guys a little later."

"I thought they didn't open until noon," Carol said. Karen turned to her, silent for a moment before answering.

"Well, I'll run over to CVS. I'm sure they must have some cheap acrylic there," Karen answered and strolled out the door, turning right instead of left, knowing that they must be watching her. The five minute walk to P & T's Corner Mart was going to take a lot longer now. She glanced once over her shoulder and saw the three of them standing around just outside Gabby's. No doubt they were talking about her. Slowing her pace, she made sure that they couldn't miss her when she stepped inside the store.

Keeping an eye on the front door, she walked the aisle slowly and deliberately, randomly selecting tubes of acrylic paints. Out of the corner of her eye, she saw Steve stop and stare at her. *Just keep walking, just keep walking.* Karen kept her head down and continued pulling tubes of paint from the shelf. After he passed by, she swallowed hard and rubbed her forehead.

A few minutes later, she stepped out of the store, looking to the left and right, before skipping across the street. She headed back past Gabby's and kept going until she reached P & T's. The bells on the door jangled loudly as Karen stepped inside. Mrs. Fargas, the plump, white-haired co-owner of the store stood behind the counter.

"Hi Mrs. Fargas," Karen said, putting on her most charming smile as she walked through the store. She picked up a copy of the Sunday paper, a two liter bottle of Coke, a package of sanitary napkins, some Midol, and a fifth of rum, and then placed them on the counter.

"Oh Karen, you know that I can't sell alcohol before noon on a Sunday," Mrs. Fargas said, nodding her head towards the bottle of rum.

"Oh gosh," Karen said looking at her watch. "I didn't realize it was so early." She let out a sigh and shook her head. "I guess I should have planned better. I'll just have to make it some other time." Karen pressed her palms against the counter and looked at the ground.

"What are you cooking this time?"

"Ham Caribbean, Steve's favorite."

"Oh, that's delicious. I've made that for Tom quite a few times."

"I was going to surprise him for his birthday, but…ah, no matter. I'll just make it some other time." Karen handed Mrs. Fargas the money for her groceries and shook her head.

"Well, I can't *sell* you any rum, but I could certainly let you *borrow* some." Mrs. Fargas winked. "Let me go get you a nip."

"Really? Oh, you're the best! Is there any chance that you could spare a little bit more? Ah…I mean, well it's a big ham. We've got quite a few friends coming over." Karen smiled, trying her best to hide the agitation growing inside of her. Mrs. Fargas looked at her a moment, but then disappeared into the back room. Karen was shuffling from foot to foot, and rubbing her temples when Mrs. Fargas reappeared with a fifth of rum. Straightening up and putting on a practiced smile, Karen accepted the bottle graciously.

"You're quite the chef," Mrs. Fargas said. "What was it you made last week? Chicken Marsala?"

Karen nodded and smiled as she gathered up her groceries. As she turned to go, Mrs. Fargas called over her shoulder.

"Don't forget to reserve some of the juice from the can."

"Huh?" Karen raised her eyebrows.

"For the ham. Make sure you save some of the pineapple juice."

"Oh, right. I've got plenty." Karen smiled and hurried out the door before Mrs. Fargas could start up another conversation.

Walking quickly down the street, Karen headed back to her apartment. She darted from one room to the next; Carol wasn't home. She tossed the bag of paints from CVS onto the floor in her room, and then dumped the contents of the grocery bag onto the table. Karen pushed aside the soda, the Sunday paper, pads, and Midol. There it was! She picked up the bottle. Her hands shook as she unscrewed the cap. Tilting her head back, she swallowed once, then twice. The amber liquid rolled down her throat, coating it with the rum's spicy sting and heat. Karen closed her eyes and exhaled slowly as it settled into her stomach. Satisfied for the moment, she recapped the bottle and set it down on the table.

Picking up the package of sanitary napkins, she tore it open and threw two pads into the trash, covering them with a couple of ads from the Sunday paper. Then she picked up the package and threw it on the bathroom counter. She peered out the window again, and then uncapped the rum once more. Another sweet swallow, another sweet surrender. Karen tipped her head back and closed her eyes, letting a calm indifference settle over her. She recapped the bottle as she walked to her room, and set it down on her dresser, but her grasp lingered on the smooth, amber bottle. Slowly, she unscrewed the cap and took one more swallow. What a sweet escape it would be to climb inside, to be hidden beneath a sea of amber.

Karen looked at her watch. They would be expecting her. Going over to the fridge, she took out a nearly empty Coke bottle, brought it to her room and poured the remainder of the rum into it. She held the rum bottle above her mouth and let the last couple of drops splash onto her tongue. Next, she grabbed her toothbrush and brushed her teeth, then rinsed with Scope. Once she finished, she grabbed the Coke bottle from the kitchen and placed it on the floor in a corner of her room next to the CVS bag. After gathering up her coat, keys, and purse, she headed for the door. Everything is in its place, she thought as she looked around the kitchen, and then froze with her hand on the doorknob. Turning quickly, she ran to her bedroom and tossed the rum bottle in the kitchen trash. It landed with a thunk at the bottom of the barrel. Karen looked into the nearly empty trash can and thought for a moment. Opening the fridge, she pulled out two Styrofoam containers with leftover Chinese food in them. She threw that into the barrel, along with a half-empty bottle of orange juice, and anything else expendable that she could find. Snatching up a section of newspaper, Karen crumpled it into a ball and tossed it in the barrel as well. Next, she emptied the small bathroom wastebasket into the kitchen trash can. Before leaving the apartment, she took one last look around. Perfect.

Karen pulled up to Fast Lanes Bowling Alley and spotted Steve's Jeep and Carol's Sentra in the parking lot. She parked her car in the empty spot two spaces over, and then jogged across the lot. Before stepping inside, she placed a piece of spearmint gum in her mouth. Steve's back was to her when she snuck up behind him and wrapped her arms around his waist. His body stiffened, and he turned to her. He wasn't smiling.

"Sorry I'm late. Did I miss much?" Karen ran a hand along his bicep, giving it a gentle squeeze.

"Where were you off to in such a hurry?"

"Nature called. I started my period." Karen smiled, but Steve's expression did not change. "I'm sorry about this morning, but you know how I get this time of month…"

"Don't I ever," he said, rolling his eyes and letting a smile slip across his face. As he wrapped his arms around her and kissed the top of her head, Karen closed her eyes and choked back the guilt.

Karen couldn't concentrate on bowling. There were just too many people inside the bowling alley. What if someone from the bar was there? Her stomach knotted up, so she excused herself and went to the bathroom. Inside the walls seemed to close in on her, and the ripe, unwashed smell in the restroom made her feel nauseous and want to shower again. Without stopping to tell anyone, she left Fast Lanes.

Some minutes later, Steve called her cell phone to find out why she left. Karen's stomach cramped up when she told him that she felt sick. *If he only knew*, she thought. It was nothing a little nap wouldn't cure she said before hanging up the phone. She set her cell phone down and pulled to the side of the road. She didn't want to go home. All she wanted to do was to forget her sins and all the lies that seemed to surround her. She wanted to be invisible.

Pulling back into traffic, Karen headed towards St. Luke's Cemetery, stopping along the way for a bottle of rum. Fifteen minutes later, she was standing over her father's grave. She shook her head. *Had he lied?* Karen sat down on the ground and leaned against an old maple tree. *Was Lillian lying?* She cracked the seal on the bottle of rum and took a swig. Above her head, the clouds collided in the sky, muting all of autumn's colors. Karen took another swallow and gritted her teeth. *He lied. Mami lied. Lillian lied.* A single tear slid down her face. Karen picked up a small stone and threw it at the headstone. *They were all liars.* She wiped her cheek with the back of her hand; she wouldn't cry for them anymore.

Karen sat propped up against the old maple until the air grew cold and unwelcoming. She took another swallow of rum, feeling strangely warm, and blew steamy clouds in the air with her breath. The sun trekked westward across the sky, its light barely visible beneath the clouds. Though she hadn't eaten since breakfast, she wasn't hungry, and although she had hardly slept these last few nights, she wasn't tired; she wasn't anything.

When the last trace of sunlight slipped below the horizon, Karen began to shiver. Staggering to her feet, she found her way through the maze of headstones, guided only by their faint silhouettes. Reaching the cemetery gates, Karen found them locked. Her car was parked on the other side of the gate. Karen kicked her foot clumsily at the gate and swore. Tossing the empty bottle of rum over the fence, she grasped the wrought iron and pulled herself up and over the gate. With all the grace of a ballerina with lead slippers, she tumbled to the ground. She pulled the keys from her pocket and began pushing buttons on the key fob—the trunk opened—the doors unlocked—then locked again—the car alarm blared and the doors unlocked again—until finally all was quiet. Karen pulled open the back door, climbed in, and curled up in a ball. Sometime in the black of night, she awoke. Sitting up, she became overwhelmed with a wave of nausea. Opening up her car door, Karen received a cold blast of air. Tumbling out of the car and shivering uncontrollably, she knelt on the hard ground and vomited until there was nothing left inside.

After midnight, Karen pulled into the parking lot of her apartment. Carol's Sentra was there, but the apartment was dark. She climbed the stairs, her legs feeling unsteady with every step she took, and made her way into the apartment. Without bothering to undress, Karen flopped down on her bed and fell back to sleep.

An insistent pounding on the front door woke Karen from her sleep. She lifted her head from her pillow and looked around. Sunlight was seeping past the edges of the shade, spilling shafts of light across her bed. The banging persisted. She sat up slowly, bringing her hand to her head to stem the pounding in her temples. The front door opened. Footsteps came towards her room. Steve stood in the doorway, his eyes boring through her. In that instance, she knew it was over.

"I went to Pete's Tavern last night, hoping to find you, but I think I found more than I bargained for. I'm going to give you one chance to tell me the truth." Steve folded his arms across his chest. His eyes never broke contact with hers. "Where did you go Wednesday when you tore out of the parking lot?"

"Steve… I never meant…"

"Never meant to what? Sleep with him?"

The room felt suffocating and hot. The pounding of Karen's heart stepped in rhythm with the throbbing in her head. She couldn't look into his eyes anymore.

"Look at me!" Steve stepped in front of her. Karen looked up, shaking her head.

"It's not my fault," she said, grabbing hold of his arms.

"Not your fault? You get pissed at me, then go off with some guy, but it's not your fault?" Steve shook her hands off his arms.

"It wasn't like that. Please, you've got to listen to me." Karen reached out for him.

Steve shook his head and backed away. "How long has this been going on with this guy? Were you with him last night too?"

"No, please listen to me. I just went to play pool and…"

"I think I've heard enough," he said, turning for the door.

"No, please." Karen grabbed onto his arm. "He kept buying me drinks, and…you should have been there for me!"

"What? You fuck somebody, like some common whore, and it's my fault?" Steve pulled the front door open and turned to her. "The funny thing is I trusted you. What a mistake that was."

Karen watched him jog down the steps and hop into his Jeep. "Please, Steve. Please, it wasn't like that…" Her words were drowned out by the squeal of Steve's tires. A flurry of leaves whirled in the wake. Slowly, Karen slid down with her back against the doorframe, sobbing.

After some time, she rose to her feet, and walked into the apartment. The front door remained open, sucking the warmth from the kitchen. Karen could feel her poison filling the room. There was nothing left for her here anymore. On a tear stained paper, Karen left a note that simply said "I'm sorry." On top of it, she placed her engagement ring, and then went to her room. She pulled a duffle bag from the floor of the closet and packed as much clothing in it as she could. When it was full, she went to the small bookshelf that stood in the corner of her room. Pushing aside her sketchpads and textbooks, she reached for a brown leather bound scrapbook. She ran her fingers across the cover, and then tucked it under her arm. With her duffle bag, scrapbook, and purse in hand, she took one last look around. She pulled the door shut behind her, determined to go where no one would know her name.

# CHAPTER FIVE

························

## *Across the Midwest*

Darkness descended upon South Dakota like bad memories and regrets. Overtaken by sleep and boredom, Robbie was slumped over slightly and nearly hidden beneath Karen's coat. Rubbing the chill from her arms from time to time, Karen cursed the heater in her truck and decided that they had driven far enough for one day. She exited Interstate Ninety, not too far from Humbolt, just after the rain changed over to sleet. Minnesota would have to wait for another day. At the end of the off ramp, Karen stopped long enough to use her sleeve to wipe the condensation off the windshield.

"And this is supposed to be spring," she muttered as she let out the clutch and turned the corner. Two miles from the interstate, she found a cheap motel that included coffee and donuts in the morning. Stepping out of the truck, she gave one tire a kick; new tires, she'd have to get those too. When would the list of things she needed ever grow smaller? Shaking her head, she walked around to the passenger side and picked up Robbie.

With Robbie slumped peacefully over her right shoulder and her duffle bag clasped in her left arm, she made her way to the office to check in. After swiping her credit card and signing her name, she collected her key and headed to room four.

She pushed the key in the lock, gave the door a shove with her left shoulder, and slid her hand along the wall to find the light switch. The room filled with a dull yellow glow from a sixty watt bulb sitting in a wall lamp. Karen laid Robbie down on one bed, then turned down the sheets on the other. Gently, she pulled his sneakers off his feet and unzipped his jacket before moving him to the other bed and sliding him beneath the sheets.

"Mommy," Robbie called to her, "Will you sleep next to me?"

"Yes my little prince." Karen kissed his cheeks and tucked in the blankets around him. Robbie let out a contagious yawn and slipped back into sleep. Karen sat on the edge of the bed. Someday, she thought, someday everything will be better. Robbie deserved a better life. She took off her tattered Red Sox hat and rubbed the brim thoughtfully. *Maybe someday we'll go to Fenway. We'll watch Ortiz knock one into the Monster seats. We'll eat popcorn, Fenway Franks, and share a ridiculously expensive soda. We'll hang a pennant on your wall, and I'll buy you an embroidered hat with a great big "R" on it. And for the first time in a long time, I won't care what it costs. Someday....*

It wasn't until she showered and changed into a pair of comfy old gym pants and a baggy sweater that she realized just how tired she was. Quietly, she climbed beneath the worn sheets and settled down next to Robbie. She kissed him softly on his nose and pulled the covers around them. Sleep came easily, wrapping her in warmth and dreams.

*The music was thumping an infectious rhythm. Everyone was laughing and dancing. Mami and Dad were dancing the tango. Carol was dancing with Paul. Steve was there, too. He stepped in time with almost a tiger-like gate towards Karen, his flirty eyes holding hers. As he drew closer, though, he evaporated and in his place stood Jimmy with his blazing eyes and his hands balled into fists. She turned around and around, but Steve was gone. Mami twirled out of Dad's arms and drifted into the thickening blackness. Karen called out to Carol, but Carol spun into Paul's arms, their faces pressed cheek to cheek. Lillian twirled past her, wagging a finger and saying "You're just like your mother" and then spun into her dad's arms. Karen felt herself yanked backwards by Jimmy's firm grasp. She twirled into his arms, where he held her tightly, making it hard to breathe. Just as suddenly as he pulled her close, he then spun her out of his arms and straight up against the cowboy, who caught her by the wrists and whispered in her ear, "Sweetness, I always got my eye on the game."*

Karen awoke with a start. She exhaled slowly and turned to see Robbie still curled up next to her. Unconsciously, she massaged her wrists. Leaning over, she planted a kiss on his forehead and caught sight of the crimson glow from the clock; it was nearly 8:30. Karen leaned her head in her hands. Sooner or later, they would have to get on the road.

"Robbie, wake up sweetie. We've got to get going soon." Karen couldn't help but smile as Robbie snuggled deeper beneath his covers. "Hey, where'd my boy go?" As she slowly pulled back the covers, a crop of sandy blonde hair appeared. Robbie squeezed his eyes shut and tugged at the covers. Karen leaned over and blew razzleberries against his neck. Robbie giggled and shrank further beneath the covers.

"Come on, Robbie. We've got to get some breakfast and get on the road," Karen said, nudging the lump under the covers. The blankets flew back, as Robbie sat bolt upright.

"Mommy, we get free donuts here. Right?" His eyes were nearly as wide as the grin that stretched across his face.

"Right! You get the donuts; I'll get the coffee." Karen laughed and nodded her head. They quickly washed, dressed, and packed their dirty laundry into a plastic garbage bag, and then raced down the hall to the dining room.

"Holy moly! Mommy, they have chocolate covered donuts with sprinkles!" Robbie jumped up and down. An old, blue-haired lady stooped over to look at Robbie.

"Boy, it sure doesn't take much to please you. Does it?"

Robbie smiled and ducked behind his mom's legs. The little old lady smiled at Robbie and his chocolate covered lips as he peeked back at her. Turning to an equally old gentleman standing by the coffee carafe across the way, the little old woman called out to him, "Carl, come on over here and see this handsome young fellow."

An elderly gentleman wearing baggy grey trousers, a wool coat, and a baseball cap that read, "Aged to Perfection" shuffled across the room to his wife.

"Hey there squirt, how's that donut? Did you save some for me?" he asked. Robbie giggled and shook his head vigorously from side to side as he popped the last bite into his mouth. Then after wiping the chocolate from Robbie's hands and face, Karen hiked their bags over her shoulder, and the two of them headed out to the open road.

It was nine-fifteen and the traffic was still bumper to bumper with no sign of letting up any time soon. The closer Karen got to Sioux Falls, the more congested the highway became. At this rate, they wouldn't make it to Minnesota until after lunchtime, and that all depended on how many potty breaks they would have to make.

Less than two hours later, Robbie began to squirm in his seat and announced that he couldn't hold it any longer. The next rest area was at least twenty miles away. Karen sighed and pulled the truck over in the breakdown lane.

"Come on, Tiger. If you can't hold it, you'll just have to go here," Karen said, helping him out of the truck. Robbie stood in between the open door of the truck and Karen, and sprinkled the pavement. Hearing a car approaching, they both turned their heads. A cruiser pulled in behind Karen's truck, causing Robbie to nearly pee on himself. He tugged on the fly of his pants, then reached his arms out for his mother. Karen snapped his jeans and lifted him into her arms. He wrapped his arms tightly about her neck and buried his head in her shoulder. An officer approached them with a smile, pausing for a moment to look at the puddle on the ground. Robbie peeked at the officer for a second, only to hide his face in Karen's shoulder again.

"It's okay. He's just a nice policeman," Karen whispered in his ear. Robbie ventured another peek, but held on even tighter. Peeing in public, the officer reminded them, was technically a finable offense.

"Heck, I got a couple of little ones of my own, and I know when they've got to go, they've got to go," the officer said with a smile. Karen nodded, and promised to be more selective with potty stops. The officer leaned over and gave Robbie a little salute before returning to his car. After buckling Robbie into his booster seat, Karen eased her truck back onto the highway. As they pulled away, Robbie strained to look behind them.

"Mommy, are we escaping?"

"Escaping? No honey. We're not escaping because we weren't captured."

"Does that mean he's going to come get us?" Robbie craned his neck again and looked behind them.

"No, Robbie. The officer wasn't trying to capture us. He just doesn't want us stopping on the side of the road for bathroom breaks anymore."

"So he isn't going to come and take you away again? Right?"

Karen's grip on the wheel tightened and she bit down softly on her bottom lip. "No honey. Nobody is ever going to take me away from you again."

# CHAPTER SIX

......................

## *The Rhythm of the Road*

As the white lines passed by the truck and the wheels whirred across the pavement in rhythm with the road, Karen thought back to that time. That day was supposed to be a new beginning for Karen. She had promised herself that she wasn't going to drink anymore—or at least not during the work week. She definitely wouldn't drink in front of Robbie, at least not more than a drink or two. But that day, she had told herself, she deserved a drink; tomorrow, she said, tomorrow she would quit.

Her shift at the diner began at 6:00 a.m. Since the sun had risen, she had to deal with every impossible customer, from the old lady that insisted Karen brew a fresh pot of coffee—despite the three pots that Karen had just put on less than ten minutes before—to the jailbait boy that kept flirting with her, calling her dear, honey, and doll every time he needed something. Karen stifled the urge to say something back, but instead brewed another pot of coffee for the prune at table four, and just smiled sweetly at the pimply-not-quite-a-man boy.

Today was Thursday, payday for many, so that meant business would be steady. Karen eyed the clock; it was one. Her feet were aching, and she just wanted to go home, but when Irene asked her if she could stay until closing, she said yes. One hour stretched into two when a carload of giddy teenage girls decided to stop in for shakes and burgers after a half-day of school. The girls, laughing and talking loudly, piled into a booth in Karen's section.

Karen stood poised over them with a pencil in hand and waited for their order: Three cheeseburgers, one double bacon, a dog with the works and a round of shakes. Less than two minutes later, a Volkswagen Jetta pulled into the parking lot. Four boys wearing Parker High School Football jerseys climbed out. Noticing the boys, one of the girls sitting at the table—the blonde with the big mouth—tapped one of her friends on the shoulder and pointed out the window. The girls murmured excitedly, then began to beckon for Karen. She looked over, forcing a smile and thinking about how a rum and Coke would be well deserved right now, and then returned to their table. Suddenly the cheeseburgers, hotdog, and shakes needed to be salads—hold the croutons—and water with lemon wedges. Karen clenched her teeth and managed to force a smile. She changed the orders, and when they were ready, served them with a well-practiced smile.

"Is there anything else I can get you girls?"

"No, we're totally good," the redhead answered, bobbing her head like a pigeon. After an hour of giggles and whispers they left, leaving behind a table covered with dirty napkins and straw wrappers, and a floor littered with lettuce and a spilled container of dressing. For the tip, they left their collective fifty-one cents in change. Violence never solved anything, Karen thought, but God it would feel good to smack at least one of them. After she cleaned up the mess and helped Irene with the prep work for the next day, Karen picked up Robbie and headed for Washrite's to do the laundry.

It was after five when they got home, and Karen was exhausted, but there was still laundry to put away and supper to make. Jimmy was sitting on the recliner with a foot propped up on the coffee table and a beer in his hand.

"You're late," he growled.

"Yes, I know," Karen answered as she hip-checked the door shut while hanging on to a basketful of clean laundry. "Somebody's got to work around here," she muttered under her breath. Jimmy threw his beer can against the TV and rose to his feet. He caught Karen by the wrist, spun her around, and struck her across the face, knocking the laundry basket out of her hands. Karen reeled backwards, falling against the counter. Robbie stood in the middle of the kitchen and started to cry.

"You've got a lot of nerve, you ungrateful bitch! I've worked my ass off for you and your little bastard kid!" Jimmy's breath was hot and steamy. The stink of stale beer and drops of spittle came out of his mouth, dotting Karen's reddened cheek. Robbie's crying grew to a feverish pitch.

"Shut him the fuck up, will ya!" Jimmy jabbed an angry finger in Robbie's direction and then stomped back to his recliner. Karen picked up Robbie and held him to her. He sobbed on her shoulder, his tears soaking her pink and blue Hardy's Truck Stop shirt. Karen squatted down with him in her arms and began picking laundry up off the floor.

"Where the hell have you been anyway? Slutting around town?" Jimmy kept his eyes focused on the TV and popped the top off another beer.

"I had to work late and do the laundry, and I stopped by Kelton Kids to pick up a pair of jeans for Robbie," Karen answered quietly, rubbing Robbie's back.

"Yah? You ought to spend some time cleaning up this shit hole, instead of putting all those hours in for that old bitch," Jimmy said, tossing another empty can towards the trash barrel, but missing it. "Anyway, you wouldn't have to put in so many damned hours if you didn't spend so much fucking money on designer clothes for a toddler. I mean what the fuck's wrong with shopping at Walmart? Huh, College?" He yanked open the fridge and stared into it. "Are you gonna make some supper tonight?"

Karen smoothed Robbie's hair back and brushed a tear from his cheek. "Hey College, I'm talking to you!"

Karen turned towards him and mumbled, "Sure."

"What? I can't hear you, College. Didn't they teach you how to talk at that big fancy school? Huh? A lot of good that did you. Waitin' tables and wipin' asses. UMASS? More like dumb ass."

Karen looked at him for a moment, wanting to throw something at him, but then thought better of it. The drunker Jimmy got the uglier he was. Since his work had slowed down, he didn't do much of anything, except sit around the house. He hadn't bothered to comb his hair or shave, and if he hadn't needed to go out for beer, he probably wouldn't have bothered to dress. Karen shook her head and carried Robbie on her hip to the counter, where she set him down. He stuck his thumb in his mouth, sniffled, and watched her every move. Karen filled a large pot with water and pulled a box of spaghetti from the cabinet above Robbie's head. When she took two steps to the right to get a can of spaghetti sauce from the next cabinet over, Robbie scooted across the counter towards her.

Feeling Jimmy's eyes on her, Karen turned to see him standing there with one hand on his hip and a tortured expression on his face. Robbie held his arms out towards Karen. She picked him up, cupping his little body against hers.

"When's he gonna talk more? The little guy don't talk much," Jimmy asked, his voice softening.

Karen shrugged and shifted Robbie from one hip to another while stirring the sauce. Robbie leaned his wet face against her chest and hiccoughed. Jimmy reached over and stroked the bright red welt on Karen's face, making her wince. He leaned into her and kissed her cheek, and then placing a hand under her chin, turned her towards him.

"Look, I'm sorry. I guess I lost my temper. I've spent a lot of time on the phone today trying to work deals, and I guess it's just grating on my nerves. I may not be out there in the field right now, but I'm still working my ass off trying to get this contracting job."

Karen nodded, but didn't look at him. "I've been working hard, too, putting in at least thirty hours a week at Hardy's, and I've got Robbie to look after on top of everything else."

"Shit, he's almost four," Jimmy laughed. "He don't eat much and he don't use a diaper anymore, so how much work can he possibly be?"

Karen shook her head and walked over to the fridge. Pushing aside Jimmy's cans of Bud, she stared at them for a moment, and then grabbed the parmesan cheese and set it on the table.

"Karen, you wait tables in a fucking diner. How hard can that be?" Jimmy tipped his head back and swallowed a mouthful of beer. Karen shrugged her shoulders as she walked over to the kitchen table and sat Robbie in his booster seat, then picked up two glasses from the dish rack.

"Look baby, I don't wanna fight with you," he said, standing in her way. "So let's just forget this whole thing. Okay?" He pulled her to him and wrapped his arms around her, pressing her arms—glasses still in hand—against her sides. He bent his head down and kissed the top of her head, then let her go. Strolling over to the fridge, he pulled out two Buds, took the glasses from her hands and placed them on the table, then handed her a beer. Karen looked at the can in her hand. *Just one*, Karen thought, *just one*. She popped the top and sipped at hers, letting the cool liquid rest in her mouth for a moment before swallowing it. *Just one more*, she said to herself as she set dinner on the table.

Halfway through dinner, Karen set down her fork and looked at Jimmy. "I've been thinking about enrolling in some classes at Black River College, you know, so I could finish up my degree." Karen waited for his response, but instead Jimmy popped a meatball in his mouth and just stared at her.

"I think we could swing it. I'm sure some of my credits would transfer from UMASS." She looked up at Jimmy hopeful, but he just shook his head and laughed.

"What in the hell would you want to go back to school for?"

"Well, if I had a degree, I could get a higher paying job. Maybe I could get a part-time job over the summer at the academy. They have some great art programs for kids," Karen said hopefully.

"Hah," Jimmy said, stabbing a forkful of spaghetti. "You wanna do something useful with your art, then paint houses. Don't waste your time painting pictures."

"I don't think I'd be wasting my time…"

"Don't think? Well, that's your problem. You don't think. We aren't gonna blow money on school just so you can paint, so just get those thoughts out of your head." Jimmy shoved his chair away from the table and grabbed his keys. "Don't wait up for me. I'm going to Billy's cabin and we're going fishing first thing in the morning."

"Jimmy, I can pay for the classes myself. They have a payment plan."

"We aint wasting money on some useless art program. You ain't going and that's that."

"But Jimmy…"

"Look, you want a job? You want to improve your skills? Then start here and clean up this place," Jimmy said kicking over the laundry basket before walking out the door.

After wiping down the dinner table and washing the dishes, Karen bathed Robbie and put him in his crib that he was quickly out-growing. Once she was sure he was asleep, she tiptoed out of his room and sat down at the kitchen table. She poured herself a shot of rum and tossed it back, then refilled her glass. Leaning her face in her hands, she could feel the welt under the palm of her hand from where Jimmy had hit her. It throbbed in rhythm with her aching head, but Captain Morgan was there, ready to save the day and make all her problems disappear. Swallowing another shot of rum, she stared down at the faded blue and vanilla colored linoleum that was marred with a week's worth of dirt. Her eyes traced one long jagged line that went up across the vanilla and into the blue crescent pattern before turning sharply downward. The crack grew bigger the further down it went, until it finally met up with the kitchen door where it gave up and peeled back in defeat.

Karen didn't hear Robbie call her name early the next morning. She didn't hear him climb out of his crib and pitter patter across the floor. When he came into the kitchen, he found her passed out at the kitchen table.

"Mommy," he called as he tugged on her pink Hardy's Diner shirt, but Karen didn't respond. Robbie tugged on her arm, but she still didn't move. He climbed onto the chair next to her and stared at his mom. Karen's head lay against her forearm on the table. Her hair hung down in front of her face. Robbie pushed the hair from her face and peeled one eyelid open.

"Mommy, wake up. Mommy, I want some pancakes." Robbie shook her once more before giving up. He dragged a chair across the kitchen and climbed onto it, then pulled himself onto the counter. He began opening cabinets until he finally found the one that held his favorite Spiderman cup. Grinning, he slid off the counter and onto the chair, before performing a superhero's leap off it. Robbie bunny-hopped over to the fridge and tugged on the handle until the door opened. He set his cup on the floor and turned back to the fridge. Grunting, he lifted a half-gallon container of orange juice out of the fridge and set it next to his cup. His dug his fingers in the lip of the carton, opened it, and tipped the mouth towards his cup. Orange juice splashed down the sides of the cup and across Robbie's bare little toes, and soon Robbie found himself standing in a pool of delicious liquid. He picked up the cup and held it up high.

"Look, Mommy. I did it myself!" His grin faded away when he realized that his mommy missed his great feat. He shrugged, and then stomped his feet in the puddle, laughing at the way the juice splashed across the floor. Leaving small, sticky footprints behind him, he went over to the cabinet and pulled out a box of Cheerios. Sitting down on the floor, Robbie scooped up cereal in his pudgy little fingers and popped them into his mouth. He licked his fingers clean, scooped up another handful, and pitter-pattered across the floor to the front door. Reaching up, he twisted the doorknob two or three times, until it finally opened, and then he slipped out the front door.

Fifteen minutes later Mrs. Bradley, Karen's sixty-two year old neighbor, stepped in the doorway with Robbie in hand, and looked at the kitchen floor, sprinkled with Cheerios and orange juice. Robbie shook his hand loose and ran outside to his sandbox. Mrs. Bradley regarded him a moment, and then turned her gaze back to the kitchen. Her eyes followed the sticky trail across the kitchen to where Karen sat with her head resting on the table. An empty bottle of Captain Morgan's lay on its side next to a glass still clutched in Karen's hand. Mrs. Bradley let out a huff of air, picked up the phone, and stood in the doorway where she could still see Robbie in his sandbox, then punched in some numbers and waited.

Less than ten minutes later, a cruiser pulled into the driveway. Karen stirred slightly at the sound of voices, one deep and calm, the other higher pitched and raised.

"Yes, I found him wandering down the street like this! Barefoot and in his jammies, without a soul around. And this is what I see when I brought him back to his house."

Karen felt a hand on her shoulder once again. Someone was saying her name, someone whose voice she didn't recognize, and then she heard the other voice say, "…poor boy has a drunken fool for a mother…" She started to open her eyes, but instinctively squeezed them shut to block out the bright morning light flooding into the kitchen. A sharp stabbing pain beat against her head as she forced herself to open her eyes and sit up. The room seemed to flick from left to right, left to right, like a malfunctioning movie. The glint of sunlight off a badge caught her attention. A man in uniform leaned towards her.

"Ms. Black, please look at me when I'm speaking to you," she heard the officer say.

"Oh God, where's Robbie? Where's Robbie?" Karen's eyes scanned the kitchen—juice spilled on the floor, a Cheerios box on its side, Mrs. Bradley in the doorway shaking her head, an officer leaning towards her—but Robbie nowhere in sight.

"Where's my son?" Karen's voice rose higher.

"Your son is in the sandbox playing, and you would know that if you hadn't been boozing it up," Mrs. Bradley said, her arms folded across her chest.

"Ma'am please," the officer said with a hand raised towards Karen's neighbor, before turning his attention back to her. "Ms. Black, is your son's father home?"

Karen looked around the house, then rose unsteadily to her feet, her heart beginning to pound faster and faster inside her chest. Jimmy's truck was not in the driveway. From the doorway, she could hear Mrs. Bradley speaking to the other officer.

"I told you so. She's a drunk. She doesn't even know where her boyfriend is, and that poor boy is all alone with her, a drunk."

Karen ran to the doorway, but the officer stepped in her path. She stopped, leaned to one side, and rose to her tippy toes, so she could see

Robbie. He was sitting in the sandbox in his pajamas. Dirt stuck to the underneath of his feet and to his juice soiled top. Another police officer crouched on the ground next to Robbie, and when he pushed a truck through the sand towards him, Robbie looked up and scooted further away. He looked towards the house and his eyes searched for Karen.

"Ms. Black, I have no choice but to place your child in protective custody until the Department of Child Services determines whether or not you can offer your son a safe environment."

The words fell upon Karen like an avalanche. The officer signaled to his partner, who stood up and reached for Robbie's hand. Robbie pulled his hand away and stepped back from the officer.

"No, no you can't do that. This is all just a mistake, a misunderstanding. I overslept." Karen tried to step past the officer when she heard Robbie call out to her, but the officer moved in front of her.

"Ma'am, please," the officer put a hand on her shoulder. Karen shook his hand off and called out to Robbie.

"Tiger, I'm right here," she said and turned back to the officer. "You can't take him away. I didn't do anything wrong."

"Ma'am, given the state we found you in, we have an obligation to place your son with Child Services until you are deemed capable of caring for him."

"Mommy," Robbie called out again, his voice panicked.

"Robbie, I'm here," Karen answered, scarcely able to keep the panic out of her own voice.

"Ms. Black, someone from Child Services will be in touch with you shortly to determine whether or not Robbie can remain with you."

Karen watched as the other officer walked Robbie over to the cruiser. "No! You can't take my son! Robbie!" She ran past the officer, but he caught her by the arm. Her hands clenched and heart beat faster. Karen jerked her arm free and ran towards Robbie, only to have the officer grab her around the waist and lift her up off the ground. Robbie began to scream and cry. The second officer pushed Robbie towards Mrs. Bradley and ran to aid his partner. Karen swung her feet up, kicking him in the chest, and then jabbed her elbow into the chin of the other officer, causing him to momentarily lose his grip on her. Two strong hands grasped her by the shoulders and a foot swept in front of her legs, kicking her feet out from under her. Karen felt the air rush out of her lungs when she hit damp grass with a thud. A knee pressed down on her back, while a hand held her head against the damp earth.

"You can't take my son," she cried. "No! You can't take my son!"

"Mommy...Mommy," she heard her son's cry and the click of cuffs being snapped around her wrists.

"Ms. Black, you are being placed under arrest for assault on a police officer. Anything you say..."

Robbie's cries grew louder and louder, drowning out the officer's words. Robbie stretched out his little arms towards Karen as the officers dragged her to the cruiser. The door slammed shut behind her, muffling Robbie's cries. Karen leaned against the window and sobbed as the cruiser pulled away. A short while later, Karen found herself sitting on a bench inside a grey windowless cell. She hugged her knees to her chest and stared down at the floor for what felt like hours. Sometime later, from down the hallway, she heard a familiar voice.

"Thanks Pete," she heard Jimmy say. "I guarantee you she wouldn't have ever taken a hand to you if she wasn't so crazy with grief. I mean, when she heard her gramma passed, she just kinda lost it. You know, her gramma raised her for most of her life, so she's got a special attachment to her."

"Well, I can understand that. But we've got to think about little Robbie's safety. She was passed out drunk when we got there, and your little fellow was out wandering down the street all alone."

"God, I knew I shouldn't have gone out last night after she got the news. But my friend Joe had a branch come down on his cabin up north and he was getting pretty worried about the rain that's supposed to be coming our way tonight. I told him now wasn't a good time, but Karen told me to go, that she'd be fine. Hell, I thought maybe she just needed some time to think, you know."

"Well, I've already put a call over to Child Services and they said that since they've never had an issue with her, and so long as you're home and she stays out of trouble, Robbie can go back home."

"Pete, you don't know how much I appreciate this. I'll keep an eye on her and see to it that she deals with her grief in some other way."

Karen stood up when she saw Jimmy and the officer come into view. He stood there smiling, her knight in shining armor. Jimmy gave her a wink, as the officer unlocked her cell.

"Now Ms. Black, you can take Robbie home with you today, but you must understand that now that a case with Child Services has been opened up, you will be subject to home inspections and unannounced visits."

Karen nodded her head quickly, ready to agree to anything that would bring her and Robbie back together. When Jimmy stepped forward and pulled her to him, she felt herself tense up momentarily until he kissed the top of her head and stroked her hair. Karen buried her face in his chest and cried.

"I told Pete all about your gramma passing, and he's agreed to drop the assault charges against you."

Karen raised her eyebrows. "Oh, right. I…ah…was pretty close to her. She practically raised me." Karen looked away. "I'm sorry about what I did. I guess I just lost it," she began, but the officer held up a hand.

"I understand," he said, giving her a pat on the shoulder. "Grief makes us do crazy things." He turned to Jimmy and said, "So I'll see you Saturday?"

"Saturday works for me," Jimmy answered.

Then the officer gave Karen a sympathetic smile and slapped Jimmy on the back. "You got a good man here."

Once Karen got inside Jimmy's truck, she leaned over and kissed him. He looked at her, shook his head, and let out a laugh.

"I still can't believe you kicked him."

"They were taking Robbie away."

"Shit. Now I gotta go help Pete hang some cabinets in his kitchen."

"Look, I'm sorry."

"Hah." He started the truck and turned to her. "It's all right. Can't hurt to have some friends on the force." Jimmy gave her knee a squeeze and pulled into traffic.

❧

When they arrived home, Karen called Child Services and was told that Robbie would be driven home in a couple hours and a case worker would be accompanying him to conduct an interview and perform a home inspection. Karen picked up a mop and began washing the floor, and much to her surprise, Jimmy began vacuuming the living room. Once the house looked tidy and welcoming, Karen breathed a sigh of relief. Jimmy stood in front of her and looked her over. He traced his finger lightly over her cheek and trailed it down her neck.

"You've got dirt on your face," he said, then lowered his gaze, "and on your shirt." He pulled her close and began kissing her, as he pulled her shirt up over her head. Karen suppressed the urge to pull away from him. After all, she owed him.

While Jimmy pumped and sweated over her, Karen's mind could only wrap around two thoughts: Robbie and Child Services. A short while later, Jimmy feeling satisfied and manly, rolled off of her and tugged on a pair of clean jeans. When Karen stepped into the shower, she found herself unconsciously scrubbing her body over and over until the skin on her thighs was streaked with red marks.

Most of the times when they were together, the sex was bearable—so long as she had just enough to drink to dull her senses. She had learned early on that if Jimmy wanted to have sex to just pretend that she wanted it too. After all, he told her more than once, a man has his needs and his manly rights. What did it matter anyway? Resisting him would only make him angry and threatening. A bottle of Bacardi washed down with Jimmy's cheap beer would let her get through another night under his grunting, sweating mass. In her dizzy state she could pretend that she was somewhere else, somewhere far from Jimmy, far from the towering trees and roughly hewn mountains of Montana. In her numbness, nobody— not the bill collectors, not Jimmy, not her pain, her guilt—nobody could get through—that is, nobody except Robbie. He was an incessant beacon that called to her.

♋

Karen stood in the center of the kitchen, listening while the case worker lectured her on proper parenting and scribbled on a note pad as she inspected the room.

"Okay, now I'll need to take a look at the bedrooms," the case worker said as she turned towards Karen's bedroom. Karen remembered with sudden clarity that she had left a bottle of Captain Morgan's on the top of her bureau. Karen stepped towards the counter, spying the half-gallon jug of milk there that she had taken out moments ago for Robbie. While the case worker's back was turned towards her, she unscrewed the cap on the jug and picked it up, knocking it against herself. "Crap!" Karen yelled when the milk splashed all over the front of her shirt. The case worker turned around in mid-stride to see what had happened. Karen set the jug back down on the counter and began dabbing her shirt with a paper towel, and then looked up at the case worker.

"Would you mind if I just change my shirt quickly?" Karen continued wiping at her shirt, and then headed towards her bedroom. Closing the door behind her, she snatched up the bottle from her bureau. Her eyes darted about the room—no, not the closet, not under the bed, or the mattress—she'll surely look there. Tiptoeing over to her window, she slid it open and tossed the bottle into the bushes, then pulled the window shut. Quickly, she pulled out a clean shirt from her drawer and changed out of her milk soiled one. Karen opened the door and jumped when she saw the case worker standing there waiting. "Sorry," Karen said as she stepped out of the room with her soiled shirt in hand. "It's all yours."

The case worker moved slowly about the room, pausing once to glance out the window, and then moved to Robbie's room. When the inspection was finally done, the case worker informed Karen that she'd be back, unannounced, to check on Robbie's well being. Losing Robbie, even for just a handful of hours, was more than Karen could handle. He was everything to her. He was the only one in this great big world who Karen could say truly loved her. He didn't care about her past. The only thing that mattered to him was that his mommy loved him. Karen held him to her and rested her cheek against his soft sandy blonde hair, vowing that she would never drink again.

# CHAPTER SEVEN

..............................

## *Painting a Dream*

On the days that Karen wasn't working at the diner, she often worked with Jimmy doing odd jobs, while Robbie stayed with a babysitter or played in his make-shift playpen in the bed of Jimmy's pickup truck. June brought about warm weekends, Junebugs, and plenty of work for Jimmy. While Jimmy rolled roofing over an addition on Wicker's General Store, Karen began painting the new siding she had helped put up. She parked Jimmy's pickup next to the side of the building and handed Robbie some scraps of wood, two small paint brushes, and a set of Crayola washable paints, and then closed the tailgate of the truck.

Karen began making careful, deliberate sweeps with her paintbrush across the siding. Robbie looked up at her, then mimicked her, moving his brush in long, slow sweeps across his scrap of wood. Karen looked over her shoulder at him and smiled.

"Hey Picasso. Get movin'. We're burning daylight," Jimmy said, while peering down at them from the roof. Picasso, Karen thought to herself, was amazing. As she dipped her paintbrush into the tray, she thought about Monet, Kincaid, and Kahlo, but none of them moved her the way Francisco Oller could with his "Hacienda Aurora" painting. Closing her eyes, she could see the rich green fields, the swaying palm trees, and feel the tropical heat of the Puerto Rican sun, her mother's homeland, pouring over her. For a moment, she even thought she could hear the sounds of the barefooted farmers padding across the dirt roads along the fields. Sometimes, she wished she could escape inside that painting and lose herself among its bright, bold colors and sense of serenity. In that painting, she imagined herself walking hand and hand with her mother, just like they did when she was little. The summers she spent there with her mother and father were some of the most carefree and exciting summers in her life.

Painting the inside and outside of buildings for Jimmy seemed to be the closest she could get to using her creativity in a way that he approved. When she mentioned Campeche, Cole, Hannock, or other artists, Jimmy sneered. Painting, real painting, shouldn't be wasted on useless pictures, he told her. Time and energy were better spent on tangible things like houses, stores, and the like. Real artists painted houses; it was that simple.

Steve, though, was so different than Jimmy. It wasn't unusual for him to show up at Karen's dorm, ready to pose for her, or go wherever inspiration called her. Karen paused with her brush in the air and smiled at the thought of him, his mild manner and easy smile. He was so easy to love.

"What the hell are you smiling at?" Jimmy loomed over her, his shadow bleaching out the colors on the wall. Karen looked up, the smile slipping from her face, and shook her head.

"Nothing. Just smiling, that's all."

Jimmy regarded her a moment before going back to work. Later that night he threw her sketchbook and pencils on the floor to make room for his feet on the coffee table.

Once Jimmy finished the addition on the general store, word began to spread even more about his construction skills, and Karen's fine color choices didn't hurt his reputation any. Jude Wicker's son-in-law was so impressed by the quality of his work that he recommended Jimmy to John Winger, the owner of Rusty's Tool Barn. Winger already had three stores around the state, but was looking to open at least three more in Montana and possibly another two in Oregon and Wyoming over the next two years. He met with Jimmy, and though impressed with his work, was worried that a small time contractor wouldn't be able to meet his deadlines. Using his charisma, Jimmy convinced Winger to at least give him a shot, telling him that he had the resources necessary for the job. A meeting was set for the middle of the month for Jimmy to submit a proposal.

"Why did you tell him that you have all that stuff," Karen asked.

"Look, I went down to Joe's house the other day and checked out ebay. I found a used box truck dirt cheap. Joe's got ladders and some scaffolding, and he's already told me that he'd be interested in working with me, so that leaves me with picking up the truck, a few more nail guns, and another table saw."

"We don't have that kind of money. How are you going to pay for all that stuff?"

"You got some stock left, don't you? Can't you just sell off some of it? And then we could get a loan for the rest."

"My stock? Jimmy, I don't really have all that much—maybe six or seven thousand dollars worth—and that's supposed to be for Robbie when he turns eighteen." Karen thought about what little stock and savings she had left. All of it had been steadily draining away since leaving Massachusetts. She remembered how Lillian refused to sign it over to her after her father's death, worried that she would spend it foolishly. After a heated discussion, though, Lillian gave in, but not before reminding Karen that her dad would've wanted her to save her money to build a secure future. She wondered what Lillian would think about all this.

"Babe, it's an investment. This is something we can do together. Come on. Just think about it. Hell, I'd do it for you if you had a shot at a gig like this," Jimmy said.

"Six or seven thousand isn't going to buy you that used truck, Jimmy."

"Well, you've got your credit card. That will help close the gap, and I can get a loan for the tools."

Karen turned away and made a face, thinking about how Jimmy scorned the idea of her going back to school. Jimmy wrapped his arms around her and rested his chin on the top of her head.

"Just think, I'd be making enough money so you could spend more time with Robbie. You wouldn't have to work at the diner or anywhere—of course, I'd love to have you work with me, you know painting and stuff."

Karen thought about the moms and kids she passed at the park on her way home from work, and how she wished she could find more time to bring Robbie there. She thought about how more money would mean they could afford to send Robbie to preschool. It would do him some good to be around more kids his age. And of course, she owed Jimmy this. If it weren't for him, Robbie might not even be home with them. He could have been living with complete strangers, with some anonymous foster family. Turning to Jimmy, she took a deep breath and nodded.

For the first time in a long time, Jimmy was sober on a Saturday afternoon and in a good mood. With the prospect of a decent income, impressing Winger became his first priority. Jimmy shaved, got a haircut, and dressed in a pair of black pants and a light blue button up shirt that he ironed himself. He even went so far as to put on a thin, black tie and traded his tan work boots for a pair of shiny black shoes.

Teasing him, Karen kissed his smoothly shaven cheek, telling him that he looked good enough to eat. Jimmy smiled, and told her that he didn't mind being eye candy for her. "You know, you and Robbie are my world," he said as he leaned in to kiss her. As he headed out the door for his meeting with Winger, Karen felt for the first time since leaving Massachusetts that she finally belonged somewhere. Maybe this was all Jimmy needed. Maybe things would change. Maybe he'd be more like the guy she thought he was when they were first together, and not so consumed with jealousy and bitterness.

Karen thought about the first few months that she and Jimmy were together. She remembered how he would step quietly into the shower with her and wrap his strong arms around her swelling belly, his hands slowly following the gentle curve to her breasts. When they slept, he often held her close, the two of them so close together that they were almost one. Karen remembered the countless times she would awaken to his kisses on her belly, his stubbly chin tickling her skin, and whenever they made love, he was always so gentle. Maybe if he got this job, he wouldn't be so stressed. Maybe he'd be happy again. Maybe she could really grow to love him…

When Jimmy came home late that afternoon, he seemed hopeful, yet nervous. Taking part of the rent money, he went into town with the used box truck he'd bought through ebay and had it stocked with more tools. Afterwards, he spent the better part of the evening on the phone recruiting guys to work with him—should he get the contract.

The following Thursday, Jimmy left the house early to meet with Winger again. After dropping Robbie off at the babysitter's house, Karen headed to work. Shortly before one, Jimmy walked into the diner with Robbie in his arms. Karen paused with her mop in mid stroke and looked questioningly at him.

"I got it babe," he yelled with a grin covering his face ear to ear.

"Really?" Karen smiled. Robbie reached over and climbed into Karen's arms. As she held him on her hip, she leaned over and kissed him once on the forehead, then both cheeks, and once more on his nose. Robbie smiled and kissed her on the nose. Jimmy took the mop from Karen's hand and dropped it in a corner. Grabbing her wrist, he pulled her towards the door.

"Come on. Let's get out of here and go celebrate," he said as he continued to pull her towards the door.

"Jimmy, I've got to finish my shift. I've still got an hour and a half to go."

"Fuck that," he said leaning close enough for her to smell the beer on his breath. "You don't need to work here anymore, not with the money I'll be making."

Irene came out from the back room with a tray full of silverware wrapped in napkins and set it down on the counter. She looked over at Jimmy and rolled her eyes.

"Hey," Jimmy called to Irene, "she quits."

"Again?" Irene held her hands out, palms turned upward.

"Yah. You'll have to find yourself some other chick to work 'cause she ain't working here anymore."

Jimmy tugged on Karen's arm once more, his smile not quite a wide as it was moments ago. Karen turned to Irene, shrugged her shoulders and offered an apology with her eyes. As she walked out the door, she turned to look over her shoulder once more. Irene simply shook her head at her and turned back to the pile of silverware.

# CHAPTER EIGHT

......................................

## *A Bottle, A Boot, and A Fist*

Karen, Robbie, and Jimmy arrived home around eight after spending the afternoon at the zoo followed by dinner at the China Star. The smile on Karen's face faded as they pulled up to their house. Cars were parked in the muddy driveway and spread across the green, patchy lawn.

"What's all this?" Karen asked.

"I called the guys while you and Robbie were watching the show with zoo lady and the snow leopard and all those other animals she brought out, whatever they were." Jimmy slid a sleek, new cell phone out of his back pocket. "Called them up on my new cell," he said and flashed her a grin.

"You bought a cell phone? With what money?"

"Relax College. We're going to have plenty of money coming in soon. I put them on your card. I got you one too—you know one of them buy one phone, sign up for two years, get another phone free plans. It'll come in handy for work."

"Let's go. They're waiting for us," Jimmy jerked his head in the direction of the house. Karen leaned into the car and unbuckled Robbie. Cake played on the new stereo inside, and their thumping vibrations rippled under Karen's feet as she crossed the lawn. She didn't have to ask Jimmy to figure out where he got money to buy a new stereo—the envelope marked "rent." Jimmy jogged up the steps and pulled the door open, but Karen stopped at the bottom step as the smell of pot filled her nostrils.

"Who's smoking that crap in our house?"

"What? That? Don't worry. They got a window open," Jimmy said waving her off. Karen shook her head and turned around with Robbie in her arms. A couple of drinks were one thing, but now this? Jimmy pursed his lips, leaned over, and reached for her arm. "Don't be such a fucking priss," he said, pulling her towards the door. Sweating beer cans were scattered around the living room. Two bottles of vodka and a bottle of rum sat on the kitchen table, along with a case of cheap beer. Karen looked at Robbie. He buried his head between her shoulder and neck, and covered his ear with one free hand, while he held onto her tightly with the other. Karen glanced out the kitchen window towards Mrs. Bradley's house. Not a light was on.

"Jimmy, this isn't good for him. I don't want this stuff around him." She watched his expression tighten. "I mean, well, what about Mrs. Bradley? I don't want to give her any reason to start trouble."

"She ain't even home."

"Well I can't chance that. If they're going to do this, I'll take Robbie to the park for a little while. There's no way I'm going to chance Mrs. Bradley showing up next door and calling the cops again." Karen turned towards the door, but Jimmy caught her by the arm and held her in place.

"No, that'd be rude. Anyway, it's getting dark out and Robbie should go to bed, so you'll stay here with me and our guests," he said to her, his tone slightly mocking. "Now, just go tuck him in bed—and then come on out and be a good hostess."

Her mouth opened as if to speak, but then closed, knowing that she had to weigh her words carefully around him. It was like trying to step around shards of glass without getting cut.

"Hey, I almost forgot. I got this for you," Jimmy said, handing her a foil wrapped package. Karen glanced at the group of strangers that sat in her living room, coughing and laughing at stupid jokes.

"Well, go on. Open it," Jimmy said as he took Robbie from her arms. Hesitating a moment, Karen looked about once more—a glance at the idiots in her living room, a glance towards Mrs. Bradley's darkened house, a longer pause at Robbie's questioning face—before absentmindedly tearing the wrapping paper off. Beneath the foil were a sketchpad and a book on interior decorating.

"If I keep landing contracts like this, you could doodle out all the painting schemes." Jimmy's smile faded slightly when Karen didn't say anything.

"What? Don't you like it?"

"Yes, of course I like it. I'm just not comfortable with all these people in our house and around Robbie," Karen said, as she placed the pad and book on the counter and reached for Robbie.

"Hey, these are our friends, babe. Lighten up."

"No, Jimmy. These aren't my friends," she said quietly, trying to slow the pounding of her heart. "My friends wouldn't be smoking pot in my house and using my kid's Sippy cup as an ashtray." Karen waved her hand towards the living room.

"Huh. Is that so? Well, honey, that's 'cause you ain't got any friends." Jimmy grabbed her by the shoulder and spun her towards Robbie's room. "Don't be such a primadona. Get him to bed and get your ass back out here," he said, giving her a little shove. Jimmy reached for a couple of beers, popping the tops off both, and handed her one. Karen held the ice cold can in her hand, but after one look at Robbie, who laced his hands around her neck and stared at her with his usual wordless curiosity, she set it down. Karen looked from Robbie to Jimmy, and choking back her fear, shook her head; Robbie was worth keeping her promise. She turned and carried Robbie to his room. As she closed the door behind her, she could feel her pulse quickening. The room was stiflingly hot and the air reeked of stale smoke. She pushed open a window, hoping for a breeze, and sat down in the rocking chair. While she was humming quietly to him, with her head resting against his, Jimmy flung the door open and stood over them. His sturdy frame blocked out most of the light flooding into the room.

"Don't you ever fucking shut that door in my face again!" Jimmy leaned in towards her. "Now, put him in the crib and get out there. We have guests here, and I won't stand for you embarrassing me." His jaw was set in a rigid line and his face reddened.

"I can't afford to have Child Services here again. I'm not going to put Robbie through that," Karen said, as she continued to rock Robbie.

"That ol' bag isn't even home," Jimmy said, reaching for Robbie. He set Robbie down in the crib he had long since outgrown and waved an arm in the direction of Mrs. Bradley's house. "She ain't even home. It's dark over there."

"Her car's there," Karen said, pointing a finger towards her neighbor's.

Robbie began crying, and stretched his arms towards his mother, but when Karen took a step towards him, Jimmy blocked her path.

"Leave him. He'll be fine in a few minutes." Jimmy made a grab for her wrist, but Karen shook him off.

"I'll come out later, after he goes to sleep," she said, trying to step around him.

"You'll come out now and be a good hostess." Jimmy grabbed her firmly by the wrist. As she remembered the look on Robbie's face as the police took her away from him, panic grew inside of her. Karen pulled herself from Jimmy's grasp and folded her arms across her chest, while shaking her head. She couldn't bring herself to meet his stare, for fear that she had already crossed some invisible line.

"Please," she said, trying to steady her voice, "I'll come out in just a little bit. Just let me get him to sleep."

Jimmy stepped towards her, backing Karen up against the wall, until his face was just inches from her own.

"He's going to cry all night if you don't let me calm him down. Please." Karen placed her hands on his chest. Jimmy opened his mouth as if to say something, but instead turned around and walked out the door after giving her a dismissive shove.

Some forty minutes later, Karen tiptoed out of Robbie's room and into the kitchen. Casting a glance into the living room, she saw Jimmy laughing with his friends and tossing back a shot of rum. Slowly, she slipped out the door, looking for a momentary escape from the chaos inside. She zigzagged back and forth across the yard, picking up the empty beer cans off the lawn and setting them in a pile under the steps where they wouldn't be visible from Mrs. Bradley's house. Karen let out a sigh and sat down on the steps. She looked towards the fence that divided her yard from Mrs. Bradley's. All the lights were off. She was probably out with her friend playing bingo at the church in town. The neighborhood was far too quiet. Of course, with only five houses on a dead-end street, it often was quiet— except for when Jimmy had parties. Karen looked at her car and then stared at the road leading away from Jimmy's house. Somewhere on the other side of the country, she guessed Steve, Carol, and Lillian were going about their business. Maybe Steve was making love to another woman? Maybe Lillian had remarried, thankful to be rid of any ties to her? Maybe Carol had another best friend, a real best friend? Did they ever think about her?

"Hey," Jimmy said startling her, "the party's in here,"

"Honey, my head is aching. I'm just not in a partying mood right now."

"I'm just not in a partying mood right now," Jimmy said, mocking her words. "Fuck you! Don't feel like partying." He stepped down in front of her and bent his long frame over her, pointing a finger in front of her face. Instinctively, Karen's muscles stiffened in anticipation of his next move. "Do you know who these people are? No? Well, I'll tell you. These guys are my buddies. They're also gonna be working with me on this job. So College, to put it in language that you can understand, you are gonna show me some respect. My friends are your friends. Understand? Now get off your ass and get inside and be a good hostess!"

When Karen hesitated too long, Jimmy threw his glass against the railing, and reaching down, yanked her up off the steps by her arm and pushed her towards the door. Karen pulled her arm free and turned towards the door. Before she could grab the handle, Jimmy grasped the back of her pink and blue Hardy's Truckstop blouse and pulled her backwards.

"You bitch! Don't you start thinking that you can pull this shit with me." His voice was low and gravelly in her ear. Karen turned towards him, her pulse pounding in her head. All at once, she wished that Mrs. Bradley was home, yet knew that if she were she would surely risk losing Robbie.

"Jimmy, please. I can't do this anymore."

"Do what?" Jimmy followed Karen's gaze towards their neighbor's house.

"I can't do this. The parties, the drinking, all this," she waved her hand towards the pile of empties under the steps and jerked her head towards the house. "This isn't good for Robbie. I don't want him around this shit. He deserves more. Please. I don't want to lose him ever again."

"Nobody's coming down here again. That hag ain't even home," he said, jerking his chin towards the house next door. Karen looked up at him and stroked his cheek. Taking a deep breath, she spoke softly and with conviction.

"I won't do this anymore. Either they leave or we leave." Karen swallowed and stood up straight, readying herself for a verbal assault. Jimmy's jaw tightened. Before Karen could utter a single word, he grabbed her by the throat and slammed her against the side of the house.

"Are you threatening me? Huh, College? You think you can just waltz over and make the rules now?" Jimmy leaned his weight against her, making it hard for her to breathe. From inside the house, Jimmy could hear one of the guys calling his name.

"Please, Jimmy. Stop," she gasped. The pounding of her heart echoed inside her head so loudly that it seemed she couldn't even hear her own voice.

"Hey, Jimmy..." a voice called from inside the house again. Jimmy glanced towards the door, and released his hold. Karen brought her hand to her throat, but didn't dare move another muscle.

"All that I've done for you, and this is how you repay me? I took you and your bastard son in and made a home for you when no one else would."

"So we're a burden to you? Is that it? Then you'd be better off without us." Karen looked up at him, her eyes beginning to tear. "I'll get Robbie and then we'll be on our way," Karen took a tentative step towards the door, half hoping that he would throw her and Robbie out, half hoping he would beg her to stay. For a moment, Jimmy just stood there speechless. His hands clenched and unclenched by his sides. Karen's hand reached for the door handle. She took another tentative step, not wanting to pause for too long for fear that she would lose the courage to leave. Suddenly she lost her grasp on the door handle, and she was spinning around to meet the back of Jimmy's hand against her face.

"Please, Jimmy. Just let us go. You can keep everything. Take whatever you want...I'll give you the rest of my savings."

"Hey, Jimmy! You comin' in or what," one of Jimmy's friends called, poking his head out the door.

"Yah, hang on," he answered, hugging Karen to him. "Me and Karen just gotta check on the kid," Jimmy called back. His friend gave Jimmy the thumbs up and disappeared back into the house. With a firm grip on her arm, he walked her into the house and around the corner of the kitchen. "Who the hell do you think you are that you can buy me? Huh, College? You think that I need your fucking money?" He spoke just above a whisper, while squeezing his fingers onto her arm and causing her to wince. "You think that I ain't man enough to run things on my own? I am the head of the household, and as the head of household I say you aren't going anywhere. Neither is Robbie. If you walk out that door," he leaned in so close that their noses were practically touching, "so help me, you'll regret it."

"Hey you two, why don't you rent a room," one of Jimmy's buddies asked when he walked into the kitchen to see them standing toe to toe. "Hell, every time I see you two, you're nose to nose." His buddy laughed, while pulling another beer out of the fridge.

"Yah, we just might do that," Jimmy forced a laugh, but didn't take his eyes off Karen. "I'm just gonna mix College here a drink, so she can forget all about her day."

"College?" Jimmy's friend raised an eyebrow as he popped the top of his beer.

"Yah, Willy. Don't you know my little Karen's nickname? You know, she's the smart one in the family," Jimmy laughed and mixed Karen a rum and Coke. He held it out to her, his eyes still smoldering, and waited for her to drink it. Karen took it from him and drank. Jimmy's friend swallowed a mouthful of beer and then held his can up as if to toast a happy couple, before leaving the kitchen. Jimmy grabbed Karen's empty plastic cup that had been warped from too many times through the dishwasher. He mixed another rum and Coke, and shoved it towards her, splashing some of it on her shirt. His eyes were unrelenting. Karen took the cup from him and tried to keep her fear from rising.

"Have another drink. Maybe it will help you to stop being such an ungrateful, uptight bitch." Jimmy reached over and popped the top off a beer. Hesitantly, Karen sipped her drink. Things were different for her this night. Most times when she drank, she could forget about things and her problems would fade away, but tonight all she kept thinking about, even as her head began to feel fuzzy, was getting Robbie and driving away. Tonight, she couldn't afford to forget.

An unrelenting fear pressed on her that kept her from drinking too much too fast, a fear greater than Jimmy; she was afraid she was going to lose Robbie, and he was the only person on this earth who she knew truly loved her. Karen took another sip of her drink and followed Jimmy into the living room, but Robbie's face—the terrified look he had whenever Jimmy stormed about the house—dominated her mind. Closing her eyes, she held onto that image. Robbie was her courage, her catalyst. She had to do this for him.

As Karen began to get up from the couch, Jimmy grabbed hold of her arm. "Where you going?" he asked, his question sounding more like an accusation. Karen showed him her empty cup, took his empty can of beer from his hands, and walked towards the kitchen. As she stood in front of the fridge, she could still feel his watchful eyes on her. She pulled a bottle of Coke from the fridge, along with two more cans of beer, and set them next to the rum on the kitchen counter. Knowing Jimmy was still watching her, she poured some Coke into her cup and then added a shot of rum. Karen brought her cup to her lips and tossed back a mouthful, loving and hating the sweet sting that lingered on her tongue. She cast a glance in the direction of Robbie's room and tried to picture his sweet, smiling face, but the image that stayed in the forefront of her mind was the look of fright and confusion he had when the police took her away from him. She looked back towards the living room. Jimmy held her gaze for a moment before turning his attention back to his company. Quickly, Karen dumped half of her drink into the sink before taking another swallow. Savoring the flavor, but keeping Robbie's image in her mind, she forced herself to drink slowly. It was almost like trying to stop an orgasm right before it happened.

Setting two cans of beer on Jimmy's lap, Karen sat down beside him. Jimmy popped the top off one can and gulped it down. Becoming somewhat uninterested in her, he turned towards one of his buddies and started a conversation. Karen got up off the couch just as one of Jimmy's friends began circulating another joint around the room.

"Hey! Where you going, princess?" Jimmy grabbed hold of her belt loops.

"I need a refill," Karen answered and pulled away from him. Jimmy leaned forward and swatted her backside before taking a drag off a joint.

"Bring me some more beers, College. And some for my good friend, Tommy. Then bring that cute little ass of yours back over here." The two men laughed and passed the joint back and forth. Jimmy leaned back and closed his eyes for a minute.

In the kitchen, Karen took two more beers from the fridge. With shaking hands, she popped the top of one beer, then another, and set them on the counter. Glancing over her shoulder, she watched Jimmy take another hit. Karen refilled her cup with Coke, and knowing he would surely look over at her again, she picked up the bottle of rum and unscrewed the cap. When Jimmy looked away, Karen put the bottle back down on the counter and went back to the living room, hoping that Jimmy would pass out soon.

Without waiting for him to ask her, she popped off the top of another beer and handed it to him. He put his arm heavily around her and hugged her to him, only a tiny trace of anger still showing in his increasingly lazy eyes. One by one, Jimmy's friends headed out the door, the last one leaving sometime around 1a.m. Karen looked over at Jimmy. He stirred slightly, his arm slipping from around Karen's shoulder, his head resting lazily against the back of the couch. Carefully Karen stood up, swaying a bit, and walked into Robbie's room. From his doorway, she looked over her shoulder to the living room. Jimmy had slumped across the couch and was snoring. With shaking hands, Karen began gathering up some of Robbie's things, taking only what was necessary—his clothes, his teddy bear, and favorite blankie.

Quietly, she slipped from his room and went out the back door. She tossed the bag of his clothes onto the back seat and returned a moment later with a duffle bag with one change of clothes in it for herself. Tiptoeing, she went back into the house, stopping just long enough to see Jimmy still sleeping on the couch. Karen quietly stepped inside Robbie's room and slowly lifted him from the crib. When he opened his sleepy eyes, Karen put a finger to her lips hoping he wouldn't start crying. He looked up at her, smiled, and snuggled up against her chest, falling easily back to sleep.

As quietly as possible, Karen slipped out of the house and settled Robbie into his car seat. She leaned into the Mustang and placed his favorite bear on his lap, and then stepped back—right into Jimmy. Turning around with a start, she looked up at him towering over her five foot four frame. His bloodshot eyes blazed, and he looked as though he was going to erupt. Before Karen could utter a single word, he backhanded her. She fell against the car and Robbie began crying. His cries set off alarm bells in her head. With her keys still clutched in her fist, she spun towards Jimmy and raked the keys across his face. Stunned, he moved away and touched his face, feeling the blood trickle down it. Quickly, Karen pulled open the driver's side door and tried to get in. Jimmy threw himself against the door, crushing her arms and shoulders between the doorframe and door with his weight. Karen cried out in pain, feeling the air leave her lungs. Jimmy backed up and watched her slide to the ground. He grabbed her arm and pulled her to her feet. Then he brought his fist hard against the side of her face, splitting open her upper lip. She fell limply to the ground, the blood from her lip pooling together with the mud on the ground. When Karen got to her knees and began pulling herself up, Jimmy kicked her in the back. She fell back to the ground and rolled onto her belly, but Jimmy wasn't through. "Please, Jimmy…" was all she could say before he kicked her in the ribs, legs, and back. Mud flew off his unlaced work-boots with each blow. The taste of blood and dirt filled Karen's mouth. She rolled over slowly, gasping for air, and struggled to stand up. He watched her pull herself to her feet, a sickening sneer spreading across his face.

"I didn't say you could get up." He watched her grab hold of the open car door and try to stand up. Lifting a muddy boot up, he held it in the air for a moment, waiting for her to meet his eyes, and then kicked her in the knee, knocking her feet out from under her. Karen's eyes widened when she felt a searing pain shoot through her knee, as though the muscles were going to tear away from her body. Robbie's screams reached a fevered pitch, and as Karen clung to the door, trying to hold herself up, she saw his face soaked with tears. Jimmy grabbed Karen by her hair and threw her backwards onto the ground, then kicked the back door of the car shut.

"Shut up, you little bastard," he shouted before turning his full, black rage back on Karen. Pushing up onto her left knee, Karen tried once again to get up.

"Where do you think you're going, College?" He reached down, and yanking her up by her arm, dragged her across the lawn and up the steps. Karen stumbled against him, her right leg unable to support her any longer. Jimmy pushed her inside the house and slammed the door behind him. "It's time to teach you a lesson," he said as began undoing his belt. Reaching their bedroom, he swung up his foot and kicked the door open, sending splinters of wood everywhere. He shoved her backwards into the room, causing her to fall against the bureau and knock over the picture frames. He pulled off his shirt and leaned his sneering face an inch from hers. His breath was foul, hot, and moist, spit dotted Karen's face when he spoke.

"So College, you think you're so smart? Huh? You think you can just walk out on me with your bastard kid after all I've done for you? It's time to show you who the man of this house is!" He pulled her towards him, then grabbing her by the front of her pink and blue Hardy's Truckstop button-up shirt, he tore it open, sending a spray of pink and blue buttons across the room.

"Jimmy, no. Please don't do this," she cried through bloodied lips. Jimmy gave her a violent shove backwards. Karen crashed against the bureau, striking her head, and then slid limply to the floor. Reaching down, Jimmy scooped her up and threw her on their bed. Blood from the small gash in her right eyebrow streamed into her eye, making her vision blur. As Jimmy straddled her hips and began unzipping his fly, Karen remembered the cowboy—his cologne, his hands clamped around her wrists, the weight of his body on hers. "No, please no," Karen whimpered and gasped for breath. She struggled under his weight, trying to get up, but everything went black and still when he brought his fist up against the side of her head. Jimmy reached down and yanked her belt from her jeans.

"You'll see who makes the rules in this house," he said as he reached the buttons on her button-fly jeans. When Karen didn't respond or beg him to stop, he looked up. She lay unmoving, her eyes closed, one beginning to swell and form a deep purple around it. Jimmy slapped her face, and she began to moan. "Yah, I'll teach you a lesson, better than anything you learned at your fancy school, College. Yah, that's right. Open those pretty green eyes," he leaned in close and watched her expression as he grabbed her breasts, but the terror, the pleading, the desperation was gone, and in its place was emptiness. He sat upright and reached down towards the buttons on her jeans, tugging and cursing at them until he pulled the last one free. Laughing, he grasped her jeans and yanked them off her.

Karen just stared up at the ceiling, through her clouded vision, even as he pinned her wrists down beside her head and climbed back on top of her. Her breath came in sharp, staggered gulps as he leaned over and pressed himself against her, the button on his jeans scraping against her bare belly. The throbbing in her lip and eye beat in rhythm with the pounding in her chest. She could see Jimmy hovering over her, and make out a blurry sickening smile on his face. Jimmy laced his restless fingers around her bra straps and slowly tugged them off her shoulders. He unhooked her front-fastening bra and pushed the cups apart, his eyes never leaving her face. He ground himself against her crotch while grabbing her breasts, and even though her eyes were open, she remained expressionless and silent, save for the occasional hiccoughing gulp of air. Jimmy's eyes slowly trailed downward from her face, and as his gaze moved, the sneer on his face evaporated. He slowly started backing away as his eyes wandered across her bare breasts and belly that were stained with his bloody hand prints. He took in a sharp breath of air, suddenly becoming aware of the smell of their struggle, her blood and sweat that tainted the air.

His mouth opened and closed, but no words escaped, and as if suddenly realizing what he had done, he took his hands off her and drew them to himself. His knuckles were smeared with blood. Slowly, he turned his hands over palm-side up; blood and dirt covered both hands. Looking back at Karen, his hands began to shake. Her eyes began to close again. Jimmy got off her quickly and stepped away.

"Oh God, oh God. Karen, oh God." Jimmy looked up at the ceiling and the back to Karen. "Baby, baby," he said while stroking her cheek. "I'm so sorry. Oh God. Karen, baby, open your eyes. Please baby. I didn't mean to hurt you." She opened her eyes and moaned as he scooped her limp body up in his arm and held her on his lap. "I'm gonna fix this. I'm gonna take care of you and make you all better," he said as he kissed her forehead and let his tears roll down his cheeks. Holding her against his chest, he carefully slid what remained of her tattered blouse off her unresisting body and then drew back the bed sheets before laying her down. When he left the room momentarily, Karen thought she could hear the fridge open, then bang shut, followed by water running. "Robbie," she whispered before losing consciousness.

Some time later, Karen felt a wet cloth dabbing at her face. She opened her eyes. Jimmy carefully washed the blood from her face, belly, and chest. Then he placed a bandage over her right eyebrow. When he tried to wipe away the crusted blood from her lip, it began to trickle again. Karen flinched at his every touch. Taking a nightgown from the bureau, he carefully slipped it over her head and laid her back down. He wrapped ice inside a cloth and held it to her lip.

"I'm so sorry. I'm gonna make it alright, baby. You'll see. I'll fix everything."

"Robbie," Karen cried softly.

Jimmy nodded his head and left the room. Karen could hear him talking. "It's okay now little buddy. Mommy fell down, but she's going to be just fine. Everything's gonna be okay." Soon after, Jimmy came in with him in his arms. Robbie's face was red and puffy from crying so long, and he continued to hiccup air in shuttered breaths. Gently, Jimmy laid Robbie next to Karen, and immediately, Robbie scooted away from him. Jimmy looked at the two of them, one beaten and bruised—the other cowering from his presence. Shaking his head, he backed out of the room, and wearing only his blood-stained jeans and dirty boots, went out the door, leaving a trail of muddy footprints behind. A moment later, Karen heard dirt kick up as his truck sped out of the driveway.

Karen awoke as the sun rose and began to stream in through her window. Rolling carefully out of bed, her body was met with pain. Hanging on the bureau and then leaning against the wall, she made her way to the bedroom doorway. Squinting to see out of the eye that wasn't swollen completely shut, she looked around the living room. Jimmy was nowhere in sight. Gingerly, she limped forward, each step erupting a fresh wave of pain in her knee. Robbie followed behind her, clutching the back of her nightgown with both hands. Karen limped into the kitchen, drawing in sharp breaths that ripped through her ribs every time she moved.

An uncapped bottle of rum still sat on the counter glimmering in the sunlight that shone through the window. Karen picked it up and swallowed a mouthful straight from the bottle. Its sting bit into her split lip, yet the amber liquid felt so good going down. She took another swallow, and then another and another, until the pain began to dull slightly.

Looking out the window, she saw that Mrs. Bradley's house was still dark. She could only wonder what would have happened if she had been home. Karen picked up the bottle and took another swig. Turning to look over her shoulder, she saw Robbie still clutching the back of her nightgown. She looked down at him. His eyes were puffy and red, his breaths still interrupted by occasional hiccupping shudders. He clung to her nightgown, staring up at her wordlessly. Karen rubbed the top of his head, whispering, "It's going to be okay, Tiger. We're leaving." Standing at the top step, she saw the glint of her keys lying in the dirt near her car. Taking Robbie by the hand, Karen hobbled down the stairs and out the door.

With shaking hands, Karen fumbled with Robbie's car seat until she heard the click of the belt. She turned around fearing that Jimmy would be standing there, his fists clenched and ready to punish her, but he was nowhere to be seen. The entire street seemed to still be asleep. Carefully, she eased herself behind the wheel and started the engine. Looking up, she caught sight of herself in the rearview mirror. Crusted blood had dried on her eyebrow, cheek, mouth, and chin. Both eyes were swollen, one completely shut, and her hair was matted with blood. She looked at Robbie, who just stared at her blankly, while hugging his teddy bear to himself. Her pulse quickened at the thought of anyone seeing them now. Karen shook her head and took in a deep breath. Grunting through the pain, she forced her right foot down on the pedal and drove away. Her vision blurred and her head kept nodding listlessly forward. Less than five miles from home, Karen's car drifted lazily across the median and off the road, hitting a parked car on the side of the street.

Resting his head against the back of his seat, Officer Taggerty was jolted awake when a fiery red Mustang ground to a halt against the side of his cruiser, snapping off his driver's side mirror in the process, and caused him to spill his lukewarm coffee all over his shirt and pants.

# CHAPTER NINE

..........................

## *Beyond the Limit*

When Karen came to, the glow of red and white lights flickered across her dashboard. Robbie, unhurt but frightened, cried as the EMTs slid him out of the car, car seat and all, and then moved him into the back of the ambulance. She lifted her head off the steering wheel and began to call out to him. A set of gloved hands gently clasped the sides of her head and a man's voice reassured her that the little boy was fine, to just stay still. A fire truck pulled up alongside of the car and one of the firefighters slid onto the passenger seat beside her. Carefully, he slid a short board behind her back, while another one placed a collar around her neck. "Damn," he said noticing the bruises on her face and arms. "Looks like someone got to her before the car crash did," he said as he fastened the short board strap in place. A sharp pain rippled through her body as they carefully slid her across the seat and moved her onto a stretcher.

Once inside the ambulance, the EMTs continued assessing and treating her injuries. A paramedic sat to her right and held her outstretched arm, palpating for a good vein to use for an IV. The medic to her left divided his time between trying to console Robbie and obtain Karen's blood pressure. With both arms stretched out to either side of her, she felt as though they were preparing her for crucifixion. Somewhere between sliding in and out of consciousness, she could hear Robbie crying. Karen tried to turn towards him, to offer a comforting word or to grasp his hand, but the plastic collar around her neck prevented her from moving her head. She tried to call his name, but couldn't tell if he could hear her or not, or if she had even been able to get the words past her bloodied lips.

Officer Taggerty stepped into the ambulance and appeared over her, leaning in close and speaking louder than necessary. She wished he would just shut up and get away from her. Robbie was crying and needed her. Couldn't any of them see that? "Ms. Black, do you understand your rights?" he was saying. Karen mumbled "yes" and began to cry.

Sometime within the fog of events, the ambulance pulled away from the scene and Robbie quieted somewhat. Karen awoke to a paramedic leaning over her with a stethoscope, listening to her respirations. As he moved the stethoscope across her chest and along her ribs, Karen tensed and wanted to push him away. Instead, she found herself a prisoner of the ambulance cot. Backboard straps crisscrossed over her, starting at her shoulders and going to her waist and down across her bare legs. Another paramedic's face peered over the cot, staring at her and saying something, his voice low and comforting. The other one leaned over her and waved a penlight back and forth in front of her eyes. He murmured something and began to scribble on his clipboard.

Despite the roaring of the diesel engine, occasional wailing of the siren, and the constant clanking of the oxygen cylinders, Karen could still hear Robbie's hiccupping sob, "Mo…Mo…Mommy…Mo…." She wanted to hold him, to tell him that everything would be all right. There was nothing in the world that she wanted more than to believe that everything was going to be all right. Her lips moved, but no sound came from her. Staring up at the ceiling, she watched the IV bag swing back and forth above her head, until all the sounds seemed to fade away into the distance and the light went from gray to black.

Karen awoke beneath the bright white lights in the emergency room to the sound of a woman's voice, "Karen, Karen,…open your eyes." A doctor was hovering over her, gently touching her shoulder. The doctor turned her attention briefly from Karen to a nurse that stood nearby.

"Let's run blood work, x-rays on the chest, right leg, her arms, and do a CT scan of her head." Turning back to Karen, she leaned in closer, smelling of perfume and latex. "Karen, how much have you had to drink today," she asked, her voice full of authority and importance.

"Robbie? Where's Robbie?" Karen asked, her eyes darting back and forth, hoping to catch sight of him.

"He's fine. He's in good hands," the doctor answered while scribbling notes on a chart. She looked up from her notes to Karen. "Karen, how much have you had to drink?"

Karen squinted against the pain that still shot through her body, and feebly answered, "I don't know. I don't know…"

"Have you taken any drugs, legal or otherwise? I need an honest answer, so we can properly treat you. Have you taken any drugs?"

Karen feebly shook her head and began to sob.

# CHAPTER TEN

·······················

## *A Second Chance*

Karen tried to shake the memory of that night from her head, but Robbie's too quiet nature and genuine distrust of people served as a constant reminder of her past. Robbie continued to peer out the rear window all through the drive across Minnesota and didn't even fall asleep once throughout the afternoon. When they crossed the Wisconsin line, Robbie's attention turned from the window to his belly.

"Mommy, I'm hungry," he said rubbing his stomach.

"Me too."

After driving another thirty minutes, Karen was beginning to think that she was going to have to stay on the road for an eternity before finding some place to eat, and that's when she saw a large Friendly's Restaurant sign looming in the distance. Easing into the right lane, Karen down-shifted and made her way off the highway.

They pulled into the Friendly's parking lot a little after one-thirty. Except for a few cars, the lot was empty. Without anyone in line in front of them, they were seated right away. The waitress handed Robbie a pack of crayons, along with a placemat to color on, and then paused for a moment. "Here," she said setting down another placemat and a pack of crayons. "Maybe Mommy would like to color, too."

"Wow! Mommy, you got crayons too! Mommies don't get crayons, but you did, so that makes you lucky." Robbie kneeled on his seat and dumped the crayons onto the table. Karen smiled at him, and thought about just how lucky she really was.

∽

Karen was lucky, the judge told her as she sat in court, her fractured ribs aching, knee in a brace, and stitches in both her upper lip and eyebrow. Yup, she was lucky. She had two choices, he told her: Go to jail, or go to rehab. Although neither appealed to her, she opted for the one that would get her back to Robbie quicker. It was funny, though, she thought as the judge went into his speech. Jimmy beat the shit out of her, and was walking free while she was being sent off to rehab. I guess Jimmy was right. It can't hurt to have friends on the force.

"…and therefore you are to leave immediately for the Percy Treatment Center for the recommended stay of eight weeks. Upon completion of your eight weeks, we will reconvene to discuss your ability to provide a safe and loving home for your young son," the judge was saying. He gave her a stern look, and then he reminded her one more time that the only reason she was being given this opportunity to go to rehab, instead of jail, was due to the circumstances of her car accident. Rehab, the judge told her, would be the best thing for her. Karen nodded, ready to do whatever it took to get Robbie back.

The Percy Treatment Center was located an hour north of Helena on a working farm. As the bus made its way up the dirt road, Karen stared out the window at the array of farm animals. Sheep dotted the fence line along the road, and in the pasture, horses munched lazily on patches of green grass. The bus, turning to the left, slowed down to make the tight curve of the driveway, its noisy engine scattering several chickens that were pecking the ground.

"You've got to be kidding me," Karen said to no one in particular. When the bus lurched to a stop at the top of the driveway, she slid her backpack over her shoulder, picked up her crutches, and hopped awkwardly down the steps.

The air was filled with the stifling smell of manure ripening under the hot, late June sun. The chickens returned to pecking at the ground and began clucking confidently as they approached the passengers. Karen wrinkled up her nose, waving a hand in front of her face, and tried not to breathe in too deeply.

"Oh, don't you worry any. You'll get used to that farm fresh smell after a couple of weeks," said a woman wearing a badge with the name Myrna on it. She introduced herself and walked Karen, along with the other passengers, to the main building. Once inside, the Admissions Counselor named Neil asked all the "guests" to bring their bags forward for inspection before checking into their rooms. Great, she thought to herself, hanging out with drug addicts for eight weeks. Exhausted and in pain, Karen leaned her crutches against the seat beside her and eased herself down in a chair.

Her ribs still throbbed where Jimmy had kicked her, fracturing one rib and bruising several others. On her right leg, she wore a brace that prevented her from bending at the knee. She was lucky, the doctor said explaining her theory of luck, that she was fortunate to only have severely strained the ligaments around her knee and not to have torn them. The ribs would heal soon enough, and the pain wasn't intolerable—so long as she didn't laugh, cry, cough, sneeze, or hiccough too hard. The only scars she would be left with were a small one through her right eyebrow, hidden by her long hair, and a small zigzag that went through her upper lip.

She leaned her head back against the wall and closed her eyes, all the while wondering what Robbie was doing, when her name was called. "Karen Black, please step forward," the guy named Neil called out unenthusiastically. Karen let out an exasperated breath and hobbled towards the desk, while he tapped his finger on the counter and waited impatiently for her. Karen slid her backpack off, pausing to press her hand against her tender ribs, and then dropped it onto the counter. With a roll of her eyes, she turned back towards her seat. An exaggerated clearing of the counselor's throat made Karen turn back around.

"Purse too," he said, again jabbing his finger repeatedly on the countertop. Karen let out a huff, hobbled back towards the desk, and dropped her purse directly in front of his narrow, pointy finger. He unzipped it and carelessly dumped out its contents onto the counter. A bottle of pills rolled across the counter, which he quickly snatched up. Holding it directly in front of his face, he looked over the top of his glasses with a frown and eyed Karen.

"Codeine, hmmm. Well, my dear, that is certainly not on our list of acceptable items. These, on the other hand, are," he said holding two sanitary napkins with his dainty fingers, his pinkies extended skyward.

"I have a prescription for that," Karen said, pointing to the bottle.

"No, no my dear. This," he said holding the bottle up and pointing to the label, "is contraband."

"Contraband? You're treating me like I'm some sort of drug addict. Look," Karen said pointing to the label. "See the label? Karen Black. Take one, three times per day as needed for pain." When his expression remained unfazed, Karen's irritation grew. "You can't take that from me! It's my prescription!"

"I'm sorry honey. It's got codeine in it. Therefore, you cannot have it. It's just not what an addict needs. Now," he said, returning all but the prescription bottle, "you may have the rest back."

"I'm not a drug addict!"

"Sweetheart," he said looking up from her intake form, "alcohol is a drug."

"I've got a fractured rib, strained ligament in my knee, and enough bruises to cover a small town, and you're going to take my prescription," Karen said, her voice elevating to a fevered pitch, while fighting back the tears that were stinging her eyes.

"Darling, you don't need this. What you need is mind over matter, and if that doesn't work, you can see the nurse for Tylenol and icepacks."

"Leo Kazokowski, please step forward," he called. Karen stood there in disbelief, and when he saw her still standing there, he waved her away with quick little jerks of his dainty hands. Karen shook her head and limped back to her seat, swearing under her breath.

The night was long and lonely. No matter what position she tried, Karen couldn't get comfortable in a foreign room. A searing pain throbbed back and forth in her ribs, and every time she tried to habitually draw her knees in close to her belly, her right leg protested. "Damn it," she groaned, wishing she had her prescription, or a shot of rum, anything to dull the pain in her body and make her forget that Robbie was living with some strange family while she was trapped here. Sometime after two in the morning, she finally succumbed to sleep, laying flat on her back with her pillow propped against her side and a blanket rolled up under her leg.

Jumping, she awoke when an all too cheery voice came over the intercom at seven announcing breakfast. Karen grunted as she rolled out of bed, a sharp pain in her ribs reminding her that this wasn't a nightmare; it was her reality. Limping into the bathroom, she turned on the shower and stepped in. Her whole body felt weak. Her hands shook when she held them in front of her. She turned the water up, but her hands still shook. One shot of rum, just one shot. That's all she'd need. Just enough to take the edge off, to stop the shaking. She would give just about anything right now to feel numb, to pretend that Robbie was just at a sleepover, not in a foster home. Oh, what she'd give to feel the sweet sting of rum rolling down her throat. Just thinking about it made her mouth water with desire.

The day started out the way Karen figured all typical rehabs began, the way they began in movies: Breakfast followed by orientation and introductions, then the all too famous self-realization, where all the residents would gather and one by one confess their deadly sins, while some counselor sat there nodding, prodding them along. The first resident in line was Mitch. He was the tough guy, a heroin addict who took to beating up anyone who got in the way of his next high. Then there was Marlene who smoked anything she could get her lips around. Next was Derek, a methamphetamine user who popped pills into his mouth like they were Tic Tacs and washed them down with Jim Beam. And then, last but certainly not least, was Lacy—a cocaine junky. Karen rolled her eyes, folded her arms across her chest, and stared out the window while they all took turns talking until, at last, the room was silent.

"Karen," the counselor turned to her. Karen turned around and saw all the expectant faces staring at her, waiting for her to spill her guts. She shook her head and said, "This is ridiculous. I don't belong here." It was as if someone let a parrot loose in the room, when one by one, they all started claiming that they didn't belong here and began snickering. The counselor held up her hand and when the group quieted down, she turned back to Karen.

"Well Karen, would you like to tell us why you're here?"

Karen shook her head and leaned back uncomfortably in her chair, her arms still folded tightly across her chest. "This is bullshit! I get beat up and sent here, while my asshole ex-boyfriend walks free." Karen stared at the floor and didn't offer another word the rest of the morning.

After lunch, all the residents were assigned to jobs on the farm. Karen followed the group out to the barn, where Gabriel, the Activities Director, assigned everyone to a task. Some went off to mend fences, some went to the chicken coup to collect eggs and replenish the water for the chickens, while others went off to groom the horses. Karen leaned heavily on her crutches and pressed a hand against her tender ribs. Smiling, Gabriel set a stool and a bucket down on the ground in front of her.

"What's this for? Am I going to husk corn or something?" Karen gave him a sarcastic smile.

"You'll see," he answered with a wink and walked away. He returned a moment later leading a large black and white cow over to her. Karen's eyebrows lifted and she covered her mouth to stifle a laugh.

"Right. A cow. You're kidding."

"Have a seat," he gestured to the stool in front of her. Then he set the bucket down on the ground in front of her. "It's simple. Grab hold here," he said taking hold of the teat, "and pull down, like so." He repeated the motion a couple more times, each pull squirting milk into the bucket.

"I am not touching that," Karen said laughing. Gabriel smiled, reaching for her hands, and placed them around the teats. Holding his hands over hers, he began moving her hands in an up and down motion as if he were teaching a five year old how to form letters: Down, up, down, up. Karen grimaced, but continued working the teat until she finally managed to get a few quick squirts of milk in the bucket. After several pulls, the bottom of the bucket was covered with warm milk. The cow snorted and slapped her tail back and forth, making Karen jump. Gabriel laughed and repositioned her hands, beginning the motion once again.

Every resident was assigned a different job each day, and each time they began, Gabriel reminded them just how important it was for them to be part of the larger picture. All their actions had consequences, and every one of the residents was given the responsibility of caring for or cleaning up after some animal, or mending and maintaining the farm in one respect or another. This, Gabriel said, would teach them patience, responsibility, and most of all, self-worth. Those who didn't keep up with their daily chores would lose nightly phone privileges. Karen didn't grumble; she just worked, swore, and sweat. Getting used to life without drinking was hard enough, but not being able to see Robbie or hear his sweet voice every night was more than she could bear.

Every Sunday Robbie came up with Irene, who had made arrangements with Karen's case worker and Robbie's foster family, to visit for a couple hours. Each time Karen saw him, she tried but failed to stop the flood of tears from her eyes. His fourth birthday was only two days away, but for the first time since he was born, Karen wouldn't be able to be with him on his big day. The thought of Robbie spending his birthday with a strange family killed her. Did they know that his favorite cake was white, not chocolate? Did they know that Spiderman was his all time favorite super hero? That he loves orange juice, but hates soda because he doesn't like the fizz? No, chances are they didn't know any of this. Still, Karen wondered if he liked them. She wondered if they tucked him in at night and read him a bedtime story, wondered if he stayed awake at night thinking about her, wondered if he did in fact even miss her.

Sitting at a table on the outside deck, Karen glanced at her watch and scanned the parking lot for any sign of them. Just beyond the bend of the road, Karen saw a small plume of dust—a sure sign that a car was bumbling its way up to the parking lot. A moment later, she saw Irene's car come into view. As the car pulled into the parking lot, Karen drew in her breath and held it there. The moment she saw him climb out of the car, Karen let out her breath and blinked back tears. Robbie was smiling and holding Irene's hand. They were laughing about something. Maybe he didn't miss his mommy. Maybe he was happier now that he was in a home that wasn't consumed by anger and violence.

When Robbie caught sight of Karen, he pulled his hand from Irene's grasp and ran up the walkway. Charging like a miniature bull, he ran with his arms outstretched in front of him until he collided with her at the top of the walkway. Karen scooped him up and covered him with kisses, unable to keep her tears from spilling onto his shirt. After a moment, she leaned over and hugged Irene, thanking her again for bringing Robbie up to see her.

"Oh no problem, honey," Irene said. "Now if you'll excuse me, I've got just about three hours to hit the shops in town. I'll see you both in a few hours." With that, Irene turned back towards her car and left.

"Hey Tiger," Karen said turning to Robbie, "I know your birthday isn't for a couple more days, but I got an early birthday present for you." She picked up a plain brown box off the table and handed it to him. Robbie opened up the box and peered in. His mouth formed a big "O" when he saw a Little Tykes farmhouse, along with a cow, pig, two chickens, a horse, and a couple sheep inside the box. "Wow!" He said when he saw the farmer and tractor that came with the play set. They walked around the farm together, Robbie stopping often to compare his plastic chickens to the brazen ones that seemed to follow them everywhere. Together they laughed and played until the bell chimed at four o'clock, signaling the end of visiting hours. Hesitantly, Karen walked him back to the deck where she found Irene waiting.

"Mommy, will you be home for my birthday?"

"No Tiger. I'm afraid I won't, but I'll be home real soon, and we'll be together again," she said, putting on a brave face and fighting back tears. Like every Sunday, neither Karen nor Robbie could ever part without crying.

"You're doing the right thing, honey," Irene whispered in Karen's ear while hugging her. "This is going to help you make a better life for the two of you." Karen nodded and wiped tears from her cheek, then hugged

Robbie to her.

"I'll be home and we'll be together again real soon. That's a promise." Karen kissed his nose, cheeks, and the top of his head before handing him over to Irene. She stood in the driveway and watched them until Irene's car disappeared from sight. After a few minutes, Karen drew in a breath and went back inside.

Missing Robbie's birthday was harder than going a month without drinking and it just seemed to add to her list of failures. If she hadn't tried to leave Jimmy, hadn't left work early that day, hadn't gotten into her car after Jimmy beat her, maybe she could have been home for his birthday. The list of what ifs went on and on. Knowing that she couldn't go back in time, she focused on the future. She'd be a better mom, get the hell away from Jimmy, and find a place for just her and Robbie. She'd never put Robbie through this hell again. Karen promised herself that she would do everything possible to get Robbie back. If it meant going to stupid group meetings, personal counseling sessions, and breathing in the stench of manure every day, so be it.

She couldn't help but notice, though, that her hands had finally stopped shaking. But still, nearly every night her cravings crept into her dreams and clouded her mind whenever things got too quiet during the day. With every Coke, she longed for rum. Anytime she cracked a bottle of soda open and heard the familiar "pssst," she thought of the sweet and sour of hard lemonade. Getting a drink in this place, though, was about as easy as breaking into Fort Knox. She couldn't even get a cup of *real* coffee. "No stimulants whatsoever," the staff reminded her whenever she complained. With a roll of her eyes and an audible huff, Karen poured herself a cup of decaf coffee and told herself, "Fine. I can do this." Robbie was all that mattered. Rum? Coffee? Who needed them?

The following Sunday when Robbie came to visit, a couple of the residents, Lacy and Derek, were walking past when they spotted Karen and Robbie sitting in the shade of a maple tree. Derek bent over and extended a hand to Robbie.

"Hey there, little guy. I'm Derek," he said holding his hand out to him. Robbie's smile vanished and he scooted up against Karen.

"I'm sorry Derek. He's a pretty shy kid," Karen said as she placed her arm around Robbie's shoulder. With a smile and a shrug of his big, broad shoulders, Derek waved and continued on his walk with Lacy.

The next morning, Karen sat in group session and listened, while those that wanted to speak about their addiction talked. Her life was her life and she didn't feel the need to spill it out to anyone here. She just sat there, picking at her fingernails and listening absent-mindedly until Lacy began to speak. Lacy talked about her addiction, how it lead to her stealing money from her own child and when her sixteen year old daughter confronted her, she slapped her repeatedly, telling her never to call her a thief or a liar. It wasn't the first time she hit her, Lacy said, but it was the last. "…and that was the last time I saw her. My ex got full custody of Jenny, and I haven't seen her in almost a year. She doesn't want anything to do with me," Lacy said with a shake of her head. Karen rolled her eyes and shook her head.

"Don't you roll your eyes at me. You're followin' right on my heels, child," Lacy pointed a finger at her.

"No. Not quite. I never hit my kid, and never have and never will do drugs."

"Honey, wake up. Alcohol is a drug. Don't try to pretend you're anything special. You're just as fucked up as the rest of us."

"I never said I was anything special. I just don't go around smacking my kid and spending his allowance on frickin' cocaine. I never stole a dime so I could have a drink!"

"No, maybe not. You're just dumb enough to sit back in some drunken stupor, while some crazy-ass man beats the living shit out of you—all while your little boy looks on! I saw that look in his eyes yesterday when we came over. He thinks every man that comes near is going to hurt you!"

"Jimmy never hit Robbie, not once," Karen leaned forward, wanting to jump up and slap this woman. Who the hell was she to talk?

"No, just scared him so damned much that your kid's a mute. Doesn't even say a single word to anybody but you. Hell, he barely even looks at anyone. Just sits there clinging to you," Lacy said. Karen sat back and folded her arms across her chest, turning her gaze towards the window.

"I mean, girl, just look at you," Lacy continued. "You come limpin' your sorry ass in here on day one, stitches barely out of your lip, tryin' to hide all those bruises on your arms and legs. You don't think you might have something to do with the fact that your kid don't want to talk? Girl, if you can't see that, then you must be high right now," Lacy sat back, mimicking Karen's body language.

Karen's mouth opened, but only drew in air that held tight in her throat. Her eyes burned. She turned away, unable to look at Lacy. Hot, wet tears slid down her cheeks and onto her arms. She wanted to hold Robbie, to make everything up to him, but because of her, Robbie was living with complete strangers.

"Hey, you ain't all that bad, just blind," Lacy said, her voice softening. "Don't be stupid and wait until it's too late. Girl, I waited. I lied to myself. Kept saying it was the world that was messed up, not me. It wasn't my fault. I was just a victim. Then when I finally got around to seeing that the problem started with me, not everyone else, it was too late. Jenny won't even speak to me now. She don't answer my calls or my letters...hell, it's like I don't even exist."

The room was quiet, and Karen could feel the uncomfortable stares of everyone in the room, but she couldn't meet their eyes. She bit down on her bottom lip to keep it from trembling and continued to stare out the window.

"Hey, you don't want to lose your kid over this," Lacy said. "A drink ain't worth this. You ain't ever going to get better until you accept that you have a problem."

Karen wiped her wet cheeks with the palm of her hand, and still staring out the window, nodded. "Okay," the counselor chimed in, "I think we're just about out of time, so we'll reconvene tomorrow." Derek and a couple other members of the group gave Karen a pat on the back as they left the room, but Lacy hung back and waited. Karen stayed in her seat, picking at her fingers, and looking down at the floor. Lacy got up from her seat and moved to the empty one beside Karen.

"It's hard to hear. I know it. I didn't want to hear it either, but I had too. It's just too bad it took so damned long for it to sink into my head," Lacy said quietly. "We ain't perfect and we never will be, but we can at least do better. Hell, this is my second time coming here, and I just got this notion in my head that if I can do this, hell, I can do anything. Maybe then Jenny would at least talk to me," Lacy said, while Karen remained silent. After a minute or two, Lacy stood up and turned towards the door. "You know," Lacy said, pausing in the doorway, "the hardest thing for me was to ask for help." Before she stepped from the room, Karen reached over and grabbed her arm. Lacy turned to her questioningly. Karen looked at her, but didn't know what to say. Lacy nodded and gave Karen's hand a gentle squeeze before leaving.

Somehow, the days that followed didn't seem quite as long. Something happened that day, and life didn't feel so impossible. Later during the week, Karen limped across the cafeteria with her tray and saw an open seat next to Lacy and Derek. Lacy smiled and pulled out a chair for her.

"How's Robbie?" Lacy asked as Karen sipped at her chicken noodle soup.

"He's good, I guess," she set her spoon down on the table and shrugged, then picked at her sandwich. "Last time he came up to visit, he told me that his foster mother—God, I hate the sound of that—well, she took him and her daughter to that big water park up north. He kept telling me how much fun it was and how they played all day long." Karen picked up a spoonful of soup and then let it roll off her spoon back into the bowl. "I don't know. I guess he's happy, happier than when he was home with me anyway." She tapped her spoon against the table.

"What? You think just because he's having some fun that he don't miss you?" Lacy shook her head and laughed.

"What's so funny?" Karen looked up at her with annoyance.

"You, that's what's so funny. Dear Jesus if you could only see how funny it looks when he comes to visit. He's like this crazed little bull charging up the walkway, and he's always got this big ol' smile on his face when he sees you. Not happy to see you? Girl, you been smoking the devil's lettuce or something? That boy's absolutely crazy about you!" Lacy patted her back and laughed. "Now go on and eat your soup and sandwich before we get called back out to the cow pen." Karen shook her head and smiled. Yes, Robbie did look like a little bull charging up the walkway.

As the weeks passed, Karen felt more and more ready to start a new life for her and Robbie. She could do this. She knew she could. When the eighth week came along and everyone packed up their belongings to leave and make space for the next group, Lacy stopped Karen before she boarded the bus.

"Hey Karen," she said holding out a small package to her, "I thought this might help you any time the rum devil tries to get you." Karen smiled and pulled the paper off. It was a handmade wooden 3½ by 5 picture frame with an inscription written in calligraphy that said, "Mommy, I love you. Together we can be strong." Robbie's picture was inside the frame.

"Wow, thank you," Karen said and hugged Lacy. "But how'd you get a picture of Robbie?"

"Hah! That's the funny part. I conned that cranky old Admissions Counselor into copying Robbie's picture from the one in your wallet. I figured you'd have one."

"Neil? You mean Captain Contraband? You actually got him to do that for you?" Karen looked at Lacy in disbelief. Lacy nodded proudly and put her arm around Karen. "Thanks for everything," Karen said as she picked up her backpack from the ground. "Promise me something."

"What's that, hon?"

"Don't ever give up on Jenny. She'll come around sooner or later," Karen said, putting a hand on her shoulder. Lacy drew in a breath and nodded. "I promise you that. I'll never give up," she pulled Karen into her arms and hugged her tight.

"Go on," Lacy said waving her towards the bus. "Your boy's waiting for you." Karen climbed aboard the bus and waved goodbye to Lacy. Soon, she hoped, she would have Robbie back in her arms—not just for a couple hours, but forever. Still, fear and doubt weighed heavily on Karen. Though it had lessened somewhat, her cravings continued to slip into her unconsciousness—the sweet sting of the rum, the dreamy feeling it gave her as it settled in her blood, the gentle letting go of things as they faded from her mind. The bus pulled away and stirred her from her daydreams, taking her away from not only the smell of manure ripening in the August sun, but also the security that she had grown so accustomed to.

Karen leaned her head against the glass and stared out the window at aspen trees and the white lines that flashed by as the bus rolled down the highway. How did it all come to this? It seemed that not so long ago she was circled in Steve's warm arms, laughing with Carol, and talking baseball with her dad. Dancing further into her memories, she thought about Mami. Every time she thought of Mami, Lillian's words invaded her mind. Her mother, the woman who brought her into this world, held her to her breast and nourished her, tucked her in at night and told her stories, bandaged her bruises and comforted her whenever she woke from a nightmare, this woman became an enigma. How could the woman who never failed to say "I love you" every single day just walk out of her life? Though it pained her, more and more she believed what Lillian had said to her. Her mother, the beautiful Cristina Maria Black, left her and Dad for another. Yes, Lillian's words cut through the perfect fantasy that Karen had held onto for so long, the beautiful fantasy that her father had kept alive for so long. Maybe we just weren't enough for her, Karen wondered. Maybe Lillian was telling the truth all along? Maybe Karen and her father's love wasn't enough to make her stay? Maybe after smoothing Karen's dark hair away from her face and kissing her goodnight, Mami left for something more fulfilling than their love, more intoxicating than the man she left with; maybe she left in pursuit of her perfect lover nestled in a sea of amber, at the bottom of her glass. Lillian once told her that she was just like her mother. Karen hoped that wasn't true.

No, Karen shook her head; she would not be her mother—not anymore. Miles away from her, Robbie was living among strangers. That was all going to change. Nothing would keep her from the one person in her life that gave her a reason to get up every morning and make a promise each day not to drink. She didn't need to promise forever, a month, or even a week. It's like getting up each morning and remembering to get dressed before going out, just to promise not to drink this day. She'd deal with tomorrow when it came around. So today she'd just worry about this day. One day at a time.

As the bus pulled into town, Karen spied Irene on the sidewalk, waving a greeting to her. Why that woman was being so kind to her was beyond her. Karen couldn't keep track of how many times she had shown up late or had been dragged out early by Jimmy, who would famously announce "she quits," for one reason or another, yet Irene and Hardy always welcomed her when she came in asking for her job back. A few weeks ago when Karen's case worker had asked her where she would be living when she returned from rehab, Karen said that she would look for her own apartment as soon as possible. On the following Sunday when Karen had asked Irene if she knew of any affordable apartments for rent Irene shook her head and told her flat out that she was not going to help her find an apartment since she and Hardy had a three bedroom home and would be happy to rent out a room.

"Welcome home," Irene said as she hugged Karen.

"Why are you so good to me?"

"Honey, I've got to find some way to guilt you into coming back to the diner. Your customers miss you," Irene chuckled and led Karen to her car. The first stop they made was at Karen and Jimmy's place. Jimmy had been served with a restraining order and told not to be on the premises when Karen came by to pick up her belongings. Karen stuffed her clothing into a large plastic bag, grabbed Robbie's favorite Spiderman cup, some of his toys, and brought them out to Irene's car. Returning to the house, she looked around. There was nothing else here for her, she thought and turned to go. Pausing in front of the closet, she turned towards it and opened the door. Buried under extra blankets, winter coats, and some hats, was a battered brown box. Karen squatted down and pulled it open. A tattered scrapbook sat underneath Karen's Red Sox hat and a small keepsake pillow with Robbie's name and date of birth on it. She brushed her fingertips across the pillow and held it for a moment before folding the flaps of the box back over. Picking up the box and without turning back, she got into Irene's car and the two of them drove away.

Before getting Robbie back, Karen needed to meet with her caseworker and agree to the conditions of Robbie's return. She was to attend regular meetings with her caseworker, be ready for unannounced inspections, hold down a regular job, and attend AA meetings. Yes, yes, yes, Karen said. If the conditions called for her to rope the moon, Karen would do it. She'd do anything to have Robbie back in her arms.

Pacing back and forth, Karen eyed the clock anxiously, waiting for the moment she would be united with Robbie. The doorknob twisted and Karen swung around as the door opened. The caseworker stepped in, leading Robbie by the hand. For a moment, Karen felt paralyzed where she stood. She saw him just last week, yet she could swear he grew at least an inch. "Mommy," Robbie shouted and jumped into her arms. He kissed her cheek and buried his head in her shoulder. Nothing could stop the tide of tears that washed down Karen's cheek as she held him close. She kissed the top of his head and ran her fingers through his soft hair. Robbie looked up at her, and scrunched his face.

"Why you crying?"

"I'm crying because I missed you so much, and I'm so happy that I have you back in my arms," Karen said, planting kisses on his cheek. A big, beautiful grin spread across Robbie's face, a grin that could out-shine the sun. The caseworker, smiling at Karen, held a packet of papers out to her. Karen set Robbie down and collected the packet of papers. "Remember," the caseworker said, "if you need help, we're here for you. You'll find a list of numbers in that packet, so don't hesitate to call." Karen looked at the first sheet containing the times, dates, and locations of AA meetings, and then nodded at the caseworker. "Okay, then we're all set here, and you two are free to go," the caseworker shook Karen's hand and patted Robbie on the top of his head. Taking Robbie's hand in her own, Karen smiled and walked out the door, eager for them to move on with their lives.

As they rode in Irene's car, Robbie looked out his window and took in the unfamiliar landscape. When the car pulled to a stop in front of Irene's, Robbie got out and stared at the house in front of him. A large L-shaped porch wrapped itself around the front and right side of the two story log cabin. Karen took his hand in hers and whispered in his ear, "Do you like your new home?" Robbie looked at her uncertainly.

Pulling her closer to him, Robbie cupped his hand between his mouth and her ear. "Mommy, are you going to live here too?" Karen's smile faded as she knelt down and placed her hands on his shoulders. "Yes Tiger. We're both going to live here with Irene and Hardy for a little while until Mommy can get us a place of our own," Karen said, smoothing his hair away from his face. Robbie looked over at Irene and then to Hardy, who appeared in the doorway. He glanced over at Hardy and then back at Karen. "Don't worry about Hardy. He's a big teddy bear," Karen said as she scooped him up in her arms and walked towards the house.

Once inside, Irene gave Karen and Robbie a tour of the house. The upstairs had two bedrooms, one was furnished with a bed, bureau, and nightstand that used to belong to Irene and Hardy's daughter who was now married and had a family of her own. Just down the hall from the bedroom were a bathroom and another small bedroom. The room was empty, except for a small bureau in the corner. Karen's gaze moved across the room. In time, she could get Robbie a big boy's bed. After all, he was too big for the crib, and quite frankly, Karen didn't want to take the crib that Jimmy had made for Robbie—despite how beautiful it was. For now, she and Robbie would share the furnished room down the hall. She took Robbie by the hand and followed Irene back down the hall.

"Our bedroom is downstairs, so the upstairs is all yours," Irene began.

"You'll have plenty of privacy up here since we really don't use the upstairs now that our kids are grown and living on their own. Home, sweet home." Karen ran her hand over the crisp, clean sheets on the bed. Home? A small smile settled across her face. Yes, this was home for now.

After a couple weeks, Karen slipped easily into a comfortable routine. Sunday through Thursday from 6:00 a.m. until 2:00 p.m., Karen waited on tables at the diner, and then she was off to get Robbie from daycare. On Monday, Wednesday, and Friday evenings, Irene dropped Karen off at AA meetings, while she ran errands and Hardy stayed with Robbie. Twice a week, Karen checked in with her caseworker. Three times a week, Karen took charge of the laundry and some other chores. Saturdays were Karen's favorite. It was the only time she really had Robbie all to herself without having to divide her attention between him, work, and household chores. When she could afford it, they would go to the movies or go roller skating, but most of the times they'd hang out at the park and play on the swings. It was funny, Karen thought, how something so amazingly simple like chasing a squealing four year old around a playground could bring her so much joy, more joy than anything else she had experienced in her life.

Each day, Karen felt herself beginning to feel a little more at home in Irene and Hardy's house. The only time shouting filled the house was when Hardy was watching baseball or some other sport. He was a Mariner's fan, and when the team faltered, Hardy let the whole world know by shaking his fist and yelling at a deaf TV. Living with Irene and Hardy was definitely a change for the better. To top it all off, there were no piles of dirty laundry or discarded work boots to trip over in the hallway, no empty beer cans on the kitchen counter, and no need to walk on eggshells here.

Even though things were getting better, Robbie still didn't talk very much. Despite this, he started to smile more. His eyes were brighter and didn't seem so weighted down with fear, yet at night he clung to Karen, unable to sleep unless he was tucked in right beside her. Whenever Karen talked to him about getting his own bed and his very own room, Robbie just shook his head. Deciding to not to fight a losing battle, Karen accepted that this is how it was to be for now. She snuggled him up against her and ran her fingers through his hair until he began to relax and finally, he succumbed to sleep.

On the days that Karen went to AA meetings, getting Robbie to sleep on time was difficult. After too many rounds of Hi Ho Cherry-O and Candyland, Hardy often gave up on getting Robbie to sleep and let him stay up to watch baseball. Tonight was no exception. When Irene and Karen pulled in the driveway at 9:15, the living room lights were still on. Irene began to open her door, but then froze, her eyes staring at the rearview mirror.

"Oh no," Irene whispered. Karen looked at her questioningly. "Karen, it's Jimmy. He's in that white box truck that just pulled over on the other side of the street." Karen looked over her shoulder and drew in a long breath.

"Come on," Irene said, placing a hand on Karen's shoulder. "Let's just go straight in the house." Karen nodded and pushed her door open. Jimmy walked over to them, taking long, confident strides. Karen froze, not knowing whether to run to him or away from him. In his hand he held a large bouquet of red roses. He nodded to Irene before turning his attention back to Karen.

"Hey baby."

"What are you doing here?" Karen asked, taking a step closer to the house.

"I just came by to talk," he said, and then turned to Irene. "Hey, wanna give us a few minutes?"

"No way in hell buddy. You just turn your ass around and march right back to your truck and get out of here before we call the cops," Irene said, resting her hands on her hips.

"Hey, this ain't any of your business. So, why don't you just butt out? I ain't here to cause any problems. I just want to talk to Karen."

At the sound of the front door opening, the three of them turned towards the house. Hardy switched on the floodlight and stood in the doorway, his sturdy shoulders filling the space around him. Behind him, Robbie poked his head out, trying to see who was out there. Hearing his mother's voice, he tried to squeeze past, but Hardy reached out a hand and blocked his path.

"No, Robbie. You stay here. Your mom is coming in," he said in a firm, yet gentle voice.

Robbie looked up at Hardy, and then spotted Karen, Irene, and Jimmy standing just a couple feet from his mom. He sucked in his breath and moved closer to Hardy, wrapping his arm around Hardy's leg.

"Girls, why don't you come on in now," he said, gently pulling Robbie away from him and stepping out of the house. "Jimmy, you go on home before you get yourself into more trouble."

"I ain't leaving until I talk to Karen. Now why don't you and your misses back the fuck off and give us a minute to talk," Jimmy answered, his voice growing louder.

"You know you're not supposed to come anywhere near her. Now go on and get out of here," Hardy answered.

Irene placed her hand around Karen's shoulder and nodded towards the door. "Let's go inside," Irene said. Karen looked at Jimmy, shook her head, and started up the walkway. Jimmy grabbed hold of her arm and pulled backwards.

"Baby, don't go. I just want to talk." His voice was soft, his eyes pleading. "I know I've done you wrong, but I ain't gonna be like my old man. I can change. I will change." He thrust the bouquet of roses towards her. "Look, I got these for you."

Karen looked down at his hand still gripping her arm and then looked back at him. "There's nothing to say, Jimmy. Let go of me please."

Jimmy twisted up his lips and blew air out his nose and shook his head side to side. "I am trying to make things right, babe. I love you and I love our boy. I want you back. Please baby," he said, pulling her closer and tightening his hold on her. "Can't we just talk about this?"

Karen hadn't even noticed Hardy come down the steps until she felt his hand on her shoulder and heard him say to Irene, "Go on inside with Karen and shut the door," he said, motioning them towards the house and placing his large two hundred twenty-five pound frame in between Karen and Jimmy. Jerking her arm free, Karen turned away from Jimmy and started for the house.

"Baby, come on!" Jimmy started towards her, but Hardy stepped in front of him. Locking his eyes with Hardy's, Jimmy clenched and unclenched his fists.

"Old man, you don't want to piss me off," his voice came out low and dangerous.

"Oh really? Or what? You'll beat me?" A small smile played across Hardy's lips. "I heard you only hit women." Holding Jimmy's gaze, Hardy yelled over his shoulder to Irene, "Honey. Go on and call the cops. Tell them I want this piece of shit taken off my lawn."

At the sight of Karen disappearing into the house, he lurched towards Hardy, his fists balled up at his sides and veins bulging along his neck.

"You prick! All I wanna do is talk to her!"

"She's got nothing to say to you."

Irene poked her head out the front door and yelled, "They're on their way."

"Son of a bitch!" Jimmy whipped the bouquet of flowers onto the ground, scattering blood red petals across the tar, and stormed out of the driveway.

That night, hours after Robbie had finally fallen to sleep, Karen still lay awake, wedged uncomfortably between Robbie's little frame and the wall. Robbie lay with his head on her shoulder and his knees drawn up to her ribs. Even in his sleep, his hands still clutched the edges of her nightshirt. She placed a kiss on his head and stared up at the ceiling. In the quiet solitude of her room, she tried to fathom why she even cared about Jimmy. She couldn't reason why she wanted to forgive him, that just for an instant, she wanted to go to him, even though the smell of his cologne and the sound of his voice choked the air from her lungs. Part of her wanted to run away from him, part of her wanted to run to him. He was all she had known of a lover for over four years. He was there for her, she admitted, when she went into labor, smoothing back her hair, encouraging her, holding her hand as Robbie made his way into the world. And there were those moments, times when he wasn't filled with rage or resentment, when he was kind and thoughtful, like when he poured his energy into making a beautiful crib for Robbie, and the times he tried his hand at making dinner for her, so she could rest for awhile. After all, Robbie had been so colicky as an infant.

As Robbie drew in another shuddered breath in his sleep, one that came with too many tears and the ever present fear of Jimmy they shared, Karen wondered, how could Jimmy be so thoughtful one minute, but so violent the next? Maybe it was her fault. Maybe she expected too much from him. Maybe supporting her and her child was too much to ask. Maybe she was unlovable. Maybe, maybe, maybe…

Living with Irene and Hardy was so different than living with Jimmy. Everybody took turns preparing meals. When Irene and Hardy were together, they laughed, they argued, and joked. Not once did Karen feel the oppression of forced silence in their house. No, if Irene didn't like something, she didn't hesitate to tell Hardy and fear his response. Yes, Karen realized, there is such a thing as love out there. If only she could find someone to love her the way Hardy loved Irene.

When sleep finally overcame Karen, it was short lived. Fractured memories pierced through her sleep—a boot, a bottle, a fist, his hands around her neck. In her sleep, she felt as if she were falling off the edge of a cliff. Startling herself awake, Karen sat up and caught her breath. Robbie still slept soundly beside her. Eyeing the clock, Karen let out a sigh when she saw that it was only four, and decided there was no point in going back to sleep. Getting out of bed, Karen stumbled over a box on the floor. Cursing under her breath, Karen picked up the box and carried it over to the closet. As Karen set the box down, she paused for a moment, and flipped open its lid. She dug her hand into the box, feeling for the scrapbook that sat beneath Robbie's first baby blanket. Quietly, Karen slipped the book out of the box and went to the kitchen.

After starting a pot of coffee, Karen sat down at the table and fingered the worn edges of the book. A long red ribbon stuck out from the pages. Karen flipped open the book and ran her fingers along the beautiful red ribbon that her mother had so often worn in her hair. Tears collected in the corner of Karen's eyes and clung to her long lashes. She stared at the picture on the first page, one of her and Mami. Karen was eight. A shiny plastic tiara sat upon her head and sparkly plastic heels encased her little feet. A yellow towel was pinned to the shoulders of her top. Karen laughed, remembering how Mami granted her Halloween wish by making her a superhero princess. Mami's smile was so wide, so carefree. Karen flipped to the next page. Mami and Dad stood side by side, her father's arm was draped over her mother's shoulder. In front of them, Karen stood in her First Communion dress and folded her hands in prayer. On the opposite page, there was a picture of Lillian and Dad. Lillian leaned her head against his chest and smiled. Karen looked back at the photo of Mami and Dad. Her father's smile looked strained, practiced. Mami held a glass in her right hand. Glancing again to the photo of Lillian and her father, she leaned in for a closer look. There was something in their smiles, a sleepy grin that exuded a sense comfortableness with each other. Karen looked back at the picture of her mother and the glass she held in her hand. Rum and Coke? The very thought of it called to her. Maybe Lillian had told her the truth. Maybe Mami and Dad were never really happy. Maybe she was just like Mami.

"Can't sleep?" Irene placed a hand on Karen's shoulder, startling her.

"No. Too much on my mind, I guess." Karen shrugged and looked down at the scrapbook. Irene patted Karen's back and then poured herself a cup of coffee. Karen flipped the page. There was another picture of her and Mami. Mami's arms were clasped around Karen's shoulders. There was a glass in her hand, an amber liquid filling up half of it.

"Is that your mother?" Irene leaned over Karen's shoulder and squinted at the picture.

"Yes, that's my mother, Cristina Camila Santiago-Black," Karen answered with a smile that quickly faded. "She was a singer and dancer from Puerto Rico. My dad met her on a business trip to Old San Juan."

"She's beautiful," Irene said, then looked at Karen. "You look a lot like her."

Karen smiled and shrugged. "My dad said she captured his heart right then and there, at Plaza de la Princessa, and danced her way into his heart. She died when I was twelve," Karen sighed.

"I'm sorry," Irene said, giving Karen's shoulder a gentle squeeze.

"She was killed in a car accident. My dad said the guy that hit her was drunk…but…" Karen shook her head and traced her finger across the picture. Her gaze settled on the glass held in her mother's hand. "It's funny. I always said that I would never drink and drive, that that's the one thing nobody could ever say about me." She brushed a tear from the corner of her eye and turned the page. There was a picture of her with Carol. They were making absurd faces into the camera and both wearing Red Sox caps.

"That's Carol. She was my best friend. I taught her how to salsa and she taught me how to play poker." A small smile played across her lips as her eyes moved across the page. In the corner of the page, yellowed around the edges, was a picture of a young boy of about three or four. He was sitting cross-legged on the floor with a red truck clasped in one hand, while he rested his head on the knuckles of his other hand. Karen froze, holding her breath for a moment, and leaned in closer to the picture. The sandy blonde hair, the knuckles pressed against his forehead, the smile…wasn't it only recently that Karen saw Robbie smile like that, only recently that she saw his eyes dance with light? She swallowed hard and chewed on her bottom lip. All this time, these more than four years, she had never considered…but they had used protection. She and Steve were always careful.

Karen stared at the picture and moved her hand away when a hot tear fell onto it. Steve had given her that picture of himself after Karen had teased him, telling him that he was acting like a silly little boy because he had scared her by placing a rubber snake in her book bag. The last time she had looked at this picture was nearly four years ago. She remembers tucking the book away and burying it under spare blankets and winter clothing after Jimmy's first outburst at the mere mention of Steve. Since then, she had made it a point to never let his name escape from her lips. She had tried to convince herself that he didn't exist, that if she buried all traces of him, the pain, the memories would all go away. She swallowed her guilt like unchewed food and felt the warm trace of tears roll down her cheeks.

"He's got a gentle smile," Irene said as she placed her arm around Karen's shoulder. She tilted her head and looked at Karen. "Don't you ever think about going home?"

Karen wiped her eyes with the back of her hand. "I don't think anyone back home would be too happy to see me," she answered with a nervous smile.

# CHAPTER ELEVEN

······································

## *Rhythm of the Road*

The sun settled below the horizon, taking any hint of warmth with it. She was going home, if she could make it there. Karen pulled into the breakdown lane and strained to the read the juice-stained map by the truck's dim dashboard light. Shaking her head and tapping the map with an impatient finger, she realized that she missed her exit. Avoiding the traffic in downtown Chicago was hopeless. Flipping on her signal light and letting out a sigh, Karen eased back into the careless flow of stop and go traffic. A yawn escaped from her, reminding Karen that the coffee she had at lunchtime had long since worn off. With her energy fading fast, all she wanted to do was climb into bed. Robbie stared up wide-eyed at the towering skyscrapers that filled the Chicago skyline. Tiring of the snail's pace on the highway and fighting a losing battle with exhaustion, Karen noted a blue and yellow billboard advertising the Windy City Motel and exited the highway.

Karen stopped at a light and looked up at the yellow and blue metal sign that lead her farther into the center of the city. A single bullet hole pierced the "O" in "Low Rates and Free Cable TV" advertised on the sign. When the light turned green, a horn blared behind her. Hesitantly, she continued through the city, taking in the bright lights and the heavily populated streets. Spying a flashing vacancy sign up ahead, Karen drove towards it and checked in. Robbie clung to Karen and pressed his ear down on his shoulder, trying to block out the screaming sirens of a police car as it raced down the street.

As soon as they stepped into their room, Karen dropped her duffle bag on the floor and fastened the chain on the door, before settling down to a supper consisting of peanut-butter and jelly sandwiches, fruit punch, and Ritz crackers. Afterwards, Karen turned on the shower and cursed the water that refused to warm, forcing her to shower at record speed. Pulling on a comfortable pair of well worn gym pants and a tee-shirt, Karen settled Robbie and herself beneath the covers.

Outside the window, sirens continued to wail intermittently up and down the street. Green and red waves of light from the bar across the street flashed through the window. A couple argued down the hall, cursing each other loudly. Something thumped against the wall. She could feel Robbie stiffen as the noise from outside seeped in through the cracked window, slipped under the door, and slid through the walls. In the hallway, two male voices could be heard accompanied by the sound of feet running down the hall.

"Fuck you!" Somebody shouted and bumped against their door.

"Mommy..." Robbie's eyes opened wide.

"It's okay, honey. It's just some noisy people in the hallway," Karen answered and glanced back at the door in the dark. Grunting and cursing, the scuffle continued with another bump against the door.

"Mommy, they're gonna come in." Robbie's eyes widened and he tugged frantically on Karen's arm.

"No, sweetie. Mommy will make sure they don't come in," Karen answered with more confidence than she felt, as she slipped out of bed and pushed a chair in front of the door. "There. Now there's no way anyone will come in."

Before slipping back under the covers, she gazed out the window at the green and red neon sign that blinked "O'Sullivan's Watering Hole." While the footfalls of the men outside their door faded in the distance, desire grew—a desire for her long lost lover, the sweet sting and amber glow found in the bottom of a glass. Karen shook her head and tugged the curtains closed before slipping back into bed. Snuggling Robbie into her arms, Karen could still see the dull red and green glow bobbing back and forth through the curtains. She squeezed her eyes shut and tried to will herself to sleep. Long after Robbie was asleep, though, she lay awake staring at the blinking glow that continued to move rhythmically through the curtains and across the ceiling.

Sitting up, she shook her head and slipped out of bed. Reaching into her duffle bag, she pulled out the small framed picture of Robbie and held it in her hands. She brushed her fingers across the picture and looked at the writing on the frame: *Together we can be strong.* Karen hugged the picture to her chest and breathed in deeply. Robbie slept soundly with his tattered teddy bear clutched in his arms. Leaning over, Karen placed a kiss on his head and lay back down in bed next to him. Still, images of rum and Coke flowing like a waterfall crept into her mind—the smooth liquid as it poured through the slow curve of the bottle, the splash and curl of it falling into a cold glass. Just thinking about it, she could taste it. The strong pull it had on her mind reminded her that she hadn't been to an AA meeting in over a week. Out here, though, halfway across the country and in an unfamiliar place, she felt so alone. She never thought she'd miss the dusty old church basement and her new friends so much.

At the last meeting Karen went to, her sponsor made her promise to seek out a meeting as soon as she got settled back in Massachusetts. With Robbie clinging to her shirttail and Karen with no idea where she would stay once she got home, she wondered if she'd ever be able to get to a meeting. After all, nobody brought their kids with them. Despite this, she promised her sponsor she'd find a way to get to a meeting and that she'd call her if she found herself falling. The meetings had provided a place for her to unload her guilt, all the rottenness that festered inside, and the meetings were where she had begun to find her voice again. Everything— Jimmy, the drinking, the abuse, that October night at the tavern, all the lies, the denial—nearly everything spilled out of her in the safety of these meetings. Karen exhaled slowly, longing for a place to purge her guilt, a place to make things right. She flipped open her cell phone and thought about calling her sponsor, but then looked at the time. It was nearly 1:00 a.m., and it really wasn't an emergency. She'd call her tomorrow.

After a nearly sleepless night, Karen awoke and began packing for the next day on the road. When traffic began to thicken about an hour later, Karen exited the interstate and followed the signs to the Waffle Hut. Pulling their coats tight against the icy wind, they jogged across the parking lot and into the restaurant. Within minutes, Karen was savoring a strong cup of coffee and Robbie was slurping chocolate milk through a straw. Ten minutes later, the waitress set down two steaming plates of waffles and crispy bacon in front of them. Robbie's eyes grew wide and he licked his lips when Karen poured golden pools of maple syrup onto his plate. While Karen began cutting up his waffle, Robbie tapped his fork impatiently and made little smacking sounds with his lips. As soon as she slid his plate back in front of him, he jabbed his fork into the waffle, popping one piece after another into his mouth. Two cups of coffee and forty-five minutes later, they were back on the road home.

Shortly before reaching South Bend, Indiana, the truck began to sputter. Glancing down at the gas gauge, Karen saw that it was still showing a half tank. Karen shook her head and looked back at the road. When was the last time she gassed up? Yesterday, around lunch time? Somewhere in eastern Wisconsin? "Unfrickin' believable," she muttered to herself. Why had she even agreed to buy this piece of shit anyway? Thumping the steering wheel impatiently, she scanned the horizon for a gas sign, but all she saw was a sign saying the next exit was two miles away.

As Karen exited the interstate, the truck let out a final sputter and cough before the engine cut out on the exit ramp. Karen put the truck in neutral and let it coast to the end of the ramp. She turned the key and pushed her foot down on the accelerator, but was answered with a low, dying groan followed by silence. Flipping on her hazard lights, Karen peered out the windows to her left and right. In the distance, she could see her saving grace—a Texaco sign.

"What's wrong, Mommy?"

"I think we just ran out of gas." Karen sighed and then unbuckled her seatbelt. "Come on, Tiger. Zip up your coat. We're going to have to walk a little way to get to the gas station." Snugging Robbie's hat onto his head, she took him by the hand, and the two of them began walking down the street. Although there was no snow left on the ground, a cold, damp wind ripped through the mid-April air.

Once they reached the station, Karen sighed and forked over money for a two gallon gas can and enough gas to fill it. As she twisted the nozzle back on the can, she looked up at the sky. Clouds bumped into each other like a traffic jam, swallowing up all the patches of blue and turning the sky a dull grey. Rain was forecast for later today, but judging by the increasing wind and dampness in the air, Karen was afraid the rainstorm that was slated to drop an inch or two was going to greet them sooner than expected. Taking Robbie by the hand, Karen urged him to walk quickly.

As the truck came into view, drops began to fall from the sky. Karen pushed the key in the lock and pulled open the door for Robbie. Once he was seat belted inside, she went to the back of the truck and began pouring gas into the tank. "April showers," Karen said and shivered in the wind.

As soon as she finished pouring the gas, she set the empty can underneath the tarp that covered the bed of her truck and then jogged to the front.

With one hand on the door, Karen stopped in her tracks. A bright orange parking ticket sat under the wiper blade and flapped against the windshield. Grumbling, she snatched it up and tossed it in her glove box. After several turns of the key, the truck finally chugged to life, sputtering but running nonetheless. Karen shifted the truck into gear and headed back towards the gas station. She shoved the nozzle into the tank and selected the cheapest grade. Watching the numbers climb made her cringe and her wallet cry. She could fill an Escort two times over with the amount of gas she needed just to fill the truck's tank! Karen looked at the bed of the truck and all the items she had crammed beneath the tarp, and then shrugged. No, an Escort wouldn't do. Before leaving the station, she checked the oil and was not surprised to see that the truck was down a quart. After topping off the oil and shaking the rain out of her hair, Karen started the truck and headed back towards the interstate.

By two in the afternoon, the rain began coming down heavily. The wipers whipped back and forth across the windshield, and the truck's tires strained to grasp the pavement. Karen reduced her speed to a modest forty miles per hour and tightened her grip on the steering wheel. Leaning forward, Karen kept her eyes focused on the white lines of the road, trying to see past the spray of water from the crazy people who zipped by in the high speed lane as if it were a beautiful, sunny day. Glancing at her rear view mirror, she saw dark clouds behind her, and looking forward, more dark clouds awaited. It seemed as though the storm was intent on following her. Every now and then, she saw a car pulled into the breakdown lane, waiting out the storm. The thought crossed her mind to just pull off the highway, but then through the grey mist she saw it: "Cleveland 20mi." Almost thirty minutes later, she crossed over the Cleveland line. Robbie gazed out the window and looked in awe at the tall buildings looming ahead. With traffic thickening and no sign of the rain letting up, Karen exited the highway and began searching for a decent place for them to stay.

Up ahead, she saw signposts for the Comfort Inn, an Embassy Suites, and a Doubletree Hotel. Karen slowed down as she passed the Embassy Suites and imagined herself falling onto the plush bedding and surrounding herself with four pillows. The mezzanine would be tastefully decorated with sparkling tile floors, bouquets of flowers would be filled with beautiful pink lilies, white daisies, and blue irises set on tall pedestals, and of course, there would be high-back cushioned chairs. She imagined the Presidential Suite would most certainly overlook Lake Erie.

"Mommy, that's a fancy place! Can we stay there?" Robbie looked at her hopefully. Karen shook her head and continued down the road. A little further down the road, Karen spotted another hotel sign. She pulled into the parking lot and went inside to check rates, only to be disappointed once again. After buckling Robbie back into his seat, she headed further down the road until she spotted another sign, this one for the Doubletree Hotel. Once again, she parked and went inside with Robbie to check rates.

"Yes, Miss, I do have a room available for $79.00 a night," the clerk told her while staring at the computer screen in front of him.

"I know this sounds tacky, but are there any other places in the area that are a little less expensive?"

"Why yes there are, but with the Indians playing a home game and the writer's conference in town, you're going to be hard pressed to find something now if you don't have reservations." He looked up from his computer screen and drummed his fingers on the countertop. "Hmmm… perhaps if you travel further east to Lakewood you might find something. Through traffic and with this rain, it'll probably take about twenty minutes or so to get there."

Robbie tugged on Karen's arm. "Mommy, I'm hungry. I don't want to ride anymore." Karen leaned her head in her hand and let out a sigh.

"Ma'am, we do have discount coupons to the Harbor Family Restaurant next door, and the food is not only good, but it is very reasonably priced."

Robbie tugged on Karen's arm once more, and looked up at her with pleading puppy-dog eyes. Turning back to the clerk, she nodded and pulled her credit card out of her wallet. The clerk began typing information into the computer and then handed her a room key. Robbie wrinkled up his face and tugged once more on Karen's arm. When his mommy leaned over, he cupped his hands to her ears and pointed to the key card. "What is that?" Robbie asked with a quizzical look on his face. The clerk, overhearing Robbie's question, answered, "That's a funny looking key, isn't it?" Robbie nodded shyly and wrapped his arms around Karen. "Ma'am," the clerk said to Karen, "our pool is open until 11:00 p.m. tonight, along with the Jacuzzi."

"Yay!" Robbie yelled out, his shyness evaporating for a moment. Karen laughed and scooped him up in her arms. "Okay Tiger, let's get unpacked and eat, and then *if* we have enough time, we'll go check out the pool." Robbie hugged her tightly, and then the two of them went back to the truck to unpack before dashing next door to eat.

Seated inside, Karen looked over the menu. Everything looked so tempting: The turkey dinner, the chicken fried steak, and the grilled honey mustard chicken, but the smell of the burgers was so overpowering and mouthwatering that she couldn't resist. So it was settled—cheeseburger cooked medium, topped with lettuce, sautéed onions and peppers, and a little bit of mayonnaise. After placing Robbie's order, Karen placed hers.

"And a drink for you?" The waitress asked, pen poised over her pad.

"Oh boy, a Bud would hit the spot right now," Karen started and then quickly caught herself. "No, wait. Make that a coffee, strong please."

Karen sipped at her coffee, cupping the mug in her hands and letting the warmth of it move through her, but it wasn't nearly as satisfying as a Bud would have been. Well, at least my hands are warming up, she thought to herself, and then began picking at the frayed edges of her coat sleeve. Once she got back to Massachusetts, she would get herself a decent job and save up enough money to buy Robbie some much deserved new clothes. Maybe if things worked out, she could take him to Fenway Park. She hadn't seen a Sox game since she watched the rebroadcast of the World Series last fall, while busing tables at the diner.

Once they were back at the motel, they went for a quick swim in the pool and then went back to the room. Karen ran a warm bath for Robbie and helped him wash his hair.

"Okay Tiger, are you ready to get out?"

"No Mommy. I want to stay in and play with my cars," Robbie said, driving a purple racecar across his knees and along the sides of the tub. Karen shrugged and sat back on her heels watching him. His smile was bright, and for the first time in a long time, he looked carefree—just like a little boy should.

After a few minutes, she left the bathroom and sat down on a chair next to the small writing table. Staring at the phone, she thought about calling Steve. Out of the thirteen numbers for Steven J. McKenzie that she had found in the North Central Massachusetts area last week, so far three of the numbers were disconnected, two of them were answered by preteens, and one man sounded to be about seventy years old or so. She had thought about calling his parents' house, but then quickly dismissed that idea. Karen flipped open her cell phone. Her palms began to sweat and her heart quicken as she began dialing the number for a Steven J.

McKenzie in Ashburnham, the town next door to where he grew up. On the third ring, a voice low and mellow answered.

"Hello? Hello?"

Karen melted at the sound, her heart pounding with nervous excitement. Oh, who was she kidding? She snapped her phone shut. She was the last person he'd want to hear from. It was funny, though, that a man who she once felt so perfectly comfortable with, so safe with, now made her go mute. The sound of his voice seeped into her heart and sang to her. After so long of an absence, more than five years, his simple "hello" awakened something inside of her, both bitter and sweet. Yes, she had destroyed his love for her, but his voice was intoxicating making her want to call him again just to hear him say hello. What an addiction! Sooner or later, though, she knew she would have to face him, and she was all too aware of how his tone would harden at the sound of her voice.

As she sat at the writing table, her cell phone still clutched in her hand, Robbie called to her from the bathroom. After helping Robbie dry off, Karen tucked him in bed and settled herself beside him. He curled up his little body against her, pulling Karen's arms around him, and soon drifted off to sleep. Karen ran her fingers through his hair, and leaning over him, kissed his cheek. Laying back and staring up at the ceiling, sleep escaped her. The sudden realization that she was almost home terrified her. What would Steve say when she told him about Robbie? Would he even believe her? Would anybody? She hadn't given anyone a chance to hear her voice, hadn't welcomed anyone's help, but most of all, she acknowledged, she hadn't accepted the truth. Instead, all she had done was run.

In the dark of the hotel room, she whispered "help me" to no one in particular. The words sounded foreign coming from her lips. Only once had she admitted that she needed help, and in the quiet of the night, Karen could taste the salt of her tears. Steve had been there for her, and so had Carol, but she couldn't—wouldn't let them help her. No, the truth was too much. At every corner, Lillian had been there, waiting, wanting to help. With the clarity of her fragile sobriety, Karen realized that Lillian had always been there, never once wavering on the truth, always pulling away the comfort of ignorance and doubts as the others had let her live in for some time. No matter how hard or unsavory the truth was, Lillian spoke it. Lillian had not lied, and Karen swallowed this truth like broken glass. Karen was a lot like Mami, she admitted. Mami drank too much, and when things had become too difficult to handle, so did she. Mami ran from the truth, so did she. Mami turned her back on her family, so did she. For the first time in a long time, as Karen lay there staring up at the ceiling, Karen wanted to go to Lillian, to tell her she knew the truth, to tell her she was sorry for all she put her through, to make up for all those lost years—but she hadn't spoken to her in over five years. After all this time, Lillian had probably given up on her. Karen hoped she was wrong.

She slipped out of bed, and sitting down in front of the writing table, she began counting her money, and then let out a sigh. She had less than fifteen hundred dollars left. First month's rent for an apartment, along with a security deposit would eat up most of that, leaving her little cash left over. Her Mastercard was nearly maxed out, leaving her only an in-store Target charge card and very little room for error. It amazed her how quickly her money went from wallet to waste, but the drinking, the parties, Jimmy's crazy get rich quick plans...all of it had eaten away at the money her father had left her. More than halfway across the country and only a day and a half from home, Karen wanted so desperately to turn the truck around and go back to the security of Irene and Hardy's place. They'd give Karen her job back; she had no doubt. Looking over at Robbie and hearing the rise and fall of his easy breathing, Karen knew she couldn't turn back. Robbie deserved better.

It was only a month ago that Jimmy cornered her in the parking lot when she got off work at four. Karen remembered trying to step past him, but he kept blocking her path. She took a quick jump to her left and tried to bolt past him, but he caught the back of her coat. Karen shook herself free from the coat and ran towards her truck. As she fumbled for the keys, he slapped them out of her hand, and then grabbed her by the shoulders.

"Baby no. Don't go. Come on, baby. I need you," the words dribbled out of his mouth in a slur, his hot breath stinking of beer. He pushed her up against the truck and leaned his face close to hers.

"Jimmy, let go of me. Hardy's going to call the cops if he sees you here," she said, trying to push him away.

"Fuck that ol' fart. He ain't gonna do nothin' cause I'll break his damned skull," he said, sliding his hands down her back until they reached her hips where he grasped them firmly. "Come on, baby. I need you so bad and I know you need me cause I'm the only one who really loves you." He pressed his groin up against her and crushed her lips under his. His hands moved up her shoulders, to her neck, and then he wrapped his fingers in her long dark hair, pulling her to him. Forcefully, but clumsily, he started kissing her neck, cheek, and lips. Karen could taste the beer on his tongue. His rough, unshaven face scratched at her cheeks. He untangled one hand from her hair and wrapped his arm around her waist. Karen pushed her hands against his chest, but her one hundred fifteen pound frame was no match for his towering, solid body. Digging her fingernails into his chest, she clawed at him, but couldn't get past his insulated flannel coat. Over the pounding of her heart, she heard Irene screaming out Hardy's name.

Hardy stormed across the parking lot and grabbed Jimmy by the shoulders, knocking him off balance for a moment. Jimmy let go of Karen, and spun around with a closed fist and struck Hardy in the face. Karen watched horrified as Hardy fell heavily to the ground. She screamed and began punching Jimmy in the back, but was answered with a hard shove backwards into the side of her truck. Jimmy turned back around and kicked Hardy in the shoulder, but before he could swing his foot back again, Karen leapt onto his back, throwing him off balance. Stumbling with her on his back, Jimmy grabbed hold of her belt and yanked her off him, tossing her as if she were a rag doll. Karen tumbled to the ground, but sprang right back to her feet. She caught hold of his coat and was dragged through the snow covered parking lot as Jimmy staggered back towards Hardy.

"I'm gonna bust your damned skull ol' man. You're gonna wish you never met me," he yelled to Hardy. Karen let go of Jimmy's coat and scrambled past him. Standing between Jimmy, and Hardy who rose unsteadily to his feet, Karen pleaded with Jimmy to stop.

"Please, Jimmy. Please just stop. I'll go with you. Just stop," she said, pressing her hands against his chest. Jimmy leaned towards her, grabbing her by the shoulder, and shoved her to the ground. Hardy held his fists out in front of him, dodging and ducking Jimmy's drunken swings. Letting out a growl, Jimmy lunged forward, knocking Hardy to the ground. Hardy rolled out of Jimmy's reach and got to his feet again, but not for long as Jimmy grabbed him by the ankle and pulled him down again. As Jimmy knelt over Hardy, ready to strike him again, Karen jumped on his back.

"Jesus woman!" He yelled, rising to his feet. "Get the hell off me!" He stood up with Karen still clinging to his back, and stumbled backwards, bumping the two of them against Irene's Toyota, causing the alarm to go off. With the sudden rush of air from her lungs, Karen lost her grip on him. Jimmy turned to her, his eyes burning, and backhanded her hard across the face, knocking her back against the Toyota. Karen brought her hands up in front of her, trying to block his next swing. He drew his fist back, but before he could swing at her, Hardy rammed his shoulder into

Jimmy's ribs, knocking all three of them onto the slick pavement. Hardy and Jimmy rolled back and forth across the tar, grunting and swinging at each other. Karen scrambled on her hands and knees across the wet tar, trying to evade flying fists, and rose to her feet again, trying to catch her breath. As Jimmy knelt over Hardy, ready to deliver another blow, Irene came running across the parking lot and began smashing Jimmy in the back and shoulder with a sauce pan.

The sounds of the yelling, scuffling, and grunting were soon drowned out by the sound of sirens approaching. Two officers ran over to the group. Jimmy got to his feet, unfazed by the officers' approach, and swung at Hardy, but missed by several inches. Before he could draw his fist back again, the two officers knocked him to the ground and jerked his arms back. Pressing his face against the ground and kneeling on his back, one of the officers read Jimmy his rights, while the other snapped cuffs on him.

A moment later, an ambulance pulled up a short distance behind the cruisers. When one of the officers signaled to them, two E.M.T.s came forward. Still kicking and struggling to get out of the officers' grasps, Jimmy called to Karen, "Baby, no! I love you! Baby, I love you!" Karen sat shaking uncontrollably, while an E.M.T. dabbed at the gash below Hardy's left eye and argued with him about the need to get checked out at the hospital. After some gentle persuasion by Irene, and after Karen promised to go too, he finally agreed to go.

Karen had gotten off easy compared to the last time Jimmy exploded. All she had to show was a bright red welt on her cheek and a sore back, but Hardy was kept overnight for ensuing chest pain. If Karen hadn't ever gotten together with Jimmy, if she hadn't returned to work at the diner, no harm would have come to Hardy. It was then that she realized she had no choice; she had to get away, to take Robbie and leave Montana. It was time to go home.

Sitting in the hotel room, she thought about the tearful goodbye and hasty planning that followed only a couple weeks after her run-in with Jimmy. When Robbie had asked his mommy why she had a big red welt on her face, Karen had said it was nothing. Robbie, though he couldn't put words to it, knew something was wrong. Words and smiles had only just begun to tumble from his lips, and then almost as quickly, he had grown silent, responding with a nod of his head or shrug of his shoulders. But how could she blame him? After all, the little boy who slept soundly right now had no concept of Massachusetts. The only homes he had known were the volatile one they shared with Jimmy and the other with Irene and Hardy. Home? What was that? All Robbie knew was that he wouldn't be playing Candyland with Hardy anymore. In the dark, Karen massaged her cheek, the welt long since gone, but the memory and sting as clear as if it just happened yesterday. Thinking about how Robbie had been deprived of a happy home, a safe, steady place to call his own, Karen leaned her head in her hand and wondered if she could ever give him that.

# CHAPTER TWELVE

·····································

## *Close to Home*

After another nearly sleepless night, Karen awoke just after dawn. Climbing quietly out of bed, she tiptoed to the bathroom and started the shower. Standing under the steady stream of water, she savored its warmth. She leaned forward and let the water roll down her shoulders and back, trying to ease the knot that had been building between her shoulder blades over the long drive. After some time, she stepped from the shower and quietly dressed.

She ran a hand through her wet hair and thought about the day of driving that lay ahead, wishing she could just climb back into bed and sleep away the day. It was still too early to wake Robbie. Going to the window, she drew the curtains open partway and watched the lights flicker on at the gas station across the street. The city began to awaken as the dull hum of a car passed quietly down the road. Little by little, the day grew brighter, though not by very much. Grey clouds still straddled the city and a light rain continued to sprinkle the ground. Karen massaged the back of her neck and looked back at Robbie wound beneath the sheets, inhaling and exhaling with long, deep sighs. It would be so easy to pull back the sheets and slip back into bed herself, but a glance at the clock told her she needed to get going. She let out a sigh and let Robbie sleep for a little while longer, as she gathered up their dirty clothes.

Around 6:45, Karen woke Robbie, and as soon as they dressed, they walked over to the restaurant next door. Karen poked at her eggs with a fork and sipped her coffee slowly. When she finished her third cup, she looked out at the dull, grey sky. At least the rain had finally stopped, but the traffic continued to thicken. Sooner or later, she knew she would have to get back on the road.

Once on the interstate, Karen flipped through the radio stations as she drove. She skipped past the rap music and the jazz before settling on pop until the frequent static became so irritating that she just shut it off. Moving her head side to side and rubbing the back of her neck, she tried to get rid of the knot that kept creeping into her muscles. To her right, Robbie slept soundly, his head resting against his worn brown teddy bear. Karen let out a yawn, feeling as though she had been driving forever, but a glance at her watch told her that she had been on the road for only four hours. She had hoped to put in at least eight hours of driving today, but her eyes felt heavy already.

Looking over again at Robbie, Karen stifled a yawn. The steering wheel followed her gaze, and when she looked back towards the road, her truck had drifted over the white line and into the breakdown lane. Jerking the wheel back to the left, she pulled the Ford back into its proper lane. Karen rolled down her window to let in the cool air, along with the exhaust fumes from the semi in front of her, blow in her face. Robbie awoke to the wind gusting in through the window of the truck, and sat up rubbing his eyes.

"Mommy, it's cold in here," he said, wrapping his arms around himself. Karen glanced over and offered him a tired smile before rolling her window back up. She stared out at the highway stretched out before her, mesmerized by the dashed white lines on the road and the rhythmic hum of the tires on the pavement. A green sign loomed over the highway up ahead, reading "Syracuse 25mi." Karen let out a groan. She had hoped to make better time on the road today than she had.

"Mommy, I'm hungry. When are we going to eat?"

Karen turned towards Robbie and then stole a glance at her watch. It was nearly one o'clock. The blaring of a horn made her look up quickly to find that she had drifted into the left lane, much to the annoyance of the driver of the silver BMW that occupied it. As the car pulled alongside Karen's truck, the young male driver lifted his leather-gloved hand from the steering wheel and flipped his middle finger up at her before speeding away. Karen brought up her own hand, but then put it back down when she saw Robbie watching her. Before long, the BMW disappeared into the traffic ahead and was soon nothing more than a mere spot on the horizon. Almost as quickly as the car faded away, so did Karen's anger. Exhaustion slipped into its place and overwhelmed her, leaving Karen's body feeling limp and weighted down.

Realizing that driving much further was not a good idea, Karen got off the next exit that noted food and lodging. She pulled off the highway, not quite knowing where she was or where she was going, and tried to orient herself. Up ahead, she saw a sign for the Blue Moon Motel, a single story concrete building that was painted blue and white.

In the office, Karen dug through her wallet for forty dollars and paid the clerk for one night's stay. The clerk slid Karen's change and a key for room six across the counter. After bringing their bags to the room, Karen took Robbie by the hand and they headed up South Avenue and then crossed over to Radcliff Road. On the corner, they spotted McDonald's. With a McNugget Happy Meal, salad, and two sodas in hand, they made their way back to the motel.

After finishing his lunch, Robbie played with a Matchbox car that he got with his Happy Meal. Karen sat on the bed with one knee drawn close to her chest as she looked over the map. Robbie drove his die-cast car up his mom's leg, turned it sharply to the right at her knee and plunged the car off her leg, where it took one bounce off the bed before hitting the floor. Robbie hopped off the bed, and as soon as he had his car back in hand, he began pushing it across the carpet. Karen watched as he drove it this way and that way, turning at a whim, then stopping and starting some more. In some ways, he was just like her.

"Mommy, can we go play at Irene and Hardy's?"

Karen tilted her head and slowly shook it from side to side. "Robbie, honey, we're a long way from Montana."

"But you said we were going home," he pouted.

"Yes, sweetie. We're going to our new home in Massachusetts."

"I don't want to go there. I want to go back to our old home with Irene and Hardy and you and me!"

"Robbie, we can't go back. We're moving to Massachusetts and that's going to be our new home."

"That's stupid. I want to go play Candyland with Hardy! I don't want to go to Massachusetts," Robbie whined and tears streamed down his cheeks.

Karen let herself fall backwards onto the bed and groaned. She rubbed her temples, wishing she could wave a magic wand and make everything all right. Maybe Robbie was right. Maybe this was a stupid idea. As Robbie continued crying, Karen couldn't help but think about how much she wanted a rum and Coke right now.

Early the next morning, Karen was pleased to see the sun spilling through the curtains. She rolled onto her side and kissed Robbie on his forehead, enjoying the peace and tranquility of the morning. His chest rose and fell rhythmically, and his teddy bear remained clutched in his arms. Karen ran her fingers through his hair and wondered what the future held for them. Quietly, she sat up and slid herself from the bed, then tucked the sheets back in around him.

Karen walked over to the small Mr. Coffee that sat on the bureau and started a pot, and then tiptoed into the bathroom. She leaned into the shower and started the water. As soon as the water heated up, she pulled off her nightshirt, gym shorts, and underwear, and dropped them onto the floor, then stepped into the shower. She poured shampoo into her hand and began massaging it into her scalp. As she closed her eyes and let the water wash away the suds, she thought about Steve and how different he was from Jimmy. Steve was gentle and sweet and so easy to love, but loving Jimmy, that was something else. Jimmy didn't love her, she realized this now. No, Jimmy just loved the idea of owning her. When Karen was with Steve, she could talk about painting, or literature, or just about anything and he would sit, listen, and share his thoughts. But when she was with Jimmy, Karen weighed her words carefully before letting them pass her lips. Art? That was useless. Literature? A hobby for fools. When Karen was with Steve and they made love, Karen felt complete. When she was with Jimmy, well, sex was just an act that needed to be performed, an enforcement of Jimmy's male rights. When Jimmy drank too much and couldn't stay aroused long enough to finish the act, the result was always the same. He'd grunt and sweat over her, and when things didn't go right, he'd grab her arm with a vice-like grip, often bruising her, and tell her it was all her fault because she wasn't able to excite him enough and sustain his interest.

The times that he was able to stay erect, usually the times when he hadn't drunk so much, his hands would push and pull at her, squeezing and parting as he thrust his way inside. He was an unwanted guest in her body, pushing harder, faster and faster, until he would finally collapse on top of her, cutting off her breath. Then when he was spent, he'd simply roll off and walk away. After the first few times they were together, Karen always made sure to dull the experience with rum, beer, whatever it took to let her escape. Most of all, she learned to fake her excitement and never, ever say no to Jimmy.

Karen stepped out of the shower and reached for a towel. As she dried herself off, she studied her reflection in the mirror. A small, pink, jagged scar about an inch long cut across her backside. She remembered how black Jimmy's mood turned at the mere mention of Steve's name. It was shortly after Robbie's birth when Karen first encountered Jimmy's temper. Jimmy had just lost a bid on a job earlier that day, and to lighten the mood, Karen packed a small picnic lunch for the two of them. Robbie slept soundly in his carriage, while they ate sandwiches in the park. Karen had stood up to admire the sun reflecting off the lake's water and noted how handsome Jimmy looked with the sun's warm glow on his face. "I should paint your portrait sometime," she remembered saying. Jimmy told her he wasn't "gonna sit for no stupid picture." And that's when it happened, when she said "Come on, please. Steve used to pose for me all the time." It came out of nowhere. He threw his bottle of beer against the tree to their right, smashing the glass and spilling the rest of the contents onto the ground. Before Karen could even utter another word, he back-handed her across the face, sending her to the ground, where she landed on a piece of glass. Karen felt it bite through her skirt and into her skin. In that moment, over four years ago, she had promised herself that she would never, ever let him hurt her again—if only she had been able to keep that promise.

Karen chuckled to herself as she slid into her jeans, amazed at how roses, tears, and apologies—along with enough rum—could make a girl forgive and forget. But now, as she tugged on her sweater and combed her hair bangs forward, covering the scar above her right eyebrow and applying makeup over the other scar that ran through her upper lip, she knew that there really was no forgetting. Forgetting was too dangerous.

Karen and Robbie stepped out of the motel about an hour later. Bright sunshine and a gentle breeze greeted them at the doorstep. Karen untied the tarp from the bed of her truck and shook the water from it, and then climbed in the back. She pulled one clear plastic container after another towards her and peeked inside, until she found the one that contained Pop-Tarts and granola bars. She grabbed a Pop-Tart for Robbie and one for herself, and then pulled a Styrofoam cooler forward and took out a juice box for each of them.

"Mommy, it's a nice day today. Can we play outside?"

Karen tilted her head and smiled at him. Sitting in the bed of her truck and looking down at Robbie, her life seemed so simple and happy. But one look at the growing number of empty containers in the bed of her truck told her that they needed to get to Massachusetts and that she needed to find a job soon.

"Robbie, we really have to get back on the road. Mommy needs to find a job and a place for us to live."

"Awww. I don't want to ride anymore."

Karen ran a hand through her hair and let out a sigh. Robbie stood next to the truck, his eyes downcast and his mouth forming a frown.

"I'll tell you what. How about we eat our breakfast outside? We can sit right here in the back of the truck and have our own adventure."

Robbie looked up at her and answered with a slow nod. Karen reached down and pulled Robbie up beside her. Listening to the sounds of the world awakening around them, they sat side by side, sipping juice through a straw and eating cold Pop-Tarts.

By eight they were back on the road again, listening to the familiar hum of the tires on the pavement. The day continued to warm up, reaching the upper fifties by mid-afternoon. Shortly before Albany, Karen exited the interstate and made her way to Troy and Route Two, which would avoid any more tolls and take them into Massachusetts. When they passed a large metal sign reading "Welcome to Massachusetts, Home of the 2004 World Champions, the Boston Red Sox," Karen's heart beat a little faster. Baseball, Karen remembered, was how she and Steve first met.

It had been a warm day in late September during Karen's freshman year at UMASS, and she and her new roommate, Carol, were sitting on the couch in their dorm watching a Red Sox game when Steve stopped over to see his sister and meet her new roommate. Like so many older brothers, his purpose in life was to harass his sibling and make her life miserable. Karen remembered how he wedged himself between the two of them as they sat on the couch and how he started showing off by anticipating plays, recalling stats, and identifying who was at bat before the announcer did.

"Hey, you remember when Wakefield rang up nine strikeouts against the White Sox? Wow, that was some game," Steve said.

"Oh really? Did you fall asleep halfway through the game? It was actually ten strikeouts against Milwaukee, not Chicago," Karen corrected him with a wink and a smile. When Carol burst out laughing at her brother's blunders, Steve gave her a playful shove.

"I think you just met your match," Carol said before officially introducing Steve to Karen. At first Karen thought he was a pompous jerk, just another guy trying to impress a girl so he could get into her pants, but after the third time he asked her out, she accepted. She loved his humor, the way he teased Carol, yet absolutely adored her. Karen and Steve had something special, something rare. He was Karen's first love and she was his. He had always been there for her. When her father died suddenly, Steve rocked her in his arms while she wept on his shoulder. And on those brighter moments, he was there too, bragging about her when one of her paintings was accepted into a regional art exhibit. But baseball, Karen smiled, it all started with baseball.

# CHAPTER THIRTEEN

.....................................

## *A Place Once Called Home*

She continued down the narrow twists and turns of the Mohawk Trail part of Route Two, suddenly becoming aware of just how much she missed her home state and the life she once knew as her own. She hungered for the days when a Sunday afternoon could be spent simply debating baseball stats and hanging out with friends.

Despite the need to conserve gas, Karen took a little detour and drove to a small town called Shelburne Falls. She remembered the time she had come here with her parents when she was little, but more vividly, she remembered when she came here with Steve. They were walking hand in hand across the Bridge of Flowers, and Karen had been talking about the Red Sox game they had gone to the night before when Steve tugged on her arm. When she stopped and turned around, Steve dropped down on one knee and reached into his pocket. Pulling out a ring, he said "Karen, will you be mine forever and help me bring more little Red Sox fans into this world?"

Karen remembered how easily the word "yes" came out of her mouth. She remembered how Lillian and her dad hugged them both, ecstatic about the news. Everybody was happy for them. That night, they celebrated together, and began planning the rest of their lives. Two weeks later, Karen's happiness was shattered when her father dropped dead of a heart attack.

Karen parked her truck on the side of the road and shut off the engine. She stared off in the distance, her gaze falling on the bridge that brought back mixed memories. Robbie sat up straighter and looked about. Small two and three story buildings dotted the winding river that wove its way through the center of town. Nearby, they could hear the rumble of a freight train as it lumbered through town.

"Mommy, is this our new home?"

"No, sweetie, it's just a little detour before we go home. Come on," she said, reaching over and unbuckling his seatbelt. "I want to show you something." They hopped out of the truck, and Karen led Robbie by the hand towards the bridge. "You see that little bridge over there? That's called the Bridge of Flowers," Karen said, pointing to the old trolley bridge that had been converted into a walking bridge some seventy years ago. "The bridge crosses over the Deerfield River, and connects Shelburne Falls and Buckland." Karen squatted down next to Robbie and pointed to the other side of the bridge. Robbie's gaze drifted from one side of the bridge to the other as his mother spoke. "I used to come out here nearly every spring with my mom and dad to see all the flowers."

"But Mommy, where are the flowers now?"

"Well, they're here, but they haven't blossomed yet. You see, every spring and summer, this whole bridge is lined with beautiful flowers," Karen told him as they walked hand in hand across it. Halfway across, they stopped and looked out at the river. Karen closed her eyes for a moment and thought about Steve. She looked at Robbie. He leaned his face against the metal fence and stared out at the river, seeming to be searching for something that was not there. Karen followed his gaze, and wondered if she could ever be family enough for him. Reaching over, she rubbed the top of his head and hugged him to her.

"Maybe next month we can come back here when all the flowers have bloomed. This whole bridge will look like a rainbow of colors," Karen told him. Robbie nodded his head and smiled, and then began to skip across the bridge. He looked over his shoulder, his eyes bright with excitement, and beckoned her to follow. Karen jogged over to him, and then grabbed his hand and skipped alongside him.

After eating at a little restaurant tucked in the corner of Shelburne Falls, they turned the truck back towards Route Two and then followed it to Route Ninety a short distance until they got to Route One-Sixteen, which would take them right into Amherst, Karen's home town. When they crossed into Amherst, Karen rolled down her window. The familiar fragrance of spring blew in, carrying with it the smell of new maple leaves and old memories. She slowed her truck to a modest twenty-five miles per hour as she drew closer to Mill Lane. Scanning the streets for the familiar, she noted the old Hansen Farm Stand, but just past it were two new large houses boasting three-car garages. Up ahead of her, a PVTA bus lumbered away from its stop and continued down the road, leaving a plume of black smoke in its wake. Farther up the road, on the corner of Route One-Sixteen and Mill Lane, stood the old convenience store with a new name. As Karen slowed down even more, a horn blared at her. In the rearview mirror, she could see a woman in an Audi waving her hands up in the air at her, as if trying to move her out of the way.

Karen rounded the corner and followed Mill Lane. As her childhood home came into view, her palms began to sweat. She pulled over on the opposite side of the road and wiped her hands against her faded blue jeans. There it stood, the same white two-story colonial with its black shutters and two-car garage. In the front yard, her favorite Canadian maple still stood tall and proud. Robbie peered out the window at his new surroundings. Two story houses, all with fresh, full green lawns lined the street. He turned to his mother and followed her gaze back to the white colonial.

"Wow! Who lives in that big house?"

"That's where I grew up," Karen answered, pointing to the house. Robbie looked up at her, his eyes wide and mouth agape, exposing two neat rows of white baby teeth.

"Mommy, you grew up in a castle?"

Karen laughed and looked back at her house. It was a decent sized house, and it was certainly more impressive than the home they had with Jimmy. She supposed to Robbie it did look like a castle. At the sound of voices, Karen leaned towards the passenger side window and looked towards the backyard. A dark haired woman was walking across the yard. It was Lillian. A small boy, who couldn't have been much younger than Robbie, ran up to her and caught her hand. Behind the two of them, a man jogged over to catch up. The man patted the boy on the head and placed his arm around Lillian, pulling her close.

Karen's face flushed. Had it been that easy for Lillian to forget her father? Karen fumbled for her keys, still hanging in the ignition, and turned them. The truck, already running, let out a high screech of protest. With a jerk of her right hand, she put the truck in gear and popped the clutch, making the tires squeal as she pulled away.

"Mommy, aren't we going to your house?"

"This isn't my home anymore," Karen answered, staring straight ahead, tears stinging her eyes.

# Chapter Fourteen

## *Starting Over*

Karen kept driving until she reached a red light and had to stop. Left, right? She didn't know. When the light turned green, she jerked the wheel hard to the right and headed up Route Nine. After a few minutes, she pulled over to the side of the road and shut off the truck. She laid her head against the steering wheel and sobbed, while Robbie stared at her, not knowing what to do or say. Tears fell onto her lap as she took in staggered breaths. Karen felt Robbie's eyes on her. She sat up and wiped her eyes with her sleeve and looked over at him. He sat silent and still, his fingers picking at the hole in the knee of his jeans. Karen reached over and put her arm around his shoulder, leaning close to him. Robbie's eyes began to water.

"Mommy…"

"I'm sorry, Tiger. I'm sorry," she said, shaking her head slowly from side to side. She wanted to tell him that everything would be alright, that life was going to be all peaches and cream from here on out, but she couldn't. She sat up and gazed out her window, and looked at the changed face of the place she once called home. During the years she was gone, stores opened, others had closed, names had changed, and people had moved on. Sometimes she felt as though she were standing in the middle of the highway, while cars loaded with happy people passed by quickly on either side of her, avoiding her as if she were litter in the road.

She looked over at Robbie. He wasn't staring at her anymore, but instead his attention was on a hangnail that he was determined to pull from his thumb. His eyes were watery and his fingers constantly picking at something.

"Hey," she called over softly to him. "We're going to find a nice place to stay." Robbie continued to pick at his thumb and didn't look up at her. "Hey, Robbie, it will be okay." Robbie nodded, but didn't look at her. She was a bad mother, a failure, and she knew it. Karen stared out at the road, and after a few minutes, she started the truck and pulled back onto Route Nine. She didn't know where to go or what to do, so she just pointed her truck towards the road and drove.

After some time of monotonous left and right turns that got her nowhere, she decided to head up towards Route Two again and toward North Central Massachusetts. As much as she wanted to turn around and face Lillian, she couldn't. The white house with black shutters no longer had room for her. Lillian had moved on—husband, child, she had the complete package. After nearly an hour of driving in silence, Karen exited the highway in Gardner and followed signs for McDonald's. Once they got inside, Karen ordered Robbie his favorite McDonald's meal—a chicken nugget Happy Meal for him, and a chicken sandwich for herself.

Sitting at the table, Robbie continued to pick at his thumb, his meal untouched.

"Robbie, you've got to eat some supper," Karen said. Robbie shrugged and picked up one nugget. He took one little bite and then began picking at his thumb again. Karen reached over and emptied out his meal onto a napkin.

"Wow! Robbie, check it out. You got another truck," she said, holding up his prize. "This is so cool!" She rolled the Matchbox car across the table to him. Robbie reached over and threw it back in the box.

"I don't want that stupid truck!"

"Why not?"

"'Cause it's just like Jimmy's," he answered, folding his arms across his chest. Karen let out a sigh, and the two of them finished their meal in silence.

When they were done, they climbed back into the truck and sat in silence for a little while. Karen switched on the dome light and stared at the map. Tracing her finger along Route 101, she followed it to Ashburnham, Steve's town. Karen didn't know if she could face him just yet, and anyway, it was getting late. Once she and Robbie were settled, then she'd work on that. They roamed around Gardner for a little while in search of a place to stay, but only found one little motel set behind a Friendly's restaurant. Karen pulled into the lot and checked in. Before going to their room, Karen picked up a copy of the local paper. Tomorrow she would search for a job, look for an apartment, get daycare for Robbie, and eventually…when they were settled…she'd call Steve. First things first, she said to herself.

Stepping inside, Karen took in her surroundings. A TV sat on a bureau in front of a full size bed that was covered with a plum colored comforter and two pillows with mismatched slips. Directly in front of the pillows sat a bag of potpourri. Karen set their bags down on the foot of the bed and plopped herself down beside them. Robbie kicked off his sneakers and sat down next to her. Grabbing hold of his teddy bear, Robbie curled up on Karen's lap. Karen brushed her fingers through his hair and wondered what the future had in store for them.

It didn't take very long for Robbie to fall asleep. Karen slid him onto the bed, unzipped his coat, and pulled off his socks before tucking him beneath the sheets. Quietly, she unfolded the newspaper and began scanning the "Help Wanted" section. Among the mere page and a half of ads were jobs for HVAC technicians, a medical secretary, long-haul truck drivers, and computer technicians. She skipped past those ads that said "previous experience necessary" and those that required certifications, college degrees, and the like, until she found one that said "no experience necessary—immediate openings." Karen's heart sunk when she saw that the call for packaging and assembly personnel was only seeking people for its night shift. Karen kept tracing her finger down the ad, stopping to circle those that she thought she could qualify for. One ad called for a receptionist, another for a dishwasher, and one for cashiers at a grocery store.

Looking over at Robbie sleeping, Karen thought about a more pressing issue—daycare. She knew that when she found a job and she had to leave Robbie at a strange house he would surely cry, as do most little children when put into an unfamiliar situation, but Robbie wouldn't just cry. Sooner or later, he would stop crying, stop talking, and just simply sink back into silence. Why should he bother to talk to adults when all they ever did was let him down? Karen opened one bureau drawer after another, until she found a phonebook. She thumbed through the pages, looking for daycare providers in the area, and wrote down names and numbers on a scrap piece of paper. Although she had the number of Irene's cousin, who ran a temp agency in Leominster—some twenty minutes from here, Karen felt unprepared for this new road in her life. A sudden fear gripped her with the realization that she was running out of money and as of this moment, she had no job, no place to live, and a young boy who depended on her. Now more than ever, she wished she could escape inside the amber bottle of rum and let it take her away from here.

She flopped back onto the bed and stared up at the ceiling that had been yellowed from years of cigarette smoke. Drumming her fingers on her belly, she wondered how she could somehow make this work. She wondered how Lillian had gotten over her father so quickly, and wondered how old her son must be. Then her thoughts drifted as her eyes scanned the room, where they paused at the small little desk. In the emptiness of the night, she wondered who had stayed here before. Was it a loving couple? Was it a business man who stopped here along his journey home? Maybe a runaway stayed here and sat at that desk, trying to figure out whether or not to call home? Or maybe it was a lonely old man who had nothing but the comfort of a bottle of scotch and faded memories to warm him? As the sound of a siren broke the quiet night, Karen wondered why she left Montana.

When she closed her eyes, she thought about the warm sting of rum rolling off her tongue and down her throat. She imagined dropping herself into a giant bottle, hiding from the world. There she'd be safe. Everything that ever troubled her wouldn't be able to get at her, so long as she sunk herself beneath the sea of rum. The harsh words of her jilted fiancé, the look of betrayal and disgust on her best friend's face, the disappointment, anger, and desperation in her stepmother's eyes—the guilt, the pain, the anger Karen felt—none of it could get to her. But then, with a jolt of realization, she opened her eyes and saw the harsh reality of it; she'd be all alone and drowning.

After what felt like an eternity, Karen fell asleep only to be woken a few minutes later. In the room next to hers, she heard the door open, then close, followed by soft murmurs and giggling. A few minutes later, the sound of rhythmic thumping could be heard. Karen looked over at Robbie, grateful that he was sleeping through the sex-capades next door. She pulled her pillow over her head as the thumping grew faster and faster, until it finally ceased. Then there was the sound of giggling again, followed by the door opening and closing again.

Karen got out of bed and pulled back the curtain slightly. A man and a woman walked together to a parked car. The man opened the car door for the woman, and then leaned over to kiss the woman intimately, while tucking his shirt into his pants. She reached out a hungry hand and grabbed him between the legs, giggling some more. After nibbling on her earlobe and caressing her breasts, he turned towards his own car, got in, and drove away. Karen shook her head and whispered in the dark, "Welcome home, Karen," and then flopped back onto the bed.

Sometime during the wee hours of the morning, she fell asleep, still in her jeans and sweater. The sound of Robbie scratching his pencil across paper seeped into her ears. Her eyes fluttered open and she saw sunlight streaming through the edges of the curtains. Rolling over to look at the clock, Karen was surprised to see how late it was. It was already ten o'clock. She couldn't quite recall the last time she had slept so late. Stopping long enough to plant a kiss on Robbie's head, she rushed to the bathroom to wash up and change into fresh clothes. She peeked out the door and saw Robbie still drawing on a piece of paper.

"Come on, buddy. We've got to get a move on," she called to him, her brush paused in mid-stroke, still tangled in her hair. Robbie put down his pencil and groaned.

"Mommy, I'm sick of all this stupid driving stuff."

"I know, honey. I'm sick of it too, but the sooner I get a job, the sooner we can settle in and relax. Now come on. Let's go," she said, pointing the brush at him.

Karen set up an appointment to meet with Irene's cousin, who worked at the Holton Temp Agency. She had hoped to get in right away, but he was booked solid, so she spent the better part of the day going from place to place, picking up applications locally and filling them out. Robbie's face bore an expression of both misery and boredom. What else could she expect from a four year old? Running around all day while Mommy tries to find a job just wasn't fun.

When they returned to the motel, Karen thought about calling her sponsor, but how could she help? It's not like she would be able to fly out here and help her get a job, a place to live, and daycare for Robbie. First, get a job, an apartment, and daycare, and then she'd call her. Karen held her cell phone in her hand. She thought she ought to call Steve, but what could she say to him? Surprise! Here I am! By the way, we've got a son. Yah right, she said snapping her phone. Surely he would hate her. She shook her head and leaned her head on her hand, accepting that sooner or later she'd have to face him. She opted later and tossed her phone onto the bed.

The following day, Karen and Robbie headed to Leominster to meet with Irene's cousin. As they drove through downtown Leominster, Karen glanced at her watch. Her appointment was in five minutes, but she still hadn't found the place. She pulled into a Shell station, gassed up, and asked for directions. The man behind the counter told her that the Holton Temp Agency had moved from Monument Square to Central Street a few months ago. If she turned around and followed Central Street down almost to the other end, she could be there in five or ten minutes, depending on traffic. Karen thanked him, and taking Robbie by the hand, got back in the truck.

Almost minutes later, Karen arrived at the temp agency. She jogged across the parking lot with Robbie, her high heels clacking loudly against the pavement. Before she stepped inside, she stopped to catch her breath and smooth out her skirt. When Karen gave her name at the desk, the receptionist looked at the clock and gave her a disapproving look.

"Mr. Hudson was expecting you at ten. It is now fifteen minutes past that, and he's with someone right now. I'm afraid you'll have to just wait," she said, peering over her red-framed glasses and glancing curiously at Robbie. She rolled her eyes and turned back to her computer screen.

Karen shook her head and took a seat in the corner of the room. Robbie colored quietly in his coloring book, while Karen bounced her knees up and down nervously.

About forty minutes later, a short man standing about five foot six, stepped out of his office and waved her over impatiently. Karen followed him into his office, Robbie tagging close behind. Mr. Hudson motioned her to sit and plunked himself down in front of his desk. Karen smoothed out her skirt and took a seat in the cracked vinyl chair across from him. Mr. Hudson looked up from his notes at Robbie.

"What? No babysitter?"

"No sir. We just arrived here a couple days ago. I haven't really had the opportunity…"

"Yah, okay. Let's just cut to the chase. First off," he swiveled his chair deliberately towards the clock and then back again. "Your appointment was for ten, not quarter past."

"Yes sir, I know but…"

"Listen, if you expect me to place you in a job, you've got to be on time," he said, pointing a chubby finger at her.

"I understand and completely respect that, sir, but I didn't realize your office was no longer at Monument Square."

"Sure, sure, sure. Anywho, you were supposed to call my neurotic cousin as soon as you got to Massachusetts to let her know that you weren't abducted by aliens or driven off the road by some crazed motorcycle gang," he said, waving his hands in the air. "She's been ringing my phone for the past two days."

"Yes sir," Karen answered with a smile. "I'm sorry. It's just that it's been so crazy since we arrived…" The ringing of the phone cut into their conversation.

"Answer that," Mr. Hudson said, pushing a few strands of hair over the bald spot on the top of his head.

"Sir?"

"Answer it. I know it's her again. I can feel it in my bones. Now answer it."

Karen reached a tentative hand over to the phone and picked it up, while Robbie looked on.

"Hudson Temp Agency, Mr. Hudson's office," Karen said into the phone, while trying to avoid eye contact with him.

"It's Holton Temp Agency, not Hudson," he said gruffly, shaking his head. "If it were Hudson, I'd be making a hell of a lot more money."

Karen felt her face flush and quickly corrected herself. When she heard a familiar voice on the other end, relief washed over her. Karen assured Irene that they were fine.

"You see, I have a gift. I can always tell when that bossy cousin of mine is going to ring my phone. Damn woman is responsible for me losing most of my hair," he said while sorting through some files on his desk. "You know," he looked up at Karen and flashed her an exaggerated grin, "I was quite a catch in my day."

Karen smiled and set the phone back in its cradle. Mr. Hudson leaned back in his chair, propped his feet up on the desk, and folded his hands behind his head, then muttered something about finally getting some peace and quiet around here.

"So, tell me about yourself Miss Black? What can you do?" Karen told him about her short stint she had done as a nurse's assistant back a little more than five years ago, and explained that she didn't stay on the job very long because she was pregnant with Robbie at the time. She also told him about working for Irene and Hardy as a waitress.

Mr. Hudson took his feet off his desk and hunched over the file in front of him, tapping his pencil impatiently and nodding.

"What else?"

Karen shrugged and bit down softly on her lip, trying to think of something that would impress him.

"Well, honestly, waitressing is what I've done primarily for the last three years, but I did some work for my ex-boyfriend. He's a contractor, and I did some light construction, but mostly painting—interiors, exteriors, whatever he needed me to paint."

"Bingo!" Mr. Hudson snapped his fingers and placed the tip of his pencil down on the paper in front of him. "I've got a dandy little number in an office. It's a nice clean job, Monday through Friday, and...oh...wait," he said, leaning closer to the paper. "Are you familiar with Microsoft Office? Banner? Oracle?"

"I've used Office before, and I'm sure I could catch on to anything they need me to do," she said, but then Mr. Hudson held up his hand in front of him.

"Do you have a degree?"

"No sir, but I did complete the first three years of a baccalaureate degree."

"No, that won't do," he said, shaking his head. "I've dealt with this company before, and they won't go for anyone without a degree or proven experience in an office setting. Hmmm...let me see what else we have," Mr. Hudson said, looking back down at the file in front of him. As he flipped through papers, Robbie tugged on Karen's arm.

"Mommy," he whispered. "I want to go back home." Karen brought her finger to her lips, and hoped he could just sit tight a little longer. Mr. Hudson looked up at Karen, then to Robbie. He reached into his filing cabinet and fished around in it. Shrugging his shoulders, he pulled out a Roledex and slid it across the desk to Robbie.

"Here kid. You can play with this. You see," he said spinning the worn cards forward, "you can spin this around and around and around." Robbie just stared at him. "Go on. Take it. It's yours. We got everything on computers now, so I don't have any use for that. Go on," he said, moving it closer to Robbie. With a tentative hand, Robbie pulled the Roledex towards himself and began spinning it. Mr. Hudson pulled open his desk drawer, took out two markers, and slid them over to Robbie. "Now you can color it too." Once Robbie picked up the markers, Mr. Hudson turned back to Karen. "Now, where were we?"

About a half hour later, after flipping through sheet after sheet and placing calls, Mr. Hudson was able to place Karen in a temp job in the dining room at a nursing home. The pay was not much more than minimum wage, but it was hers for eight weeks while another employee was out on maternity leave. The nursing home was only about twenty minutes from Leominster, and the hours were from 5:00 a.m. until 1:30 p.m. Now she had three days to find a place to live and seek out daycare for Robbie.

They stopped on the ride back to the motel to pick up a loaf of bread and a jar of peanut-butter. Once back inside their room, Karen made peanut-butter sandwiches for the two of them. While chewing thoughtfully on her sandwich, Karen looked through the paper and circled apartments for rent. She thought she should find something in the same town as Steve if possible, but then shook her head and looked at other towns nearby. When she and Robbie were settled, then she'd get in touch with him. She flipped open her phone and started dialing Lillian's number, but then snapped it shut after the first ring. What could she possibly say to her? Letting out a sigh, she turned back to the newspaper and continued looking through the ads. A glimmer of hope rose inside of her when she found an apartment immediately available in Gardner. The price was right and heat and hot water were included. She dialed the number and was met with disappointment. The apartment had just been rented out this morning. She tapped her finger on the next ad for another place in Gardner, and called right away. The landlord would be happy to show them the place and could meet in two hours.

As Karen strolled through the simple, yet clean and roomy apartment, the landlord asked her about her work history. After explaining that she just moved into town and would be starting a new job in just three days, the landlord lost his enthusiasm. He wanted a tenant with a steady work history and good credit. Driving away disappointed and disheartened, Karen headed back to the motel. By late afternoon, she and Robbie had visited three more apartments. Each visit brought more disappointment.

Giving up on apartments for the moment, she began calling around to daycares and scheduling visits for the following day. She stuck the piece of paper with appointments on it inside her purse. Too tired and discouraged to panic anymore, she walked over to the door and opened it. Leaning against the doorframe and watching the traffic build on Pearson Boulevard, Karen didn't know what she had left to offer Robbie. Why on earth had she even left Montana? She had a job, a place to live, even a few friends. What the hell was she thinking?

Robbie laced his hands around Karen's arm, pulling her out of her daydreams. She looked down at him and smiled weakly.

"Hey, what do you say we go for a little walk? Would you like to share a pizza?"

Robbie nodded, and the two of them walked down the boulevard and cut through the parking lot of the mini mall next door. As they walked, a box truck drove past them. Large sweating bottles of Miller beer stuck in an enormous bucket of ice decorated both sides of the truck's panels. Karen watched as it slowed and made a right turn into the parking lot of a liquor store just beyond the motel. One, just one drink, that's all she wanted—just enough the kill the knot building in her gut. She could do it. She could. Just one.

Robbie tugged on her arm and looked up at her. Karen turned to him and chewed on her bottom lip habitually, then looked back up in time to watch the truck disappear behind the liquor store. Another yank on her arm stirred her back to life and they continued their walk across the parking lot, where they were met with the wonderful smell of Chinese food, pizza, and best of all, coffee! They stepped inside the pizza place and ordered a small pepperoni pizza, along with a side salad.

Back at the motel, Karen chewed on a slice of pizza and looked through the newspaper some more, while Robbie ate in front of the TV and watched SpongeBob Squarepants. Near the bottom of the page, Karen found an apartment available in Fitchburg. It was listed as a weekly rental, so chances were good that the landlord wouldn't require perfect credit. Her credit wasn't horrible, but it was less than appealing. With all the times Jimmy charged tools on her credit card, and the times that she felt a desperate need for a drink, and all those times she fooled herself into thinking that she could afford nice things for Robbie—trips to the zoo, the movies, new clothes—well, coming up with the minimum payment by the due date had become a problem for some time.

The landlord had someone scheduled to see the apartment tomorrow, but he could show it to them tonight if they wanted to come down within the hour. After scribbling down the directions, Karen hung up the phone and urged Robbie to finish his pizza. While he washed down his last slice with chocolate milk, Karen counted her money one more time.

Twenty minutes later, they arrived in downtown Fitchburg and pulled up in front of a four-story apartment building. The occasional wail of sirens and steady hum of traffic filled in the space around them. Robbie pressed himself against his mother, and when the loud blast of a fire engine's air horn burst through the night, he jumped and covered his ears. Karen waited in front of the main door and watched as people filtered in and out. A Cadillac Escalade pulled into the parking lot, and a neatly dressed man stepped out. He introduced himself as Martin Weaver, the landlord. Pulling open the front door, he ushered them in and led them through a dimly lit hallway. Karen looked up at the wooden stairs that continued for four stories.

"The place is this way," the landlord said, jerking his head in the opposite direction, and then jogged down the stairs to the basement. He pushed a key into the lock of a door that sat at the foot of the stairs, turned the knob, and waved them inside. Karen stepped in with Robbie and looked about. The ceiling was peeling in places and the paneling was warped in a couple spots. A fluorescent light fixture with a cracked covering sat above the sink and cast its pale white light onto a small, but new fridge. Next to the fridge sat an electric stove. Burnt pieces of food were embedded in the burner rings, and one of the knobs was missing, leaving only a metal prong sticking out. The floor was made up of self-stick black and white checkerboard tiles. Scratch marks gouged the tiles directly in front of the stove.

"There are some coin operated machines for laundry here. Just go out this door and skip across the hall."

The landlord waved them towards the bedroom. It was a modest size of ten by eight feet. The closet was small, too, measuring only about two feet deep by three wide, and the door was missing. It certainly wasn't paradise, but she couldn't afford paradise anyway. Karen chewed on her bottom lip and looked around. Robbie's bed should fit, and when she could afford to buy a bureau, that should fit, too.

The living room had a worn, stained blue-grey carpet, and it wasn't much bigger than the bedroom, but it would do. The bathroom was small. It had a shower stall, pedestal sink, and a row of make-shift shelves that ran from the floor to ceiling. Well, at least she'd have plenty of room for towels, toiletries, and the like.

"So, the place is four hundred a month. That covers your rent, me taking care of the parking lot in the winter, and trash removal," the landlord said matter-of-factly. "You cover heat, hot water, electricity. Security is another four."

"Wait. I thought the ad said rent was weekly," Karen said, digging the ad out of her purse.

"Well, paying weekly is an option; however, it would be one hundred per week, which would leave you paying a hundred dollars more a month on those months that have five Fridays. You see, payment is due the first Friday of every month, or in the case of a weekly plan, every Friday."

Karen looked around once more. A glance at Robbie's face told her that he didn't like it here, but he'd have to adjust. It would only be temporary—she hoped.

"So, you interested?"

"Do I have to sign a lease?" Karen asked, and looked around once more.

"No. If you decide to move, you need to give me one month's notice," the landlord said.

Karen nodded and walked around the apartment once more, with Robbie hanging on to the back of her coat.

"Hey, if you need more time to think about it, that's okay, but I do have someone coming to look at it in the a.m.," he said, moving towards the door.

"No, wait. We'll take it," Karen answered.

"Great. Okay, that means four hundred tonight for May, plus security," he said as he flipped open his receipt book.

"I'd like to move in before May. Is that possible?"

"Sure. I can let you have the rest of April for two hundred and the electricity will be on me for this month."

"Two hundred? There's barely a week left of the month," Karen said holding her money in her hand and stopping in mid-count.

"Hey, like I said, I'll cover the electric bill for the rest of this month, and remember, this place heats with electricity. So I'd say you're getting a pretty good deal, but of course, if you want to think about it some more…"

Karen shook her head, sighed, and counted out one thousand dollars. With a flick of his pen across paper, he wrote out a receipt and tore off her copy, then handed it to her. Reaching into his coat pocket, he pulled out two keys—one for the main entrance and one for the apartment door. The landlord took the money from her, wet his thumb, and counted the bills again.

"Okay, so your next rent will be due on the first Friday of June. I'll need a bank check dropped into the box that in the front hall marked with my name on it. If it's not there by 5p.m. on the first Friday, there will be a late charge of thirty dollars," the landlord said as headed out the door. "Oh, by the way, I wouldn't go carrying around that much money with you, not in this neighborhood anyway. I mean, there are a lot of great people here, but there's few that I wouldn't make friends with, if you know what I mean," he said as he climbed the stairs back up to the main entrance.

"Mommy," Robbie whispered once the landlord was out of sight. "It's scary here. Can we leave now?"

Karen let out an exasperated sigh and pulled him close. "Tiger, this is where we're going to stay," she said. "But it's only temporary, just until we can find a better place." Karen forced a smile and let her gaze wander slowly over the apartment. "Home sweet home," she whispered to herself.

After spending one last night in the motel, they packed up their belongings and headed back to Fitchburg. As they drove, Karen thought about how she might actually miss the little motel with its mismatched sheets and plum comforter. The first trip consisted of unloading the nearly empty plastic containers, the Styrofoam cooler, their two duffle bags, a small box of toys and keepsakes, and a plastic bag of dirty laundry from her truck. Robbie clung to Karen every step of the way, making it much slower to unload everything.

Once all the light stuff was out of the truck, they headed for the Salvation Army store on Route Twelve to see what kinds of deals they could find. Robbie's mood perked up when Karen found an unbelievable deal on a bed frame. Karen couldn't believe her luck—a Lightning McQueen racecar bed frame for only fifty bucks! Lightning McQueen was one of Robbie's favorite characters from the movie "Cars." Robbie tugged on her arm and walked her around the bed frame, pointing out every detail on it. "Whoe, Mommy, this is so cool!" It was funny how a plastic bed frame could make his whole world seem right again.

In addition to the bed frame, Karen picked up a small folding table, two folding chairs, some summer clothes for Robbie, and two dresses for herself, all for a small sum. After sliding everything into the bed of the truck and tying down the tarp, they drove to a discount furniture store to look for a mattress for Robbie's bed and an inexpensive futon for Karen to sleep on. Karen picked up a set of red and blue sheets for Robbie's bed, promising that she'd buy him real Lightning McQueen sheets when they had a little more money.

Despite being exhausted, Karen knew they still had a full day ahead of them. After a quick lunch at a sandwich shop, they stopped at the local grocery store and carefully selected store brand and sale items from the shelves. Karen jotted down prices as she went, stopping once or twice to see how much she was up to so far, and then pushed the carriage to the checkout. Grimacing, she handed her credit card to the cashier, charging $115.00 on it, and pushed the carriage outside. With Robbie seated in the carriage, Karen pushed the cart, hopped on the back, and rolled it across the empty parking lot. Robbie began laughing hysterically and pointed at her, thinking his mother was the craziest and funniest mom alive. At the sound of his carefree laughter, after so many days of riding in near silence, Karen began laughing too. She discovered something wonderful that day; Robbie's laugh was contagious.

Before heading home, Karen stopped to visit three different daycares in the area. Although all three daycares were run by women who seemed very loving and attentive, not one of them could bring a smile to Robbie's face. Feeling desperate, Karen got a cash advance on from her credit card and chose the daycare that she got the best vibes from, then paid for one week of care. Robbie remained silent, refusing to acknowledge the daycare provider when she said hello to him. His laughter had died away soon after they had left the store. Karen sighed, and for a moment, considered going back to the grocery store and riding the cart across the parking lot, just to hear him laugh once more.

After Karen had taken all of the groceries out of the truck and put them away, she jogged back up the stairs to unload the rest of their belongings. Like a shadow, Robbie ran up the stairs behind her, following her every move. When Karen slid the folding table out of the truck and turned around, she practically knocked him over.

"Honey, why don't you wait downstairs for me?"

Robbie answered with a fervent shake of his head and wide eyes that seemed to question the sanity of his mom's suggestion. Karen rolled her eyes, and carried the folding table down the stairs, then returned for the futon and folding chairs. Exhausted and breaking into a sweat, Karen stopped in the living room long enough to strip off her heavy pullover, and then jogged back up the stairs in her Red Sox shirt, enjoying the blast of cool April air on her skin. As she jogged up the stairs, a man with dreadlocks and smooth, dark skin jogged past her with a laundry basket in his hand and yelled "Go Sox" as he passed by. Karen smiled and continued up the stairs, Robbie hot on her heels.

Karen slid the mattress out of the truck, tucked Robbie's big yellow dump truck under one end of the mattress and rolled it towards the door. Robbie walked alongside of her, fascinated that his yellow dump truck could carry such a big load. When they reached the door, Karen lifted up one end of the mattress and asked Robbie to pick up his truck and carry it down the stairs. With his truck in hand, he stepped down one step and waited for her.

"Robbie, you need to go all the way down," Karen said, but was answered with another shake of his head. Karen groaned and thumped the mattress down one stair at a time. "Robbie, you need to move before I accidentally knock you down," Karen said, waiting for him to move. Hesitantly, Robbie backed down the stairs, his attention divided between his mom and the open door to the laundry room. When the man they had just passed a few minutes ago came through the door, Robbie ran up the stairs and grabbed onto Karen.

"You need a hand with that?" The man with the dreadlocks stopped on the stairs. Karen hesitated for a moment, and then nodded her head. The man grabbed the other end of the mattress and the two of them walked it down the stairs and into the apartment.

"Thanks um…"

"You're welcome. And the name's Kenny," he said while extending his hand. "And you are?"

"Karen, and this is my son Robbie." Karen shook his hand and smiled. Kenny jogged back up the stairs with her and helped her bring down Robbie's bed frame, all the while Robbie following close behind. Karen thanked him once more. He turned towards the door and then stopped with one hand on the doorframe.

"Hey, you ain't from around here, are you?"

"No, not this part of Mass."

"Well, welcome to the neighborhood," he said before jogging back up the stairs.

Karen smiled and closed the door after he disappeared around the corner. After setting up the bed frame and pulling the plastic wrap from the mattress, Karen made his bed up and then set up her futon in the living room. She opened one of the plastic containers, dug through it, and tossed a couple of fleece blankets on the futon. Karen looked around the apartment. Plastic crates, some empty, some not, were scattered around the kitchen. Karen pushed them into a corner, leaving the cleanup for another day, and dug through the cabinet in search of something for supper. Spaghetti and sauce was quick enough, she thought as she put on a pot of water to boil.

"Mommy, can we get a TV?" Robbie looked up at her from his plate of spaghetti. Karen shook her head and pushed her pasta around with her fork. Running numbers through her head, she didn't know if she was going to be able to manage rent, groceries, daycare, and gas on a job that barely paid above minimum wage, let alone buy a TV. Despite the worry that was beginning to consume her, Karen was thankful she still had two days before starting her new job and sending Robbie off to daycare.

Robbie, despite having a new bed and his own room, insisted on sleeping next to Karen. Too tired to argue and realizing that it was going to take some time to adjust, she pulled Robbie into her arms and snuggled him to her. The next morning, Karen awoke early feeling stiff and tired. Slipping out from under the covers, Karen tucked the blanket back around Robbie and tiptoed to the kitchen. By eight she had the floor swept and mopped, the stovetop cleaned, and the counter wiped down. She massaged her head and cursed herself for not buying a coffee pot and a couple of mugs. Shrugging it off, she set about unpacking the rest of the plastic crates. Inside one crate, there was a box with a note stuck on top of it. It was Irene's handwriting. Karen picked up the note and read it: "I thought you could use these for your new home. Love Irene and Hardy." Karen looked quizzically at it and opened the box. Inside the box was another box that held a brand new set of plate settings for four. Best of all, there were four coffee mugs too!

After washing the new set of dishes and cleaning the bathroom, Karen scrambled eggs for herself and a very sleepy Robbie. With his hair sticking up in every direction and his teddy bear clutched in his hand, Robbie slid onto his chair and rested his head on the table. At the sight of scrambled eggs, he perked up a little and started eating, but reminded his mom that he didn't like this place.

"Robbie, this is our home now," Karen answered.

"I don't like this stupid ass place!"

Karen's eyes widened. "Watch your mouth," she shouted, pointing a finger at him. His gaze dropped to the floor and his fork clunked down on his plate. Karen blew air out her lips and dropped her hands to her sides. "Honey, please don't say words like that," she said, her voice softening.

"But you and Jimmy say that word," he said, causing Karen to cringe. She opened her mouth to say something, but then just shook her head.

# CHAPTER FIFTEEN

. . . . . . . . . . . . . . . . . . . . . . . . . . . . . .

## *Not Enough*

After nearly two weeks of setting places, passing out plates of food, wiping down tables, and washing dishes at the Beacham Nursing Home, Karen had settled into her new job easily; Robbie, though, was not settling in quite as easily. Every morning, he sobbed on Karen's shoulder when she dropped him off at daycare. Maria, his daycare provider, assured Karen that he always settled down once she was out of sight. She even invited Karen to sneak around the back side of the house and peek in to see how he would settle himself in front of the chalkboard or a coloring book once she left. Just as Maria said, sure enough, Robbie found something to do once she was out of sight. It was just his way of dealing with her departure, Maria told her. Still, it didn't make Karen feel any better. She hated to see him cry. He had already experienced too much sadness in his life, that if she had a magic wand, she'd wave it over him and grant him eternal happiness.

By the third week at work, Karen came to the conclusion that her paycheck just wasn't going to cut it. Daycare expenses sucked up $180.00 per week, absorbing two-thirds of her paycheck, leaving her a small fraction each week to put towards gas, food, and rent. She sat down at the kitchen table after Robbie had finally fallen asleep, and began counting her money, what little was left. She thought about calling Lillian, and picked up her phone, but then put it down. Lillian had her own family to worry about.

She didn't need Karen in her life, and Karen didn't need Lillian in hers.

Instead, Karen dialed Steve's number, knowing that the caller ID would only show "private number" on the display when she called. At the first ring, though, she flipped her phone shut. "What the hell am I even going to say to him," she asked out loud to the empty kitchen. "Hey, it's me, your fuck up ex-fiancé. You have a son and I'm broke," she said sarcastically and banged her phone against the table. "What the fuck!"

On her way home from work, Karen stopped to pick up a local paper and a coffee pot, justifying the expense as a money saver in the long run. As good as Dunkin' Donuts' coffee was, she couldn't afford to keep buying it every day. She collected her mail and walked down the stairs with Robbie. Rifling through the mail, she tossed the junk into the recycle bin and set the bills on the table. Robbie needed new sneakers. She needed a haircut. The fridge was bare. She couldn't continue this way. Combing through the paper, she wondered if she could get a job for a couple hours each day and keep Robbie in daycare just a little bit longer. Looking over the ads, she couldn't find anything that would work with her schedule, until she saw an ad for delivery person for a local florist in the next town over. The ad was specifically for Saturdays and personnel would be compensated for mileage, earn a minimum rate, plus tips. Karen called the number, but was greeted with the disappointing news that they had just hired someone. The man asked her to fill out an application online anyway, just in case something else opened up. Sure, Karen said to herself after she snapped her phone shut. I'll just hop on my computer and do that right now.

Karen set her phone down and continued looking through the paper. She needed another job soon. There were only five weeks left of her temporary position, and although her boss loved her work ethic, he didn't have any other positions available. All Karen could do was keep looking for another job and pray that Kristie, who was still on maternity leave, would suddenly want to stay home fulltime.

With the passing of each week and each failed attempt to find a better paying job, Karen found it harder and harder not to want to drink. Every morning, though, she made the promise that just for that day, she wouldn't drink. By the end of each day, the desire for rum, the desire to just escape the loneliness and failure that seemed to surround her grew. Karen thought about going to an AA meeting, but then shook her head, unable to justify spending more money on a sitter when she couldn't even figure out how she was going to manage the bills she already had. The meetings were in the evening, and other than paying for a sitter, she had nowhere to bring Robbie. She was alone. Staring at the four walls that surrounded her, she walked over and peered out the tiny ground level window that barely let any light into the kitchen. Shaking her head, she whispered "This is no home."

The ringing of her cell phone pulled her from her thoughts. She flipped open her phone and looked at the caller ID. It was Irene. Karen answered, her mood lifting at the sound of Irene's voice. Irene always had a way of lifting Karen up when she was down. Irene talked about the diner, the customers who still asked about Karen, and how the new waitress had some big shoes to fill. Karen smiled, and walked to the living room with the phone in hand. Robbie was constructing a tower out of Legos when Karen walked in.

"Someone wants to say hi to you," she said with the phone held out towards him. Robbie took the phone from her and held it to his ear, but didn't utter a single word. "Go on and say hello to him, or he's not going to talk," Karen said leaning towards the phone. When Irene said hello, Robbie's face lit up. They talked for a few minutes and then Hardy got on the phone.

"Mommy, it's Hardy! He's talking to me from way far away!"

Karen sat on the futon, smiling, as Robbie chatted on with Hardy. After a few minutes, Robbie handed the phone back to Karen. Before hanging up, Irene told Karen to keep an eye on the mail for some gifts that she and Hardy boxed up for them: A dozen of Irene's famous homemade chocolate chip cookies, a Lightning McQueen storybook for Robbie, and a phone card for her. Karen set the phone down on the table, feeling a little less alone in the world.

After a late supper of hotdogs and beans, Karen sat on the edge of Robbie's bed and opened the book he had picked from the Fitchburg Public Library. As Karen read to him, Robbie lay across her lap and yawned. When Karen finished one book, Robbie begged for just one more story, so she picked up "How Mr. R. Bitt Found His Way Home: Tales of a Toad Lost in the Woods." Karen had only read the first three pages when she looked down at Robbie and saw him fast asleep. She picked him up and tucked him beneath the covers. For a while she sat by his side and just watched him, her beautiful boy. Someday, somehow, things had to get better.

# CHAPTER SIXTEEN

## Confronting the Past

The last week of May brought flowers in bloom, longer days, warmer weather, and more worry for Karen. As her shift drew to a close at the nursing home, Karen asked her boss one more time if there was anything available in the kitchen.

"I can cook, prep, stock shelves, whatever you need me to do. I just need a job," Karen said in the cheeriest voice she could muster. Her boss frowned and shook his head, apologizing once more that there just weren't any positions available in the kitchen. Karen nodded, saying that she understood, and turned back to the pile of silverware in front of her. She wanted to call Mr. Hudson again at the temp agency, but he'd likely tell her the same thing that he already told her yesterday and the day before. The fulltime positions he needed filled at present were for a nightshift packager in Littleton, a nightshift janitor at a factory in Leominster, positions that were part-time evening, and a handful of fulltime day positions that she just didn't qualify for. He promised her he'd keep looking, but didn't have anything at this time. With less than two weeks left of work in front of her, Karen felt as if everything she had just accomplished was about to be ripped away from her. She hadn't been able to save up anything over the last six weeks. Every cent went to one bill or another—daycare, rent, gas, food, leaving her with no room for error. Being out of work, if even just for a week, could destroy everything she worked so hard for.

The next morning while Karen was working, her boss told her the manager of the nursing home wanted to speak to her right away. Looking confused, Karen nodded her head and went to the manager's office. The administrative assistant motioned Karen to have a seat, telling her that Mrs. Madigan would be back in a moment. Karen rested her elbows on her knees, and leaning forward, began massaging her temples. She counted the weeks she worked in her head. She should have at least another week after this week. They couldn't just ask her to leave early, could they?

"Ms. Black?" Mrs. Madigan's question jolted Karen from her thoughts. Karen sat upright and nodded. "I see that your temporary position with us is to come to a close by next week; however, we'd like to pull you from that early," she said, and in the single moment of a pause, Karen could feel her chest tighten with panic. "You see, Harold has been telling us that you're a hard worker and in need of a job, but we just do not have anything available whatsoever in the kitchen with Kristie returning from maternity leave," she said, looking over the rims of her glasses. "But I'd like to make mention of another position we have available, if you're interested in it." Mrs. Madigan picked up a sheet of paper, reading it over, and then looked back up at Karen. "This is the job description for a janitor's position that we are going to advertise in next week's paper. One of our janitors has just accepted a job out in Boston and he's starting tomorrow. Not very much time for us to replace him, don't you think?" Mrs. Madigan handed the paper to Karen. "Normally I would advertise this, but we're in a bit of a jam, and Harold promises me that you have great work ethic and that you have a good rapport with the residents here. Is this something you're interested in?"

"Absolutely. I am very interested," Karen answered. Mrs. Madigan went on to discuss Karen's new pay, benefits, and hours. Starting tomorrow, she would be working 7:30 a.m. until 4:00 p.m.

"Now, you'd better get back to the dining room before Harold has a conniption fit," Mrs. Madigan said, rising to her feet. Karen extended her hand and thanked Mrs. Madigan over and over again. At the end of the day, Karen left work feeling hopeful about the future.

The next morning, Karen was introduced to her immediate supervisor, who walked her around the nursing home, showing her where the supplies were kept, and went over daily duties and hazardous chemical precautions. Shortly afterwards, she was left to do her work.

As she went from room to room mopping floors and scrubbing toilets, she considered how many times she had been left to clean up after Jimmy. He was a toilet seat up kind of guy, and his aim was often less than perfect, but she couldn't recall their bathroom ever being quite as pungent as some of the ones she was cleaning now. Karen shoved the bowl brush into the throat of the toilet, wrinkling up her nose as she did. It wasn't until she was kneeling in front of the toilet with the brush in hand that she realized she hadn't had a drink in almost a year.

After she finished scrubbing the residents' rooms, she dragged a vacuum cleaner out to the lobby and began to look for an outlet to plug it into. On the far side of the lobby, a small boy sat on his mother's lap. The two of them were talking to an elderly woman that sat directly across from them. Though Karen couldn't hear what they were saying, she knew by their laughter and mannerisms that they must be a very close family. A man appeared in the entrance of the lobby, and the boy hopped off his mother's lap and ran into the man's arms. Carrying the young boy in his arms, the man walked over to the women. He leaned forward and kissed his wife, and then placed a kiss on the elderly woman's cheek. Karen knelt on the floor to plug in the vacuum. Before switching it on, Karen listened to the boy's giggling as his father tickled him. Flipping on the vacuum, she tried to drown out the voice in her head that told her she needed to call Steve. Robbie needed his daddy.

Over the weekend, Karen drove to Ashburnham. She pulled over on Main Street to check the map one more time. Her finger traced an "L" shaped path across the map, and stopped at Center Street. She looked at the road that cut across Main Street and knew that his house wasn't very far from here. Not knowing whether or not he was home, she sat staring at the map as if it held the answer to her question.

"Mommy, what are we doing here?" Robbie looked at her before turning his attention back to his surroundings. Karen turned to him for a moment, her eyes seeming to ask the same question.

"Umm...I need to see someone," she answered while staring down the road.

"Who?"

"Just somebody. You don't know him yet," she answered. Robbie shrugged and went back to looking out the window. Karen picked up her phone and stared at Steve's number. Her palms began to sweat as she dialed.

"Hello?" His voice was low and mellow. "Hello? Are you going to speak?" His voice grew louder, impatient.

"Steve..." Karen answered, her own voice barely audible beneath the pounding of her own heart.

"Who is this?"

"Steve, it's me...Karen," she responded. Time seemed to stop, making the few seconds between the question and the answer stretch out like a long fly ball that drops foul, just before the pole.

"What do you want?" Steve answered with an edge to his voice that Karen barely recognized.

"I need to talk to you," Karen answered, rubbing a sweaty palm against her jeans.

"We don't have anything to talk about."

"Please, can I come over for just a minute? I really need to talk to you." Karen waited for his response, wondering for a moment if he had hung up.

"Look, whatever you need to say, just say it."

"Please, just hear me out. I'm in town and I'd really rather talk to you in person."

"Fine. You have my number, so I assume you have my address," he said and then hung up. Karen closed her phone, took in a deep breath, and started her truck. She took a left turn through town and followed it to Center Street. Spotting his house number, Karen slowed the truck to a stop on the side of the road in front of a small red cape. A bright yellow Nissan Xterra sat in the driveway, mud caked on its body and tires. When Steve stepped out of his house, Karen's breath caught in her throat. He stood at the top of the steps with his arms folded across his chest.

"Stay put," Karen said, turning to Robbie. "I've just got to go talk to this man." Robbie looked out his window at the stranger with the sandy blonde crew cut. When the stranger made eye contact with him, Robbie unbuckled and crouched down in his seat.

Before walking up the steps, Karen ran a hand through her hair, pulling her bangs forward over her scar. As she walked up the steps, she turned back to look at Robbie, who kept peeking and then ducking from view. When she turned back around, Steve stood just a couple feet in front of her. His hair was much shorter than the last time she saw him, and he sported a Fu Man Chu mustache. He wore a pair of ripped jeans, dotted with wet paint, and his button up shirt was open, exposing sweat and hair on his chest.

"Painting?" Karen asked, smiling nervously.

"What's this about? I've got work to do," he answered, his attention divided between Karen and the little boy peeking at him every now and then from the truck. Steve looked from the boy to Karen, his eyes narrowing and lips parting.

"I…okay. When we broke up…before we broke up," Karen hesitated, then cleared her throat. Steve looked at her with an eyebrow raised in expectation. "That's Robbie," Karen said turning her gaze towards the truck, and then looking back to Steve. "He's our son," she said, her voice dropping to almost a whisper.

Steve's mouth opened, but nothing came out at first. He looked at her, then to Robbie, and back to her again, erupting in laughter.

"You're funny. You know that," he said, shaking his head. "Oh Karen, you're a real piece of work," he said.

"Steve, please. Don't do this. Not here, not in front of him. He's your son." Karen turned to Robbie and then back to Steve. "Look at him, just look at him. He's got your hair, your sweet nature, and…and…he even rubs his knuckles just like that," she said, pointing at him frantically. Steve stopped and dropped his hands to his sides. He took a step towards the truck and then looked back at Karen, a small laugh coming out as he shook his head.

"Hey, look I don't know what kind of trouble you got yourself into, but he's not mine. He can't be. We were careful."

"Yes, we tried to be, but…"

"This is bullshit. Come on, Karen. Be honest. What happened? Did your bar buddy dump you, and now you need to find a daddy for your kid?" Steve stared at her, his sarcasm and anger betraying the doubt in his eyes.

"Steve, please." Karen stepped closer to him and put her hand on his arm. "I swear to you. He's yours. He is," Karen said holding his gaze. Steve shook her hand off and turned away. Karen grabbed his arm again, her grip firm and unyielding. "Just look at him! Look at him Steve!" Karen pulled on his arm and stepped in front of him, pointing to Robbie. Steve let out a huff of air and turned back around. He took a step closer to the truck, staring at the crop of sandy blonde hair and hazel eyes that peeked out the window from time to time.

"If he's mine, then why the hell didn't you come to me and tell me this, what…" he counted the years and months in his head, "…over five friggin' years ago?"

"I didn't know. I swear I didn't know."

"You're something else. How could you not know?"

"Steve, please. I…"

"Save it! You haven't changed a bit. You're still a liar hiding behind a bottle," he said as he turned around and began walking up the stairs.

"I'll prove it," Karen shouted, causing him to stop halfway up the stairs. "We can get a blood test," she said to his back.

"Look, what is it exactly that you want from me," he said turning back around. He looked over at her truck, his eyes following the splinters of rust the raked through the rear quarter panels. "What do you want? Money?"

"No, Steve. I don't want your money, and I didn't come here with the intention of messing your whole life up, and I know that's hard to believe, but please, please believe me that all I want is for Robbie to know he has a good man for a father."

"Why now? Why all of the sudden do you show up here and tell me all this now?"

"I couldn't come to you before. My life was…I just couldn't come…I didn't know…" Karen squeezed her eyes shut and pressed her fingers against them. "I just want Robbie to know his father. That's all. I swear. Look," Karen said, pulling out a piece of paper from her purse and handing it to him. "Here's my number. Please, when you're ready, just come see him." She held out the paper to him. He stared at the ground and then looked back at the boy in the truck. Turning back to her, he shook his head, snatched the paper from her hand, and then walked away.

Karen watched him disappear into his house and heard his door slam shut. She took in a staggered breath, fighting back tears, and went back to the truck. Robbie stared at her with his quiet curiosity.

"Come on, sweetie," Karen said patting his seat. "You've got to get back in your seat and buckle."

Robbie climbed on the seat beside Karen and threw his arms around her. Holding him in her arms, she cried softly. Robbie's little hands patted her back. Karen wiped her eyes and settled Robbie into his seat.

"Mommy, who was that man that was yelling at you?"

Karen looked at him a moment before answering. "Oh, he's just somebody I used to know," she said, wondering where the Steve she once knew went.

After two days passed without word from Steve, he finally called and left a message on her voicemail: "Fine. Let's get this done with." The following week, Karen left work an hour early and took Robbie to the lab at the hospital to get a blood test. Karen sat with Robbie in the waiting area just outside the lab and waited for the technician to call Robbie's name. It was just before 4:00 p.m. and the waiting area was empty except for the two of them. The occasional sound of heels clicking across the industrial tile floor and announcements over the speaker broke up the emptiness.

Karen listened to the click-clack of the women's heels as they passed by. She missed her heels, her nice clothes, and the way people used to look at her, like she was someone special, someone with class. She stared down at the floor and looked at the sneakers on her feet. The rubber sole was peeled back near the toe of one sneaker, and the heel cracked on the other. Her laces were threadbare and in need of replacement. She looked over at

Robbie's feet and marveled at his relatively new sneakers she had found for him, another bargain at the Salvation Army.

When Robbie's name was called, Karen took him by the hand and walked in the lab. "Now, remember it's just a blood test. You'll feel a little pinch just for a minute, and then it will be all over," she said to him. Robbie looked about nervously, his hand gripping his mother's tightly. A technician spoke softly to Robbie while he tied a tourniquet around his upper arm and washed his skin with an alcohol swab. When the technician pressed the needle into his vein, Robbie let out a piercing cry, but then fell silent. With his mouth open and tears streaming down his face, Robbie watched horrified as his blood traveled from his body into the small tube the technician held. Karen stroked his head and felt the sting of tears pulling at the corner of her own eyes. She pressed her face against the top of his head and kissed him, wishing she could just kiss away his tears.

When the technician was finished, he pressed a piece of gauze against Robbie's arm and secured it with a bandage. With wary eyes, Robbie watched as he pulled something from a box and then turned back towards him. Robbie pulled his arms close to his body and pressed up against Karen when the technician stopped in front of him.

"Here you go buddy," he said, handing Robbie a couple of stickers. Robbie looked up at his mom and nudged her. She took the stickers from the technician and thanked him, and then handed them to Robbie. At the end of the appointment, the lady at the desk handed an information sheet to Karen, along with an invoice. Glancing down at the numbers, Karen swallowed hard. After the bill she had just racked up, Karen hoped that Steve would follow through with his test and that it would confirm what she knew in her heart to be true.

Days passed and Steve still hadn't called. Privacy laws prevented Karen from finding out anything on her own. Everything hinged on Steve.

With each passing day, Karen wondered if maybe she had it all wrong. She did the math in her head, counting back to when she and Steve were last together. She couldn't recall missing a pill, but then again, some mornings she had been too hung over to remember much of anything.

When Steve finally called, he didn't bother to say hello. His voice was sharp and bitter.

"I can't believe I even have to ask this. What's his name?"

"His name is Robert. Robert Joseph Black," Karen answered.

"How could you keep him from me all this time? You had no right."

Before Karen could answer, he hung up the phone, leaving Karen listening to dead air until the phone began beeping loudly in her ear.

# CHAPTER SEVENTEEN

......................................

## *New Beginnings*

Over the past two weeks, Robbie shot off a thousand questions for Karen about his daddy since she broke the news to him. Why didn't he live with them? How did he get all the way out here? Was his daddy mean? Did he yell a lot like Jimmy? Was he going to live with them? Did he like to play Candyland? When was he going to meet him? Some questions were harder to answer than others, but at least she could answer one of them with a degree of certainty. He was going to meet his daddy soon.

It was a hot summer day in late June. Robbie held his mother's hand tightly as they walked over to the park. Winchester Park abutted the public library and a small building that held the police and fire stations. A young mother chased her toddler around the playground and said a quick hello as she passed by Karen and Robbie. Two other women sitting on a bench near the sandbox chatted while their children played in the sandbox. It seemed like Ashburnham had the typical small town comfort, charm, and an air of friendliness about it, but with police cruisers parked nearby, none of that mattered to Robbie. He gripped Karen's hand even tighter. His eyes darted from Karen to the cruisers and back again. Tugging on her arm, he pulled her to the opposite side of the park. Karen looked over at her son, holding her hand tightly and turning a deaf ear anytime anyone said hello. While other children played, Robbie remained worried and suspicious. Karen wished Steve would just hurry up and get here. Maybe once Robbie had a chance to meet his daddy he'd relax a little more.

After about fifteen minutes and Karen promising him for the fourth time that nobody was going to take him away from her, Robbie finally worked up enough courage to go down the slide by himself. After each time down the slide, he ran over to Karen and hugged her, performing this act like a sacred ritual that would protect them both. Whenever a car pulled up, Robbie would point to it and ask "Is that my daddy's car?"

Steve pulled up in his Xterra a little past 4:30 p.m., about a half hour past the time they had agreed to meet. As he walked towards them, Robbie froze in his tracks, his eyes focused on the badge on Steve's chest. Robbie ducked inside the tube slide and refused to come out when Karen called him. Steve stopped next to Karen, his eyes hard and questioning.

"For God's sake, why couldn't you have told me sooner?"

Karen looked up at him, but then looked away. Steve folded his arms across his chest and shook his head. Karen drew in a breath, and measured her words. "I didn't know. There's been so much chaos in my life. I just didn't think it was possible that he was yours," she said.

"You just didn't think? That says a lot about you."

"Please, please, Steve. I know you have every right to be angry, but please let's just not do this, not here, not now in front of him," Karen pleaded, holding her hands out in front of her. Robbie peeked out at them, but then ducked back inside the slide and climbed to the safety of top of the slide, where Steve couldn't see him.

"Fine, but we're not through," Steve said. Karen nodded and called to Robbie again. She ducked her head inside the tube slide and called to him again, but Robbie shook his head.

"I'll go up and get him," Karen said turning towards the stairs that led to the top of the slide.

"No," Steve said, touching Karen's shoulder. "I'll go to him."

"No, that's not a good idea," she said, catching his arm. Steve looked at her questioningly. "He's really shy and doesn't do well around strangers." Karen poked her head inside the tube and called to Robbie, but was greeted with another fervent shake of his head. "Please come down and say hello," Karen coaxed. "Come on Tiger, please." Robbie slid down the slide and peeked out at the man in black pants, black leather boots, and a white button-up shirt and a badge that glinted in the sun. He shook his head and scooted back up the slide.

Karen turned to apologize to Steve, but he was already climbing the stairs to the top of the tube slide. "Steve," she called to him, but he waved her off. "It's okay. I got this," he said he approached the top of the slide. Robbie watched from the top opening of the tube slide with wide eyes and then ducked back inside. When Steve sat down on the landing and peeked inside the slide, Robbie took one look at his badge and then slid down and away from him. Reaching the bottom, he jumped out and ran to Karen.

"Mommy, my daddy is a cop," Robbie said in a panicked voice, while tugging on her arm. Karen glanced over at Steve's truck and noted the small red light that sat on the dash.

"No, he's not a cop. I think he's a firefighter," Karen said as she tried to coax him back in the other direction. "Go on over and say hi. He's a nice guy."

"He doesn't seem very nice. He's a big dumb dumb meany! He yelled at you before," Robbie said, standing in front of her and folding his arms across his chest. He turned around and watched with surprise as Steve squeezed himself into the tube slide and slid down. As soon as Steve reached the bottom, Robbie ran back up the stairs and ducked inside the slide. Karen started to go up the steps, but Steve caught her arm.

"It's okay. I can wait. I don't have to be anywhere right now," he said and stood next to Karen. Robbie peeked out at Steve and saw him standing next to his mom. When Steve waved to him, Robbie ducked back inside. After a few minutes, Steve climbed back up the steps. Robbie poked his head out the top and stared at Steve as he approached the landing. A wide smile spread across Steve's face. Robbie started to back down the slide, but Steve held up one finger and reached into his pants pocket. From the bottom of the stairs, Karen watched as Steve held out a small die cast fire truck in front of him. Robbie looked from the fire truck to Steve, but didn't take it. Steve set it down on the lip of the slide and rolled it towards him. Robbie backed away, his eyes darting from the fire truck to Steve and back again.

"It's for you," Steve said, pointing to the truck. Robbie regarded him for no more than a second or two before retreating down the slide. He ran over to Karen and tugged on her arm. She squatted down and looked him in the eyes, telling him that it was okay to take the fire truck. Robbie looked towards the slide and then to Steve, who remained sitting on the landing. A moment later, Robbie saw the little fire truck roll out of the tube and bounce onto the ground. First glancing up at Steve and then to Karen, Robbie took a few tentative steps forward and picked up the fire truck. Running back over to Karen, Robbie held up the fire truck to her. The sound of someone coming down the slide caused Robbie to turn around. When Steve reached the bottom of the slide and let himself plop onto the ground with a thud, Robbie giggled and ran back up. After some hesitation, Karen moved a couple feet away and sat down on a bench. Steve sat down next to her and waved to Robbie.

"He really is pretty shy, huh?" Steve asked, watching Robbie peek at him from the top of the slide.

"He just needs some more time to get to know you," she answered.

"I just don't get why you didn't tell me about him sooner. I mean why in the hell would you keep him a secret from me?" Steve asked while trying to keep a smile on his face whenever Robbie looked over.

"Please, can we just talk about this some other time?" Karen looked back up at Robbie and smiled. Steve opened his mouth to say something, but then stopped when he saw Robbie duck into the tube and heard him slide down. Robbie climbed out of the slide, gauging the distance between him and his mom, and then ran over to her. He jumped onto her lap and pressed his head against her chest, feeling safe enough to study the strange guy called daddy that was sitting next to his mommy. Steve smiled, but stayed right where he was. After a moment, Robbie held up the fire truck and smiled.

"Do you like it?" Steve asked. Robbie nodded, one hand grasping his mother's shirt, the other holding the fire truck.

"That's called a pumper truck. Its job is to take water from a fire hydrant or pond or lake and suck it up into the fire truck's tank and shoot it out the front and onto the fire." Steve pointed to the back and then the front of the fire truck. Robbie turned the fire truck over in his hand and studied it.

"So," Karen said, attempting to make small talk, "how did you go from studying natural resources to being a firefighter?"

Steve looked at her, any trace of a smile gone from his face. "Let's just say that my life changed directions."

Karen nodded quickly and then glanced at the time on her cell phone. "Oh, it's getting late. I've got to get Robbie home and get supper started," she said. When Karen stood up with Robbie in her arms, Steve got up too.

"I'd like to see him again, you know, get to know him better," Steve said and walked alongside Karen and Robbie.

"Yah, okay. I think he'd like that," Karen said and opened the door of her truck. Reaching in and patting Robbie on the head, Steve said "I'll see you later." Robbie looked up at him, but didn't respond. After Karen buckled Robbie in his seat and shut his door, Steve walked with her to the driver's side of the truck.

"Maybe he'll talk to me next time," Steve said, shrugging his shoulders. Karen assured him that after a spending a little more time with him Robbie would open up a little more. They planned to meet at the park every day for the rest of the week.

On the ride home, Robbie inundated Karen with even more questions. As soon as they left the park, Robbie's silence was overtaken with curiosity. He wanted to know again how his daddy got all the way across the country, wanted to know if his daddy liked chocolate ice cream, if he liked Spiderman, if he had ever watched the movie "Cars," and if he liked kids. The list of questions went on and on. Karen smiled, knowing this was the most Robbie had talked since arriving in Massachusetts.

With each visit, Karen was greeted with a hard stare, but Steve made it a point not to let Robbie see his anger. Every time Robbie saw his dad, he ran to the top of the slide and waited for him. They played a game of cat and mouse, Robbie sliding down the slide and Steve coming up behind him, hot on his trail. On the last Saturday of June, one week after their first meeting, Steve showed up at the park. It was his day off, and he wanted to spend more than an hour with Robbie. Steve wore shorts, a tank top, and sneakers, a strange sight to Robbie who wasn't used to seeing him out of uniform.

Again, they started their routine. Once Steve reached the top, Robbie slid back down again, satisfied that he evaded him once more. Again, Steve slid down the slide and let himself land on the ground with a thud, sending a spray of wood chips in every direction. Robbie burst out laughing, surprising Karen with the sound of his voice. Steve got to his feet and started to run towards Robbie, but suddenly stopped short and began hopping up and down on one foot. Giving Robbie a playful grimace, he sat down on the bench next to Karen and pulled off his sneaker, dumping a handful of woodchips out. As Karen watched Robbie double-over with laughter, she couldn't help but laugh too. Seeing his mother laugh while sitting next to his daddy, Robbie ran over and hopped up on her lap. Reaching over, Robbie poked Steve in the arm and smiled.

Robbie poked him again and then hopped off Karen's lap and ran back up the stairs, glancing over his shoulder once or twice to see if Steve was coming. "Okay pal, as soon as I get my sneaker back on, I'm going get you," Steve said, making a face and giving his sneaker another shake. When Robbie disappeared into the top of the slide, Steve spoke to Karen, but kept his eyes on the slide.

"Okay, so if I've done the math right, I figure he must have been born in late July or early August. Is that right?"

"His birthday is in two weeks. He came three weeks early," Karen said. Steve shook his head and got up off the bench. He shot Karen a look, and then put on a smile as he jogged up the stairs to Robbie. There was a time, Karen remembered, when Steve's face used to light up whenever he saw her.

Before they parted ways, Steve told Karen that it was time for the rest of his family to meet Robbie. Karen hesitated, wondering if by "family" he meant a wife and kids. Surely he must have someone in his life; she hoped she was wrong. She knew, though, that this moment was inevitable, and didn't respond right away.

"They have a right to know their own flesh and blood. Damn it Karen, my sister and parents have a right to know him." Sister and parents? Karen felt immediate relief, though she knew that even if Steve didn't have a significant other in his life, it didn't make him hers. It didn't erase the past or take away the pain. Karen thought about how much she didn't want to face his parents or Carol, but knew that meeting them would make

Robbie feel even more secure. Realizing that there would never be a perfect time, Karen hesitantly nodded her head and agreed to meet Steve at the park again tomorrow.

The next morning, Karen took more time than usual applying her makeup and doing her hair, doing her best to make her scars go unnoticed. She applied her foundation and lipstick slowly and deliberately, trying to eliminate any evidence of the scar that ran through her lip and just beyond. Carefully, she parted her hair to one side and combed her bangs so they hung over her right eyebrow. She dug through Robbie's clothes and pulled the tags off the new shirt and shorts she bought for him at Target with her Target charge card the night before. Standing in the apartment, with one hand on the door, Karen wished she had a shot of rum to subdue the dread building inside of her. She shook her head, took Robbie's hand in hers, and left the apartment. As she pulled up to the park, her heart began to race. She wished somehow she could just hide somewhere and be safe from the arrows that would soon come her way.

Just five minutes after they arrived, Steve's family began showing up. First to arrive were Steve's parents, who simply stepped out of their car and walked over to Steve and Robbie, without even giving her a second look. Then Carol pulled up with another man, who Karen guessed must be her husband. Karen stood some distance away and could feel Carol's eyes on her as she walked towards Steve and Robbie. She turned away and sat on the bench closest to her, which thankfully, was the furthest from Steve's family. She wished she could close her eyes, click her heels, and disappear from view. Robbie ran over to her and hopped onto her lap. Cupping his hand to her ear, he whispered "Mommy, did you see my new grampa, gramma, auntie, and an uncle?" Karen nodded, kissed his cheek, and hugged him to her. "Mommy," Robbie said, hopping off her lap and tugging on her arm, "Come on over with me." Karen shook her head and brushed her hand against his cheek, telling him this was his special time with his new family.

Steve jogged over and squatted down in front of Robbie. "Hey Robbie, Gramma and Grampa have a little present for you. You want me to fly you over there like an airplane?" Steve looked at Robbie, his expression hopeful and encouraging. Robbie looked at Karen, his eyes questioning.

"Go on. It's okay," Karen said and nodded towards Steve. Robbie held his arms up to Steve, and Steve lifted him into his arms for the very first time. For a moment, Steve just held him there and planted a kiss on the top of his head. He had fallen in love already. Steve hoisted Robbie in the air, and with Robbie's arms outstretched like wings, they flew off to the other side of the park. Karen turned away, feeling the tug of the beginning of tears at the corners of her eyes. She didn't even notice Carol walking towards her until she heard her familiar voice.

"I don't know what you're trying to pull here, but you just better think about what you're doing," Carol said, pulling off her sunglasses and staring intently at Karen with her brown eyes. Karen didn't know what to say. After all, what could she say to this woman, who she once called her best friend? Resting her hands on her hips, Carol leaned closer, her voice hard but low. "You put my brother through hell, and I'm not going to just stand by and watch you do it again."

"Carol, I have no intentions of doing anything to hurt him," Karen answered.

"Really? What do you call keeping his own son from him for nearly five years?" Carol shook her head and turned on her heel.

While Steve's family gathered around Robbie and fawned over him, Karen felt smaller and smaller, almost nonexistent. Steve's parents never turned her way, not even once. It was as if she were invisible. Robbie even seemed to forget she was there, too, but what else could she expect with all this excitement? Be glad that he's settling in so well, she reminded herself. In fact, she had never seen him smile so much. He seemed so happy, so content. His face was flush with excitement as his new family presented him with little gifts. It was like Christmas in July.

Within a week, Robbie had become comfortable enough with Steve to walk with him from the park to the ice cream stand with Karen following along at a distance. Steve told Karen that he would like it if Robbie could come over for supper on Saturday night. Robbie jumped up at the mention of it, but when the time came for Karen to leave him alone with his daddy, unease replaced excitement.

"Mommy, why can't you stay?" Robbie whispered in her ear. Karen smoothed his hair back and kissed him on the forehead. "This is special time for you and Daddy. I'll be back soon. I promise," Karen said as she stood up to go. As Karen stepped out the door, Robbie ran to her and caught her hand. Steve stood in the doorway and shrugged his shoulders. Karen knelt down and pulled her watch off her wrist. Handing it to Robbie, she said "Here, you keep this with you. You see this?" She pointed to the hands on the watch. "When you see this big hand point to the eight," she looked up at Steve who nodded in approval, "I'll come back and pick you up. I promise." Karen kissed him once more and headed down the stairs. Stealing a quick glance up after she started her truck, she saw Robbie wave to her and then reach for his father's hand. Karen blew Robbie a kiss and watched him disappear into the house.

With three hours of free time on her hand, Karen returned to her apartment and folded the pile of clean laundry she hadn't gotten to earlier. She sat on the futon and listened to the certain stillness that crept in during Robbie's absence. The apartment was far too lonely and quiet for the first full hour. Later when the noise started up from the Saturday night partiers directly above her, Karen welcomed the intrusion. She put away the folded laundry and went to the kitchen. Taking a seat at the kitchen table, Karen poured herself a bowl of cereal and stirred it absently. Above her, she heard the sound of laughter and footsteps walking back and forth. From the hallway, she could hear the clink of a bottle being tossed into the recycle bin. Her mouth began to water. What would one drink hurt?

Abruptly getting up from her seat, Karen opened up the cupboard and began rummaging through it. She set down a mug on the counter and brewed a pot of coffee. Then while it brewed, she filled the sink with hot water and washed the handful of dishes that were in it. Over the sound of the running water and the gurgling of the coffee pot, she could hear the rhythmic thump, thump, thump of the bass coming through the ceiling. Doors opened, followed by the sound of more bottles being tossed into the recycle bin. Karen peered out her window and watched two guys carrying a couple of cases beer towards the entrance. The new people above her, she soon found, were party central.

Karen sat down on the futon in the living room and pulled her pillow over her head, but still the noise only grew louder as more and more people showed up at the apartment above her. The stereo bumped up another notch and so did the voices. Soon, an argument broke out, followed by shouting and feet scuffling across the floor. As lonely as she was, she felt relieved that Robbie didn't have to sit through another noisy night. Tonight, the people upstairs started up earlier and noisier than usual. The scuffling continued and was coupled by the sound of breaking glass, followed by laughter and curses. Karen peeked out her front door and looked up the stairs. Two guys were pushing and shoving each other, one asking the other where the money was. Karen closed her door and locked it, not wanting to draw any attention to herself. Last weekend, some guy banged on her door and insistently asked for someone named Johnny D. The apartment complex became a regular stop for the police, which wasn't helping Robbie at all. Each time the police showed up to deal with the people upstairs, Karen felt a knot build in her stomach. All too vividly, she remembered the utter terror on his face when they took him away from her. She wondered if she could ever provide him with a happy home. He was so much better off at his dad's.

Karen flipped open her phone and checked the time. Although it was only about a ten minute drive to Ashburnham, Karen decided to leave early. As soon as the hallway was empty, she pulled her door shut and jogged up the stairs. She reached Steve's house early, so she just shut the truck off and sat in it listening to music until it was time to get Robbie. At eight o'clock, she went up the stairs and knocked on his door. Steve opened the door with Robbie by his side.

"Mommy," Robbie said, wrapping his arms around her. Karen scooped him up and kissed him on the nose. Robbie leaned close to her and whispered in her ear. "My new daddy is nice. I like him."

"I knew you would," she said, kissing him once more.

"Hey squirt, why don't you go get your stuff," Steve said. As soon as Robbie disappeared around the corner, Steve turned to Karen. "So tell me, why is he so quiet? I mean, he doesn't say much beyond yes and no."

"Well," Karen said, knowing that the truth couldn't be explained in just one or two words, "maybe he just needs to get to know you more. I'm sure after he spends a little more time with you, he'll start talking more. He's pretty shy."

"I'd like to get to know him more, too. I'd like to spend more time with him, more than an hour at the park," Steve said, looking over his shoulder at Robbie who was picking up his brand new Matchbox cars and stuffing them into a plastic carrying case. "I've got five years of catching up to do."

Karen nodded, trying to ignore that certain something that squeezed at her heart. Wasn't this what she had wanted all along? Robbie came back to the doorway, lugging a carrying case for his cars and a Matchbox fire station play set. He looked up at Karen, his face beaming, and put down the fire station play set.

"Mommy, look!" Robbie opened up the fire station play set to reveal a three-bay garage, and he showed her how to put a fire truck in the bay, press on a lever, and roll the trucks down the ramp. "And daddy got me these trucks too!" Robbie opened up the plastic case, pointing out each and every truck to her. "Daddy says this one is called an ambulance and it brings hurt people to the hospital, just like the one you rode in," Robbie said, holding the ambulance up. Karen caught a glance at Steve, who gave her a curious look. "And this one puts out fires," Robbie said, holding up a pumper truck. "And this one, see the gigantic ladder? Daddy says it has a big ladder so the firefighters can reach tall buildings. It could probably reach way up over the top of our house, Mommy."

"Wow. This is the most I've ever heard him talk," Steve laughed. Karen smiled and nodded. Steve squatted down to eye level with Robbie and helped him put his fire trucks back in the case. "Robbie, your mommy and I were just talking about you and I spending more time together. Would you like that?" Robbie nodded his head. "Maybe you could sleep over some night," Steve asked and looked up at Karen.

Karen looked from Steve to Robbie. Her shy little boy, the one who never wanted to leave her side was nodding his head vigorously. Steve looked up at her, any trace of anger or resentment gone from his face. Hesitantly, Karen nodded her head. Three hours without Robbie was long enough, and now she was agreeing to a night? But Steve had every right to ask for and expect time with his own son. After all, he was a good father, and that's what she always wanted for Robbie. Still, a voice nagged inside her head—a voice that made her wonder if she was doing the right thing. What if Steve wanted Robbie to stay with him all the time?

After work on the following Thursday, Karen made a quick trip to Walmart before picking up Robbie from daycare. She walked quickly through the aisles, not wanting to take any more time than she needed to because daycare was expensive enough without adding late charges onto weekly charges. Karen picked up a Lightning McQueen remote control car for Robbie's birthday that was coming up this weekend, and found a Lightning McQueen birthday card to go with it.

When she arrived home from work with Robbie in tow, she put away her groceries and plugged in her phone to charge. When the phone blinked on, she saw that she had four missed calls and two voicemails. The first message was from Steve, apologizing for the last minute request, and saying that he wanted to throw a birthday party for Robbie this Saturday, and he would like Robbie to spend the night with him. He had a very special day in mind for his soon-to-be-five year old. The second message was from Carol asking Karen if she and her husband could take Robbie out for ice cream on Sunday. Karen sighed, knowing that Saturday and Sunday were typically the only days she really got to spend any quality time with him. The rest of the week was spent running to daycare, to work, back to daycare, to the store, to the laundry room, and it seemed, about a hundred other monotonous things. She blew out a huff of air, and gave the kitchen chair a kick as she walked by, reminding herself that she should feel happy that Robbie had such a loving family.

Hesitantly, she called Steve back and told him that Robbie said he would love to spend his birthday with his daddy. When Steve offered to pick up Robbie at noon on Saturday, Karen looked around her apartment that always seemed to be in a state of disarray, and insisted that she would drop him off. Before hanging up, Steve asked Karen to send over a bathing suit and towel with Robbie. Karen told him she would be sure to pack his stuff, and then called Carol and told her that she was sure they could work a time out for Robbie to go with them. When Karen hung up the phone, she sat down and stared at the phone in her hand, dreading the all too lonely weekend coming up.

On Saturday morning, Karen sang "Happy Birthday" to Robbie and let him have birthday cake before lunch. She handed him his present and sat back on her heels watching him with amusement as he ripped the paper from his gift. Robbie picked up the Lightning McQueen car and began jumping up and down. He threw his arms around her and kissed her over and over. Karen put in the batteries and spent the rest of the morning watching Robbie jump over his car as it sped back and forth through the kitchen and living room. After a while, Karen looked up at the clock and told him it was time to go.

A short while later, Karen arrived at Steve's house. Steve's parents' car, as well as Carol's and a couple others, lined the street. The mailbox was decorated with balloons and streamers, and in the backyard, Karen could see a trail of curious family members looking her way. Karen raked her bangs down over the scar above her eyebrow and quickly checked her makeup one more time before getting out. Karen reached over and lifted Robbie out of the truck as Steve came down the walkway to them. "Hey squirt, do you want to see what I have for you in the backyard," Steve asked Robbie. Karen set Robbie down and watched him run hand-in-hand with his father. Leaning back into the truck, Karen slowly gathered up Robbie's favorite blanket, his teddy bear, a pillow, and a plastic bag with his change of clothes in it. Standing alone on the walkway, with Robbie's things in hand, she turned and walked slowly across the lawn, following the sound of laughter.

When Karen reached the backyard, Robbie was already driving a ride-on Jeep around the yard and squealing with delight. A yellow and white party tent was set up with three long folding tables beneath it. Off to the right a Slip 'N Slide stretched out across the grass. The smell of burgers and dogs cooking on the grill filled the air. Karen watched Robbie zoom around the yard in his new Jeep. In just a matter of weeks, Steve had given Robbie everything a boy could want.

"Can I take that inside for you," Carol asked, holding her hands out for Robbie's belongings.

"Sure. Thanks. Well, tell Steve that if he has any problems to call me," Karen said, then hesitantly handed Robbie's stuff to her.

"I'm sure they'll be fine," Carol said, her face serious and unforgiving. Karen nodded and then called Robbie over to say goodbye. Robbie turned his Jeep and drove over to Karen.

"Mommy look," Robbie said, pointing out the horn, the gas pedal, brake, and gearshift.

"Wow! That's so cool," Karen said, beeping the horn. "Well Tiger, I think I should head out now. You'll have a great time with daddy." Karen kissed the top of his head, ruffled his hair, not wanting to go, but not wanting to stay.

"Mommy, you can't go! It's my birthday," Robbie said. Steve turned at the sound of Robbie's voice, so loud and so clear. Robbie tugged on Karen's arm, urging her to stay. "Mommy, I don't want you to go," Robbie said again, stirring up a guilty satisfaction in Karen. His daddy had just given him the coolest gift in the world, but he still wanted to be with his mommy.

"Karen, you're welcome stay, you know, so he can get a little more comfortable," Steve said.

"Steve, I really don't think…"

"Please," he said, touching her shoulder. "This is the most I've ever heard him talk. If you leave, he's not going to want to stay."

Karen agreed to stay for a little while, even though she couldn't feel anything but uncomfortable beneath all the curious and probing eyes. She sat in a lawn chair at a distance from the rest of the family, not wanting to intrude, yet wishing so much to be a part of the circle of warmth that surrounded Robbie. From where she sat on this hot day in July, though, all she could feel when their gazes fell her way was cold.

After about an hour, Karen quietly got up and headed back to her apartment, stopping for a large ice coffee along the way. She returned to her apartment and paced back and forth. The quiet was just as stifling as the hot, steamy July air. Here it was, a hot summer afternoon, and all Karen could do was pace the floor. She was probably the only twenty-six year old in the whole state of Massachusetts that couldn't find something better to do on a Saturday night.

When the phone rang the first time, Karen jumped up and said hello without even stopping to check the caller ID. There was no one there. Karen hung up and scrolled through the calls only to find the number listed as "unavailable." Not thinking too much about it, Karen flipped her phone shut and sat down at the kitchen table with a book in hand. The phone rang once more, again, listing the number as "unavailable." Getting a little irritated, Karen snapped the phone shut and tried to begin reading again. At 9:30 p.m., the phone rang again. Karen picked it up and looked at the caller ID. Steve's number came across the caller ID. Apologizing for calling so late, Steve said that Robbie was feeling a little nervous being away from his mom for so long. With her keys in hand, Karen headed out the door and back to Ashburnham.

In just ten minutes, Karen was at Steve's doorstep. Robbie sniffed back tears and held up his arms to her. Reaching down, she scooped him into her arms and kissed his little red nose. Steve looked utterly crushed, but rubbed Robbie's back and told him it was okay if he wanted to go home. When Karen looked at Steve, he looked back at her and shrugged his shoulders, traces of bitterness and disappointment lined his face.

"I was hoping he'd want to stay, but…" he said, dropping his hands by his side. He locked his eyes on hers and then shook his head.

Karen turned away from Steve's gaze and kissed the top of Robbie's head. "Tiger, what if I tuck you in and tell you a bedtime story?" Karen stroked Robbie's hair. "Would you stay here with Daddy if I tucked you in?"

"Will I have to stay here forever?" He whispered in her ear, his fingers absently playing with her hair. Karen shook her head and promised him that she would pick him up right after breakfast in the morning.

"So what do you say? Do you want to give it a try?" Karen asked as Steve looked on. Robbie tilted his head and scratched it, then nodded. A smile spread across Steve's face. It was his smile, with all its tenderness, that Karen loved so much, the same smile he had at one time given to her. Robbie took Karen by the hand and showed her to the new room his daddy had cleared out just for him. Karen pulled back the sheets and snuggled Robbie beneath them before telling him a story. She began telling him a tale about a gallant prince and a beautiful princess, and drew her hands in an arc across an imaginary sky. With her words, she painted a picture of a world from another time, when men cherished their women and fought savage beasts with nothing but a sword, a suit of armor, and the courage of a lion.

After finishing one story and then beginning another, Karen watched Robbie's eyelids flutter and grow heavy with sleep. Soon he was drawing in contented breaths, his raggedy brown bear tucked under his arm. Karen stayed seated on the edge of his bed for a few minutes, running her fingers through his hair and listening to his deep, easy breathing. She leaned over and kissed him, then drew back the sheets a little to ward off the summer heat. Sensing someone behind her, she turned around and saw

Steve standing in the doorway. Karen flushed a little, unsure how long he had been standing there. She stood up and dug in her pocket for her keys. Steve stepped into the room and kissed Robbie's forehead.

"Well, I'll guess I'll be going," Karen said as she stepped past Steve. Before she stepped out the door, he caught her hand.

"Thank you. This really means a lot to me," he said, still holding her hand in his. Karen felt an old familiar rush of heat, and fought the urge to throw her arms around him. Then just as quickly, Steve let go of her hand and said goodnight.

The early morning phone call Karen had hoped for never came. When she called Steve's, he told her that Robbie was doing great and that they were going for ice cream right after lunch. Steve offered to drive Robbie home around three, but Karen needed to get a few things done and said she could just pick him up on her way home from running errands. Steve gave her Carol's address and asked her to meet them over there in the afternoon.

When Karen turned down Hunter Avenue, she slowed her truck to a conservative twenty miles per hour, wary that where there were bikes, skateboards, and basketballs, there were children. She made a left turn onto Williams Passage and followed it around the sharp curve where it turned into Lincoln Avenue. Carol lived in the picture perfect neighborhood, a small subdivision that only had one road connecting it with Route Twelve. Modest houses, some with swimming pools in their back yard, lined the streets. Kids frolicked about in the summer sun, riding the bikes, tricycles, and skateboards down the center of the road. She pulled her truck over on the side of the road, not wanting to stain Carol's new blacktop with oil leaking from her engine.

When Carol opened the door and waved her in, Karen paused at the welcome mat to wipe her feet. A small TV sat on the kitchen counter and was broadcasting a Red Sox game.

"They ran to the store. Steve wasn't expecting you for another twenty minutes or so," Carol said, while wiping down the counter with a wet cloth. She stopped, and looking out her kitchen window into the backyard, placed both hands on the counter.

"So what's your agenda Karen?" Carol asked over her shoulder. Karen's focus moved abruptly from the TV to Carol, a look of confusion coming over her.

"My agenda?" Karen asked.

"Yes. Your agenda. You must have one. Suddenly you show up after over five years without a single word from you. You're here, now." Carol turned to face Karen and leaned against the counter, her arms folded across her chest. She stared at Karen, her eyes unblinking like a child in a staring contest.

"Carol, I don't have an agenda," Karen said, tired of trying to defend herself. "All I want is for my son to be able to spend some time with his father."

"And it took you over five years to figure this out?" Carol let out a sarcastic laugh and shook her head.

"I didn't know he was Steve's," Karen said, shifting from one foot to the other and tracing a pattern on the linoleum with her toe.

"How the hell can you not know? How many guys did you sleep with that it took you over five years to figure this out? You honestly couldn't keep track of whose bed you were in where and when?"

"That's not how it happened," Karen said, feeling the heat rise in her face. "I didn't set out to hurt him…"

"Hurt him? Well you did! You've got a hell of a lot of nerve coming back here after all the shit you've put everyone through, especially what you've put my brother through! You've hurt a lot of people! Don't you realize that? Or were you just too damned drunk to figure that out?" Carol slapped the counter and looked away from Karen. "And now you're here," she said, her voice quieter, but firm. "And you've got the gall to tell me that you didn't know Robbie was Steve's kid? Have you looked at your son? Are you blind?" Carol spun around to face Karen again, her arms spread and palms turned upwards in a question.

"I swear to God I didn't know. I thought…well, that night…I was…I…Jesus, if I had known, right then and there, I would have told him. I wouldn't have left!"

"Oh come on. Skirting the truth is something you've turned into an art form." The room fell silent for a while. "I just don't know why you didn't tell him sooner. I don't understand why. You were my best friend. I trusted you, and you just threw us all away. Just left without a word."

"But I'm here, Carol. I'm here now and I'm trying to make things right!"

"Are you really? Your timing is so convenient. You're down on your luck, Daddy's money has run out, you're saddled with a kid, and Steve's finally divorced," Carol said leaning back against the counter.

"Steve was married?"

"Like you didn't know that," Carol said. Karen's gaze seemed to dissolve and move to somewhere inside of herself. She looked around the kitchen, her eyes stopping at the TV. The Yankees were at bat. A shot flew above the head of an unfamiliar Red Sox centerfielder, and the ball was relayed to home plate. Sliding into second was a player Karen recognized, but something wasn't right. Johnny Damon had shaved his face, cut his hair, and was playing for the other team. Everything had changed, was still changing. When did Damon start playing for the other team? When did Steve get married? When did her best friend become her enemy? Her life, her lover, her friend, her home team had turned their backs on her.

Everything she once knew had been dismantled. Nothing was the same.

"Karen," Carol said as Steve pulled in the driveway, her voice suddenly hushed and pleading. "He's been through enough. Please don't make things any harder for him than they already are."

Karen nodded, and without saying a word, gathered up Robbie's things and put them in her truck. She forced a smile, said goodbye, buckled Robbie in his seat, and backed out of the driveway. As she drove down the road, her phone rang. Karen pulled over and picked it up. When she said hello, there was no one there. Staring at the phone in her hand, she could feel goose bumps rising on the back of her neck.

The following Friday after supper, Karen dropped Robbie off at Steve's for the weekend. Never venturing beyond the entryway, Karen kissed Robbie on the top of his head, the tip of his nose, and his rosy cheeks before leaving him. She restricted her conversations with Steve to only what he needed, not making any attempt at small talk, and picked up some extra money on the weekends for a painting company. Waking up early Saturday morning, Karen slid on a pair of faded cut-off blue jeans and an old UMASS tee shirt, and headed out to work. She showed up at 7:00 a.m. sharp, ready to work, and arrived only second to her boss. Two other young college guys, Nate and Ryan, showed up an hour late, clearly hung over, and held their heads while, Cal, their boss, screamed at them. Once Cal set them all on a task, he left for a couple hours to set up appointments with more customers. Without hesitation, Karen climbed the scaffolding and set to work with her brush in hand. At noon when Nate and Ryan invited her for a beer and sandwiches they had packed in their cooler, she politely declined and sat in the bed of her truck, sipping on ice coffee and eating a peanut-butter sandwich.

Karen worked ten hours on Saturday and another ten on Sunday, and at the end of the weekend, her boss handed her half her pay in a check and the other half in cash. Other than splurging on a large Dunkin's ice coffee, she deposited every cent into her savings account, determined to save up enough money so she could move to a bigger apartment in a better neighborhood. She continued to work every weekend, and even some Friday nights painting interiors of houses. Whatever her boss threw her way, she took. Her days were spent working at the nursing home, evenings with Robbie, and weekends outside painting. Life began to have a mundane routine to it that Karen welcomed, yet she longed for something more, something beyond a weekly paycheck that would just be consumed by every damned bill that found its way into her life, and even though Steve offered more than once to give Karen money towards stuff for Robbie, she refused. The last thing she needed was more guilt, more reasons for Steve, Carol, and his parents to question her motives. After all, hadn't she taken enough away from Steve already?

Karen shook her head, unable to comprehend how life had changed so dramatically while she was gone. Carol was happily married, and surely had a new best friend. Steve had been married and divorced. Karen wondered if she knew the woman, wondered if Steve had held her close the way he once held her, wondered why they divorced, but most of all, Karen wondered if somewhere deep inside himself Steve still loved her. Somehow she doubted it.

Kneeling down on the scaffolding and painting trim under the scorching hot August sun, Karen wished she could just escape her thoughts and couldn't help but crave an ice cold beer. Watching Nate and Ryan wash down their sandwiches with ice cold bottles of Coronas didn't help anything. She climbed down the scaffolding and took a sip of her ice coffee, watching them twist off the top of another beer. They must have mistaken her gaze for one of interest because it didn't take long for one of them to hop on the tailgate of her truck and ask her out. After Karen politely turned down Nate, Ryan slapped his friend on the back and made his attempt, which she turned down also. The two dangerously handsome boys, talking loud enough for Karen to hear, came to the only possible explanation; she must be gay! Karen rolled her eyes at them, and forcing a laugh, hopped out of the back of her truck and climbed into the front seat. She closed the door behind her and shut her eyes. She could practically taste the beer, feel its chill as it rolled down her throat. Opening her eyes, she threw her empty plastic cup against the passenger side door, spilling the ice onto the floor.

After work, Karen returned home and set her cell phone down on the table, before skipping across the hall to start a load of laundry. When she returned, she noticed the light on her phone blinking. She checked her voicemail. The first two were hang-ups and the third one from Irene: "Hi Karen. It's me, Irene. I don't want to alarm you, but I thought you should know that I heard through a couple of customers that he's been asking about you. It's probably nothing to worry about, but I just wanted to let you know. I hope everything's going okay for you over there. Give me a call sometime."

Karen was still digesting Irene's message when the next one began. Another hang-up was followed by a deep sigh and then his voice: "Baby, it's me. Come on. Pick up the phone. I know you're there. I just wanna talk. Shit, come on Karen. Pick up the phone, please."

His voice trailed off and was followed by a definitive click. Karen held the phone to her ear, frozen for a moment, in time. Looking at the door, Karen quickly walked over to it and clicked the deadbolt in place. Taking a step backwards, she regarded the lock for some time before going into the living room. She held the phone in her hand and wanted to call someone, but didn't know who to even call. For the rest of the night, every little sound, the drop of a shoe on the floor above, the sound of the entryway door opening and closing, and the thumping of tenants going up and down from the laundry room made her jump. She double-checked the lock, shook her head, and folded the laundry. He was all the way across the country, but even so, she checked the lock one more time before getting in the shower.

After she dried off, slid into an old tee-shirt and gym shorts, and slipped under a single sheet on the futon, the phone rang. Karen froze, waiting until the third ring to pick it up and check the caller ID. Breathing a sigh of relief, she saw Steve's name on the display. When Karen answered, Steve said "I'm sorry for calling so late, but Robbie is insistent that he cannot go to sleep until he says goodnight to you. We tried earlier, but just got your voicemail," Steve explained before handing the phone to Robbie. Karen listened as Robbie told her all about his fun day with daddy. He got to climb inside all the fire trucks and even blew the horn. They talked for a few minutes, and then Robbie kissed her through the phone. Karen blew kisses in the air and sent them his way. After saying their goodnights, Karen hung up the phone and settled herself back down on the futon. Not even a minute later, the phone rang again. With a smile still on her face, Karen answered the phone, laughing and thinking that Robbie needed to say goodnight one more time.

"Don't hang up, baby. I just want to talk," Jimmy said. At the sound of his voice, Karen felt the skin on her arms bump up.

"We don't have anything to talk about," she said, her legs suddenly feeling leaden.

"Hang on a sec. I just want to know how you are. You okay?"

"I'm fine."

"Good. I'm glad to hear that, baby. Listen, I'm sorry about everything that's happened. I really am," Jimmy said. When Karen didn't respond, he cleared his throat and asked about Robbie.

"Jimmy, please don't do this."

"Don't do what? Karen, baby, I miss you guys so much. You can't just honestly expect me to up and forget you. Can you?"

"Jimmy, it's late and I can't ignore the past."

"Oh? I didn't realize it was so late where you are," he said. Karen snapped her phone shut and cursed her stupidity. She held the phone in her hand, worried that he would call again, and then decided to shut off her ringer. Sleep evaded her that night as thoughts of Jimmy clouded her mind and choked off her breath.

The next morning, Karen forced herself out of bed and got ready for work. She flipped open her phone and scrolled through the missed calls. There were seven of them, all listed as "unavailable" and another seven messages too. In each one of his messages, his voice grew louder and more insistent, until finally his words were reduced to curses slurred over the phone.

After doing her best to ignore the calls that had started again just past noon, Karen had finally given up and shut off the ringer on her phone. Even though it meant less money for her, she was glad when her boss called it a day and had them stop work early because rain was forecast for late afternoon. Karen climbed down the scaffolding and helped her boss load up the back of his truck. Before getting into her truck, she flipped open her phone and saw that no more missed calls or voicemails were received. She flipped back on the ringer, not wanting to miss Robbie or Steve if either one called. After stopping to take a quick shower and change first, Karen arrived at Steve's a couple hours earlier than usual. As she carried Robbie's belongings out to the truck, her phone began to ring again. Without realizing Steve was watching her, she flipped open the phone, jammed her finger down on the button, and snapped it shut.

"Something wrong?"

"Uh, no," Karen said, a little startled. "Just a wrong number," Karen answered, waving a hand in the air. Karen reached over and buckled Robbie in his seat, trying her best to not let her concern show. She hopped in, started up the truck, and headed home.

The next day, after Karen returned home from her fulltime job, she flipped open her phone to see if he had called again. No missed calls, no messages. She breathed easier, hoping that Jimmy had gotten tired of his little games. During supper, she and Robbie talked about the start of kindergarten. She couldn't believe that he was going to start school in just a few weeks! Her little boy was growing up fast. Around seven o'clock, Robbie let out a yawn and laid his head on his mother's lap while she read a story to him. Five pages into the story, Robbie fell asleep. Karen was setting the book down on the floor when someone knocked at the door. She slid Robbie off her lap and went to the door, expecting it to be a neighbor from the third floor returning the laundry soap he borrowed. When she opened the door, Jimmy was standing there. She swung the door shut, but not fast enough. He wedged his foot in the opening.

"Hey, hey, I just came by to talk. I aint here to start anything," he said. "Come on, baby. I flew all the way across the damned country just to talk to you, to make things right. The least you could do is hear me out," Jimmy said, pushing his hip against the door and forcing it open a little more. Karen kept her hand on the door and tried to swallow her fear.

"Jimmy, we don't have anything to talk about. Now I want you leave us alone," she said with one hand still on the doorknob. The voice in her head screamed *run* away, contrasting her memories with the man who stood in front of her, smiling sweetly at her. Sporting a clean shaven face, a new pair of blue jeans, and a short sleeve button up shirt, he stretched his muscular arms out and brought his elbows above his head, resting his forearms against the doorframe. Jimmy kept one foot planted half in, half out of her apartment, while he rocked on the toe of the other.

"Karen, baby. I want you to come home."

"I am home," Karen said, still hanging onto the door.

"Honey," he said, casting a glance over her shoulder. "I don't like the thought of you and Robbie living all the way out here by yourselves. I want you to come home with me."

"No Jimmy. We're not going anywhere with you. It's over," she said, keeping her voice low and even, hoping Robbie wouldn't wake up.

"Please baby. Don't say that. Look, I know I fucked up a lot, but I've changed."

"Jimmy, no. This is our home now, and I can't...I won't put Robbie through all that chaos again."

"It won't be like that no more. And I never, ever laid a hand on our boy."

"He's not your boy. You may never have laid a hand on him, but he's heard and seen enough," she said and turned away from him, her fingers unconsciously massaging the small scar above her lip.

"Karen, honey," he said, touching his hand to her face. "I'm telling you, I'm a changed man. I'm not the same any more, and I'm here to prove to that to you. I'm ready to make a commitment to you and to Robbie." He reached into his pocket and dropped down on one knee. Withdrawing his hand out of his pocket, he held up a ring to Karen. "I want us to be a family again. I want to do things right. Karen, I want you to marry me."

"What?" Karen shook her head, unable to believe what he had just said.

"You heard me. Marry me," Jimmy said, taking hold of her hand. He caressed the back of her hand with his thumb. Seeing him down on one knee and his eyes warm and inviting, stirred up old memories in her. His cologne, his presence began to awaken her, forcing her to recognize her empty, lonely world. She looked into his eyes and held his gaze, remembering a distant time when his touch was gentle and loving. But now, here, she saw something different in his eyes, the way he looked at her as if she were something to possess, to control. She shook her head, breaking away from his gaze, and looked over her shoulder towards the living room.

"Jimmy…I can't. I have to do what is best for Robbie." Karen turned back to him.

"Is what's best for him livin' in the city in this cellar hole of an apartment? I can offer you two so much more."

"Jimmy, we're better off this way."

"Hey," he said, standing up, "you ought to try and remember where you came from. When I found you, you were pregnant and all alone, but I didn't care. I loved you anyway. I didn't judge you. No, I took you in. Remember, I was the one that held you at night when you had no one. Hell, I even helped you raise Robbie, just like he was my own, even though you didn't even know who his daddy was. So now you're gonna just throw me away? Like some piece of trash? I took you in. I loved you, Karen, just the same," Jimmy brushed his hand lightly against her face. Karen drew in a deep breath and closed her eyes, and without looking at him, shook her head.

"Damn it Karen," Jimmy said, pounding his fist against the doorframe. "Can't you see that I love you?" He lifted her chin with his fingertips, and looked her in the eyes. Karen looked away. He moved closer to her. She could feel his breath on her face, smell his aftershave, and felt a longing to have someone in her life again, but it was quickly cut off by a fear that squeezed air from her lungs. Karen looked over her shoulder towards the living room once more. Jimmy ran his hand from her waist and traced it up her ribs until his thumb rubbed against the underside of her breast. Karen flinched and stepped away from him.

"No," she said pushing her hand against his chest. "Jimmy, we're through."

"Karen, baby. I love you," he said pulling her back towards him.

"Your version of love is a brutal one," she said just barely above a whisper, pulling away from him. "I won't put Robbie through that again." Karen reached for the door and cast a glance back at Robbie still sleeping on the couch.

"Okay, I know I lost my temper at times," Jimmy said, catching the door and holding it open. "But I've changed."

"Lost your temper? You broke my ribs," Karen said, her voice rising.

"For God's sake, Karen, when are you going to forgive me? I mean, Jesus, when I took you in I became an instant father. Do you know how hard that is?"

"I guess I was your own personal pressure valve," she said, the bitterness of their past crept into her voice.

Jimmy thumped his fist against the door, causing Karen to jump. He let out a sigh and grasped her hand. "Alright, I admit it. I let my temper get the better of me, but I've been working on that. What'll it take to convince you? Tell me what you want, and I swear to God I'll make it work. That's the God's honest truth. I promise."

"Jimmy, we're just not good for each other," Karen said as she glanced back over her shoulder. "Please, just leave before you wake him up. He's been through too much already."

"For Christ's sake! What's with you? Nothing I ever do is good enough for you! I crossed the fucking country just to be with you, and this is how you repay me? I worked my ass off to provide for you and Robbie, and I'm willing to do it again. I gave you a home when you had no one. When you gave birth to Robbie, I was there, not these fucking people you came back here for. I took you into my world."

Shaking her head quickly and taking a step back, she said "I'm sorry, Jimmy. I can't be part of that world anymore."

"Fine. Be that way," Jimmy said, shoving the engagement ring back inside his pocket. "So you got somebody else now? Is that it?"

"Please just go," Karen pleaded. Jimmy slapped his hand against the wall and leaned close to her. "Fine, College. I'll go. But you're losing the only person who gives a fuck about you. Don't fool yourself into thinking that anybody back here in Massachusetts gives a shit about you. Not your ex, not your stupid stuck up college friends, not even your fucking stepmother," he said, giving her a dismissive shove. "You remember that. When you want somebody to hold you at night, you remember that I crossed the fucking country for you when no one else would even cross the street for a whore like you!" Jimmy kicked the door with enough force to splinter the wood and stomped up the stairs.

Karen quickly pushed the door shut and slid the deadbolt into place. Her hands shook and eyes stung with tears. From behind her, she heard sniffling. Robbie stood in the kitchen, his teddy bear dangling from one hand and tears streaming down his cheeks. Karen pulled him into her arms and they sat in silence, holding each other long into the night.

The next morning, Robbie was so groggy that Karen let him stay in his pajamas for the ride to daycare. She packed a change of clothes and his lunch, and then gave him a piggy-back ride out to the truck. Karen stopped dead in her tracks when her truck came into view and she found a fresh dent in her door. She let out a sigh and tugged the door open. Robbie scrambled across the seat and waited for Karen to help him with his seat belt. During the five minute ride to daycare, Robbie didn't say a single word until they arrived. Robbie, who hadn't cried about going to daycare in over four weeks, suddenly burst into tears.

"Mommy, is he going to come back again?" Robbie's was face red and streamed with tears. He brushed his knuckles against his nose and sniffed as the two of them stood on the doorstep of his daycare.

"No. I told him not to come back," she said as she dabbed his face with a tissue. "Everything is going to be alright. Just try to forget about him. Okay?"

"Why can't we just go live with daddy?"

"Oh sweetie, that's just not possible, but Mommy's been saving up money so we can move sometime soon," Karen said and ruffled his hair.

"Mommy, I don't want you to go to work," he said, wrapping his arms around her neck. Karen drew in a breath, her heart breaking as she walked him inside. "Mommy has to go to work," she said, kissing the top of his head. "I'll take you home just as soon as I get done my shift." Robbie shook his head and clung to her. He didn't want her to leave, and he definitely didn't want to go home. For the rest of the week each day was a battle, Robbie never wanting her to leave, but never wanting to go home.

On her way home from work Friday, Karen listened as Robbie talked about wanting to go to his daddy's house. Robbie's eagerness was even more evident when he pushed aside his favorite supper of chicken nugget and fries, saying he wasn't hungry despite the audible growling of his stomach. Karen threw her hands in the air, shook her head, and just put his meal in the fridge. Since Monday, Robbie had grown terribly quiet and preoccupied once again, asking more than once if he had to wait until Friday to sleep at his daddy's house. An incessant fear began to grow inside, one that Karen could not ignore; she felt as if she was only one mistake away from losing Robbie.

For the first time all week, Robbie was smiling. He was thrilled to be going to his daddy's house. Karen wished so much that he wanted to stay with her, that he could feel happy and safe. "Hey, how about you and I go to the movies tomorrow?" Karen asked Robbie when they pulled up in front of Steve's.

"Am I still going to sleep at Daddy's house?" Robbie asked, his expression serious. When Karen told him yes, a small smile spread across his face.

As Karen sat alone in her house on a Friday night, she wondered if Jimmy was right. Maybe he was the only one who would ever love her. Maybe she had only been fooling herself by coming home. Wanting to kill the hurt inside, having a heart full of self-doubt, and longing for a drink, Karen did the only thing she knew to do when feeling this way; she buried herself in the mundane routine of work, taking on more and more hours, until she had no space left in her life for anything else.

Bright and early on Saturday morning, Karen met her boss at a house set back in the woods of Ashburnham. After setting up the scaffolding, Karen and her boss set to work, just the two of them since the twins, as Karen affectionately called the two college boys, called in sick and apparently the only cure for the guys was the beach. By ten, the late August heat had risen to ninety degrees. Under a broiling sun and feeling dead on her feet, Karen continued to work, stopping often to wipe the sweat from her brow. By noon, the humidity had grown and the heat climbed another five degrees. With a thunderstorm and heavy rain predicted for late afternoon, her boss hesitantly called it a day.

After helping her boss pack up his truck, Karen drove towards the center of town and decided to stop for a sandwich at the local pizza place. As she sipped on an ice cold soda and ate a chicken salad sandwich, she skimmed through the headlines of the newspaper. It was only when she caught sight of the date on the top of the paper that she realized today was her father's birthday and she had forgotten to have flowers delivered to his grave. Every year without fail, Karen had put money in an envelope addressed to Lillian along with a note asking her to put flowers on her parents' gravesites on their respective birthdays. She never included a return address, never asked after her, or offered anything about her own life. This was the first time she had forgotten to send money to Lillian for the flowers.

Not bothering to finish her sandwich, Karen paid her bill and drove to Amherst under a rapidly graying sky. She made a quick stop at a florist shop and found enough money in her wallet to buy a bouquet of daisies. With flowers in hand, she headed to the cemetery. Bringing her truck to a stop just outside the gates of the cemetery, Karen crossed the lawn under the darkening sky. The storm, Karen guessed, wasn't going to wait until late afternoon. She walked between rows upon rows of gravestones, not quite remembering which row he had been buried. After searching for about twenty minutes, she finally found it in a back corner next to her mother's, just a few feet from some tall evergreens. She knelt down and ran her hand slowly across each of the headstones and traced their names with her fingers.

Sitting back on her heels, she turned to her father's grave. "Hey daddy," she said, propping up the small bouquet against the headstone. "Happy birthday." She drew her hands into her lap and bowed her head, unable to comprehend how the years seemed to have slipped by so quickly. As she knelt on the ground, she wondered if everything Lillian had said about her mother and father was true. Had Mami tried to leave? Had Dad lied to her, to protect her from the truth, a truth that she had every right to know? The air grew still, leaves curled up, ready to catch the impending rain, and a distant rumble rolled across the sky. Hot drops rolled from Karen's eyes and down her cheeks, and were soon followed by cool drops of rain from the sky. The rain started out slow and light, but gathered intensity quickly. Still, Karen remained on her knees, her fingers tracing and retracing her father's name on the cold stone.

Death was a dark, mean thing that left only loneliness and heartache in its wake. Among all these stones scattered across sacred ground, Karen felt the ache of absence. Was there even a god? If so, why had he left her so utterly alone? Why was she forced to live a life without a mother, without a father? She didn't have a lover to call her own, didn't have the comfort of a friend, or a single shoulder to lean on.

Instead, she could feel the familiar tug of her only faithful friend. She could feel its fire, the sweet burning it left in her throat, the splash of it in her belly. One, just one drink is all it would take to ease the pain. She could stop at one; she had gone a whole year, one month, and twenty-two days without a single drop. She could handle one drink.

Karen looked up from the headstone to the sky. Why?" She screamed and clenched her fists, beating them against her rain soaked jean shorts. "What the fuck! Why couldn't you just tell me?" She looked around the empty graveyard and to the barren streets that paralleled the cemetery; not a soul was in sight. Was she so impossible to love? She bowed her head into her hands, nodded, and rose to her feet. Her father had lied to her. He didn't want her to know about Mami, but she thought, she was just like her.

Ten minutes later, Karen pulled up to her childhood home. Not seeing a car in the driveway, she stepped out of her truck and crossed the street. Peering through the garage window, she saw that it was empty. Lillian wasn't home. Karen breathed a sigh of relief and jogged up the walkway. She tried her old key in the lock, but found that it no longer fit. She peered in the kitchen window and noticed a crock pot sitting on the counter. Moving over to the dining room window, she saw a bottle of pinot noir on the hutch. Karen shivered in the rain and walked around to the back of the house. After finding the back door locked, too, she went around to the cellar door, and found that locked as well. Coming back around to the front, Karen squatted down and ran her hand under the matt in front of the door and then underneath the potted plant that sat on the steps.

The sound of a car caught her attention. Karen looked up and saw a patrol car come to a stop in front of the house. An officer stepped out and walked towards her, pausing to look at the Montana plate still hanging on the front of her truck.

"Miss, is there something I can help you with," the officer asked with a raise of his eyebrow.

"No sir."

"That your truck?" He jabbed his thumb in the direction of her truck.

"Yes sir."

"What's your business here?"

"I just came by to see my mother," Karen said, pushing her wet bangs out of her eyes and shivering in the rain.

"Mother? Well then, would you mind telling me your mother's name?" He cast a glance at her truck with its gaping rust holes in the quarter panel, dented door, and out of state plate.

"Lillian Black," Karen said, hugging her arms around herself. The officer looked at her skeptically and jotted down her plate number.

"Really? I didn't know Lillian had any children. Okay, Miss…" he paused, holding out his hand expectantly.

"Black, Karen Black," Karen answered.

"Good, then you won't mind showing me some ID and your registration, will you?"

Karen shook her head and muttered under her breath. The officer looked up at her, his eyebrows turned up in question. Karen pointed to her truck, opened the door, and leaned over to the glove box.

"Well, you certainly have come a long way, Miss Black," the officer said, pointing to her Montana plate. Karen backed out of her truck and handed him her license and registration. He took them from her, looking at her license and then her.

"Black is a common name. You don't look a bit like Lillian," he said without a trace of a smile.

"She's my stepmother," Karen said while rubbing her hands up and down her bare arms.

"Hmmm. And you don't have a key to your stepmother's house?" He looked at Karen, waiting for a response. Karen threw her hands up in the air and shook her head. "I guess you two can't be that close if your own stepmother doesn't allow you to have a key to the house," he said, scrutinizing her and the truck parked on the side of the road.

At the sound of an approaching car, the officer looked up. "Well, it looks like we're about to meet Lillian right now," he said, nodding to the car pulling up the street. Karen swallowed hard and watched as Lillian slowed in front of the house and pulled in the driveway. The officer cocked an appraising eyebrow at Karen and told her to wait right there, as he approached Lillian's car.

Karen folded her arms across her chest and leaned against her truck. She could hear the officer talking to Lillian: "Good afternoon Lillian. This young lady has been snooping around your house and claims that she's your stepdaughter," he said with a jerk of his head in her direction. Lillian stepped out of her car and looked in Karen's direction. Lillian's mouth opened, and she shook her head. Was it disbelief or disgust? Karen couldn't be sure.

"Oh my God. Karen?" Lillian pressed her fingers to her lips.

"I didn't know you had a daughter," the officer said, his eyebrows upturned as he looked at Lillian, who only gave a slow nod in response. "Well, if you're all set here, I'll be on my way," he said with a polite nod and then returned to his patrol car. Stopping with one hand on the door of his cruiser, he said "Oh, Miss Black, your license plate is hanging by a single screw. I suggest you get that fixed before you lose it."

Karen nodded absently and chewed on her bottom lip, her attention still on Lillian. They stood, as if locked in time, and looked at each other from opposite sides of the street. Karen hugged her arms around herself, trying to control the shivering that overtook her. She slowly exhaled, her breath stuttering in her chest. Lillian was looking back at her, not saying a single word. Maybe Jimmy was right. Maybe she shouldn't have come.

After a moment, Lillian held a hand outstretched towards Karen. "Would you like to come in and get out of the rain?"

Karen hesitated a moment, and nodded her head. Lillian pushed her key in the lock, pausing to look at Karen, and then opened the door. They stepped inside and were greeted by the cold blast of the air conditioner. Karen's lips trembled and she rubbed her arms.

"You're soaked. Let me find you something dry to wear," Lillian said, disappearing up the stairs. Karen stood on the welcome mat and looked around the foyer. Lillian's usual collection of glass bells and decorative plates were displayed prominently in a glassed in cabinet. She looked for any sign of the little boy she saw walking hand in hand with Lillian a few months ago, but didn't see any.

"Here you go," Lillian said coming down the stairs with a dry change of clothes and a towel in her hands. Karen looked at her, wanting to say something, but the words caught in her throat. "You better get out of the wet clothes and dry off before you catch a cold," Lillian said and nodded towards the bathroom. Karen pulled off her wet sneakers and socks, then wiped her feet before tentatively taking the clothes from Lillian.

Karen's eyes watered as she opened her mouth to speak, but words remained trapped inside her. Lillian patted her on the back. "Go on and get changed. I'll put on some hot tea."

Inside the bathroom, Karen tugged her wet clothes from her body and slipped into dry ones, her skin still shivering. Outside, the rain continued to spill from above and drum a rhythmic beat against the windows, while thunder rolled across the sky. A streak of lightning cut through the darkened clouds, momentarily lighting up the sky, and was followed by a loud clap of thunder. Karen looked out the window at the backyard. The lawns were always green in this part of town, even in August.

Bunching up her wet clothes in a ball and wrapping them in a towel, Karen carried them downstairs and placed them on top of her wet sneakers and socks. Lillian emerged from the kitchen and shook her head at Karen.

"They'll never dry that way," she said, picking them up off the mat and disappearing down the cellar stairs and into the laundry room. Karen stood in the foyer and waited for Lillian to return. A moment later, Lillian came back up the stairs. "I have a small cranberry pork roast in the crock pot. There's enough to share if you'd like to stay for dinner," she offered.

"I'd like that," Karen said softly.

"Good, then it's settled, so long as you promise to give me my clothes back this time," Lillian said with a smile. Karen nodded, remembering the last time she had seen Lillian and borrowed clothes from her. "We have a lot to talk about," Lillian said as she turned towards the kitchen. Karen followed her into the kitchen and stood near the entryway, while Lillian took two plates from the cupboard and picked silverware from the utensil drawer. Lillian handed them to Karen and asked her to set them on the dining room table, while she sliced up the pork roast. Going to the dining room, Karen set the plates down on the dining room table and stared at the bottle of pinot noir that sat on the hutch.

"Can I get you something to drink?"

"Huh?" Karen turned to her.

"Would you like something to drink? Coke? Water? Coffee?" Lillian asked. Karen nodded and Lillian went to the kitchen. She sat down at the dining room table, staring at the bottle of pinot noir that seemed to be mocking her. She bounced her knees up and down nervously, not quite sure what to do or say. Suddenly aware of Lillian's presence, Karen stopped and looked up at her. Lillian forced a smiled and sat down in the seat next to her. For the first fifteen minutes or so, they ate in an uncomfortable silence. Karen bit into the tender roast, letting the taste of the cranberries and nutmeg linger on her tongue.

"This is delicious," Karen said, trying to break the silence. Lillian smiled again, and then her expression grew serious.

"I knew you were here. I had been worried about you," Lillian said. "Every year since you left, you've sent me money for flowers for your parents' on their birthday, but I checked the mail every day last week, but there wasn't anything from you. I didn't know what to think, whom to call," Lillian said and then looked out the window. "I bought some flowers and went to your father's gravesite on my way here, and that's when I knew you must have come home. I saw the daisies," Lillian said, her eyes meeting Karen's.

Karen couldn't hold Lillian's gaze. How could she be so calm and so quiet after everything she had put her through? For a fleeting moment, Karen wished that she would just scream at her, call her names, bang her gavel in judgment, just get it over with, but instead Lillian remained quiet and offered her a slow, gentle smile. Karen cleared her throat and pushed her fork back and forth across her plate.

"I came by here in April," Karen said, registering the surprise on Lillian's face. "You were walking across the yard with a little boy and a man," she said still shuffling her food back and forth across her plate.

"Wait, you were here? But…you mean to tell me that you've been back for what," she paused counting the months in her head, "for four months, and you never bothered to come by, to let me know that you were here? Karen, I've sat here day after day worried sick about you. I even hired a private detective to try to find you!"

"I'm sorry. I'm so sorry," Karen said, trying to hold back tears and brace for Lillian's storm, but instead she just sat back and drew in her breath. Karen looked up at Lillian and continued, "I came back here," Karen said, her voice unsteady. "And I saw you and the little boy and the man…and I…I just couldn't face you…not you, not Steve, not Carol." Karen shook her head and stared at her hands in her lap, "And I saw you with your new family and…"

"My new family?" Lillian thought for a moment, and then letting out a laugh, shook her head vigorously. "No, no, no. Oh Lordy, a little boy? Me? No. Karen, that little boy is Peter, Gary's nephew." Lillian tilted her head and her voice softened. "After your father passed, you weren't the only one that was a wreck. I was too. Once he died, so did any thoughts of having another child. That man you saw me with is Gary, my fiancé. We've been seeing each other for the past six months, and he proposed to me two weeks ago." Lillian reached over and touched Karen's shoulder. "Karen, I loved your father very much, and I know it was very hard for you to lose your mother and have me go from being a friend of the family to your stepmother, but you need to know that your father meant the world to me. You mean the world to me. God, you've been a part of my life for so long that when you left, it hurt. When you left, I felt like I had failed you, failed your father, your mother."

When Karen looked up at Lillian, she couldn't stop the flood of tears that began falling from her eyes.

"Where have you been all this time?" Lillian looked over at her and brushed the tears from Karen's cheek." Karen drew in a breath and said "Montana" so quietly that Lillian leaned in closer. "Montana? That's a long way from home," Lillian said leaning back in her chair. She smoothed her fingers over her linen napkin and stared off at some distant space in the room. The sound of the rain beating against the windows and the ticking of the grandfather clock echoed in Karen's ears, stretching the silence into an eternity.

"Well, you're here now. You're home and that's all that matters," Lillian said and picked up a forkful of pork.

"Lillian, I have a five year old son," Karen said. Lillian's fork slipped from her hand and fell onto her plate.

"A son? You have a son?" Lillian swallowed her pork in lumps.

"Look, I know I should have told, told Steve...I just..." "He's Steve's?" Lillian shook her head and leaned her head in her hands. "Why wouldn't you tell me this? Why didn't he?" Lillian's voice reached a fevered pitch. She threw her hands in the air and looked at Karen.

"Steve didn't know. All this time, I just thought Robbie..."

"You gave him your father's name." A small smile came across Lillian's face. Karen nodded and reached for Lillian's hand.

"I wanted to tell you, really I did, but I felt so ashamed after what happened that night at the bar, and I...hell, my life just sort of fell apart in front of me."

Lillian pulled her hand away from Karen, leaned over, and wrapped her arms around Karen's shoulders. Karen let her head rest on Lillian's shoulders and cried a hushed, breathless cry. Lillian held her tight, letting Karen's tears spill onto her shoulder and soak her peach top. When Karen exhausted herself of tears and quieted, she said "Why are you so good to me?"

"Because you came home," Lillian said, kissing the top of Karen's head.

# Chapter Eighteen

......................................

## *Truth and Pain*

Fixing her eyes on the pinot noir that sat on the hutch, Karen said, "I haven't had a drink in a little over a year." Lillian glanced from Karen to the bottle and back again.

"Would you like me to move that?" Lillian asked. Karen let out a laugh and nodded. "Yes, please." The two of them laughed, and Lillian put the bottle in a cabinet. "You know, you were right. You were always right, but I...I just couldn't...wouldn't listen to you," Karen said and shook her head. "God, I always hated it when you were right."

"What was so bad that it took you five years to come home?" Lillian asked Karen, holding her gaze. Drawing in a deep breath and closing her eyes, Karen replayed the last five years in her mind. After awhile, she told Lillian about how she met Jimmy, about how lonely and desperate she had become.

"He was someone to come home to at night, someone who cared about me...or so I thought," Karen said as her gaze drifted off elsewhere. "He didn't care if I drank. In fact, he preferred me to drink—'cause I wasn't such a stuck-up bitch' when I drank." Karen turned to Lillian and shrugged her shoulders, and then began to talk about Irene and Hardy.

"Wait, wait," Lillian said. "Did he always talk to you like that? Did he hurt you?" Karen looked away and let out a little laugh. "Karen, don't look away from me. You always run away when you can't deal with something,"

Lillian said, placing her hand on Karen's shoulder. Karen began to bounce her knees up and down, and checked her watch.

"Oh God, it's after six. Shit! I was supposed to pick up Robbie from Steve's at 6:30 and take him to the movies," Karen said, standing up. Lillian caught her arm.

"So call Steve. Tell him you're not going to make it on time. But don't run out of here. At the very least, you owe me the courtesy of an answer. Anyway, your clothes are still in the dryer and I'm holding them hostage," she said, handing her the phone.

Karen nodded and sat back down. She called up Steve, explaining that she was an hour away and wouldn't make it on time. She could hear Steve talking to Robbie in the background and asking him if he wanted to go to the movies with daddy instead. Her heart sank a little when she heard Robbie yell out with excitement. After talking to Robbie and blowing him kisses over the phone, Karen said goodnight to him and hung up.

Karen let out a sigh and watched as Lillian put on a pot of coffee. "I think Robbie would rather stay with Steve than me," Karen said with a frown.

"I wouldn't be so sure of that. After all, you are his mother, and kids just don't ever forget their mothers," Lillian said as she set the cream and sugar on the table. "So what happened with this Jimmy guy?" Lillian asked, and poured them each a cup of coffee. As if feeling her way through a darkened room, Karen stirred her coffee and began telling Lillian about Jimmy, about his possessiveness, his jealousy, and how he had hit her for the very first time shortly after Robbie was born.

Lillian leaned her head in her hands, and Karen stared out the window. The rain continued to pour down as another wave of thunder and lightning rolled across the sky. Sometimes she wished she could just let everything out, and be like the rain, just wash away all the hurt and shame. But maybe it was just too much to ask. Karen was staring out the window, lost in her thoughts, when Lillian suddenly asked, "Just tell me, please, why in God's name you would stay with a man who hit you."

Karen shook her head and looked away. Lillian stood up and paced the floor, then suddenly stopped in front of her. "How can you let a man hit you? How can you let some son of a bitch hit you? For God's sake, you had a baby to think of!" Lillian fell silent for a moment and continued pacing, but then stopped again. "Why didn't you come home? All you had to do was call me, and I'd be there. Didn't you know that?"

"It didn't happen all the time," Karen said just barely above a whisper.

"Once is too much!" Lillian shook her head vigorously. "Why would you let him hit you? I just don't understand how you could just allow it to happen?"

"You don't understand! He was there for me! He was there when no one else was! I mean, he didn't do that all the time. Things just got to him after a while!"

"So what are you saying? That it was your fault? That you asked for it?" Lillian bore an incredulous expression on her face.

"Well, no, not that I asked for it, but…I mean I was pregnant and he was willing to take me and my baby in."

"So what, now that makes him a saint because he accepted you, a pregnant woman?" What kind of crock of shit has he given to you? That if a woman is pregnant, she's got to be accepted, and then in turn, understand why some overgrown brute, who doesn't even deserve to be called a man, beats her?"

Karen's eyes began to water again and her face flushed. She shook her head and said "I think I just pushed him too much, and there he was, taking care of not only me, but paying for diapers, formula…he was an instant father."

"I don't understand you," Lillian said, shaking her head again. "You mean to say that you're going to just shoulder the blame? I mean, who are you? Eve?"

"Eve? Who's Eve?" Karen said with a tilt of her head and raised eyebrows.

"Adam and Eve, that Eve."

"What's she got to do with this?" Karen couldn't help but smile a little at how worked up Lillian was getting.

"I'm going to tell you what she's got to do with this. They say that she's the blame for Adam getting chased from the Garden of Eden."

"Well," Karen suppressed a smile, "she did tempt Adam."

"Right, but if she told him to jump off the Brooklyn Bridge, would he do it? Should he do it?"

"I don't think there were any Brooklyn Bridges back then," Karen laughed.

"Look, I'm being serious, and you're not helping," Lillian shook a finger at her.

"I'm sorry. I just don't know what Adam and Eve have got to do with this, and why you're so worked up over them."

"It's not about Adam and Eve. It's about you letting some jerk convince you that you're the blame for his life, that you're the reason he can't control his temper and has to hit you. It's about him convincing you that he has some innate right to rule over you and your body, that he can hit you whenever he wants or have sex with you, that anything he does is your fault and you're the reason for anything that goes wrong in his life."

The smile on Karen's face faded. She stared out the window and folded her arms across her chest as a single tear rolled down her cheek.

"The problem is, Karen, that you've let the mistakes from your past curse your future, just like so many women do. You see, Eve may have tempted Adam, but he was the one who was weak. Nobody forced him to eat the apple. Nobody forced this Jimmy," Lillian said with a sneer, "to become an instant father. He made the choice, and you deserve better than what you've accepted. It's time for you to take a good look at your life and all you have to offer. You're a good person, and don't you dare let anybody tell you otherwise." Lillian touched her hand to Karen's cheek. "When are you going to stop beating yourself up over the past?"

Lillian drew Karen into her arms and held her. The rain continued to beat against the windows, and as day slipped into night, Karen and Lillian talked on and on. For the first time in a long time, Karen could say that she was home. Realizing that it was getting late and she needed to work in the morning, Karen stood up and hugged Lillian.

"Oh, wait," she said, remembering that she still had on the clothes Lillian had loaned her. "I'd better go change."

"It's late. You can bring them with you on your next visit." Lillian held open the door for Karen and then put her hand on her shoulder. "You are going to come by again real soon, right? I'd love to meet Robbie."

"Yes, I'll come by soon, and I'll bring Robbie."

"Promise you won't disappear on me again?"

"I promise," Karen said as she stepped outside. Before getting into her truck, Karen looked back at Lillian and thanked her.

"For what?" Lillian asked.

"For letting me in," Karen said, and then waved as she drove off.

# CHAPTER NINETEEN

## *Things That Go Bump In The Night*

After making the hour and ten minute drive from Amherst to Fitchburg, Karen arrived at her apartment. She picked up her cell phone off the seat of her truck, almost forgetting that she had left it in there earlier, and flipped it open. A chill went through her when she saw "unavailable" listed several times on the missed call menu. It had to be Jimmy again. Hesitating a moment, she checked her voicemail. There were a couple of hang-ups and then a message from Robbie saying goodnight. Then the fourth message began. It was him again.

"Baby, come on. Pick up the phone. I know you're there," Jimmy slurred into the phone. "Pick it up! Come on you slut! You fucking whore!" The message ended and then the next began. It was Jimmy again: "College! College! Pick up the fucking phone! You can't just wipe me out of your life," he screamed, and then there was a pause followed by a click. The next message began: "Baby, I'm so sorry. Please, Jesus, please baby pick up the phone." Jimmy droned on, asking for forgiveness from Karen and from God, his voice pleading and desperate, until he suddenly exploded with rage. "Karen! You ain't walking away from me! You're screwing somebody else! I know you are!" He drew in a long breath before going on, and his voice softened. "Please…" Karen snapped her phone shut and looked around the parking lot. There was no one in sight. Quietly, she walked to the front entrance, opened the door, and peered down the stairwell. It was empty.

Karen stepped into her apartment, locking the door behind her, and then took a long hot shower before stretching herself across the futon. Just as sleep began to overtake her, her cell phone rang. She sat upright and flipped the phone open. Just ignore him, she told herself and closed the phone. It rang again and again. After awhile, Karen picked up her phone and listened to Jimmy's routine again—the begging, the pleading, the apologies, and professions of his love, all followed by a swelling rage that filled her ears and pounded her head.

"You ain't walking away from me! You and Robbie belong with me!" Jimmy's words reverberated inside her head, the mere mention of Robbie's name sending charges of electricity up and down her spine. Karen set down the phone, her hands shaking, and looked around. This place was no good for Robbie. She needed to move, not next week, or next month, but now. She double-checked the lock on the door and dialed the police. Within a minute, a patrol car pulled up and an officer was listening to the messages left on her phone. He nodded and jotted things down on his pad, telling Karen that she should file a restraining order first thing in the morning. After assuring her that he would have regular patrols in the neighborhood, he took his leave.

Hours ticked on, but sleep only came in short respites counted in minutes. Despite the stifling August heat, she slipped under the covers and pulled them tightly around her. Throughout the night, the slightest sound awoke her—the door opening on the floor above, the hum of the refrigerator, the dripping of the bathroom sink. Sometime after four in the morning, Karen's eyes could no longer stay open. Her head was so heavy with sleep that the nagging buzz of her alarm clock failed to wake her at six.

She awoke with a start to the sound of a fire truck's wailing sirens a little after seven. Springing out of bed and reeling against a throbbing headache, Karen pulled on fresh clothes, brushed her hair and put it up in a ponytail, then ran up the stairs. As she pushed open the front door, she was greeted by a gorgeous, clear blue sky and a light breeze. The previous day's thunderstorms had ridden out on the clouds and taken the humidity along for the ride.

With no time to make breakfast, Karen made a quick stop at Dunkin' Donuts in downtown Fitchburg. As she pulled out of the parking lot, she could have sworn she saw Jimmy across the street. Pushing her foot down on the pedal, she headed through town, glancing at her rearview mirror from time to time. Later, as she drove up Route Twelve towards Ashburnham, she thought she saw a white box truck. But there were lots of men with his muscular build and dark hair, she told herself. It could have been anybody.

Despite the beautiful blue sky and pleasant breeze, Karen couldn't take her mind off Jimmy. Standing up on the scaffolding and dunking her brush into a can of evergreen paint, she carefully applied a coat of paint to the window trim. A Honda Civic slowed down in front of the house and then moved down the road. Karen squinted against the sun, trying to see who was driving it, but couldn't tell with the glare of the sun reflecting off the windshield. Every car that passed by caught her attention. Jimmy, after all, wasn't one to let things go easily.

"Hey Karen," her boss called up to her, "I've got to take off early. You think you can finish up the trim and cap everything up?" Karen nodded, figuring she could be done in another hour or two. Her boss gave her a salute and hopped in his pickup truck. At five o'clock, the twins began their "end of the workday" dance, making Karen laugh.

"Ah hah!" Ryan yelled, "You like what you see. One look at my moves and you're ready to convert." Ryan continued dancing on the roof of the porch as his portable stereo blared out a dance tune. Karen rolled her eyes and laughed. "I don't think so," she said and shook her head, secretly glad for their company. The three of them began rinsing out their brushes and putting them away in the equipment trailer. As Karen set her brushes and trays down in the trailer, her phone began to ring. She flipped it open and looked at the caller ID, then snapped it shut again.

"Ooh burn!" Nate said, looking at her. "Did you just break another guy's heart?"

Karen shook her head and forcing a smile, said "It's just some prank caller." She climbed back up the scaffolding, and paused to look around the neighborhood. It was quiet, quaint, and peaceful. Was he out there somewhere? As she put a hand up to her eyes to shield the sun and watch a pickup truck move down the road, she accidently kicked the lid of a paint can off the scaffolding.

"Hey heartbreaker," Nate called up to her. "Anything you need help with? Putting away the paint cans, locking up the trailer, someone to run you a hot bath? 'Cause Ryan and I've got to jam."

"No thanks, I think I'm all set," Karen said, laughing as she climbed down the scaffolding. Standing on the tips of her toes, Karen reached up to grab the open can of evergreen trim from the scaffolding. She turned at the sound of another car coming down the road. The can of paint slipped from her fingers, a stream of evergreen splashing down her arms, and landed with a bounce onto the lawn. Cursing out loud, Karen threw her hands up, and shook drops of paint from them.

"Now how about that hot bath?" Nate asked and burst out laughing. Ryan handed Karen a rag, trying his best not to laugh.

"Oh, go ahead and laugh," Karen said as she flicked paint their way. She had paint on her knee, dribbled down both arms, the front of her shirt, and a little even made it into one of her sneakers. After she capped the last can of paint and put it in the trailer, Karen flipped open her phone and glanced at the time. It was just past 5:30. Karen jumped into her truck and headed to Steve's.

When she knocked on the screen door, Robbie greeted her with an expression of surprise.

"Mommy, you're all green," he said, standing in the doorway with chocolate ice cream dripping from a cone clutched in his right hand.

"And your lips are all brown," Karen said and kissed the top of his head.

"Woe. Green's not your color," Steve said, startling her as he came up the walkway behind her, carrying a couple cucumbers and some tomatoes in a basket. "Did you dump the entire can on yourself?"

"No—only half," Karen laughed.

"Are you going for a punk look?" Steve asked, fingering a clump of hair matted with paint.

"Oh no, do I have it in my hair too?"

"Yah," he said, holding a strand of her hair out. Karen looked at him and felt her face flush. He was so close to her that she could feel the heat radiating from his body. Suddenly she remembered, all too well, what it felt like to be in his arms, and with that came a longing for him. Even though he was standing only a foot away from her, in an instant—when he cleared his throat and moved his hand away—it seemed like miles.

"Well, I'll get his things," he said, brushing past her and disappearing into the house. When he returned a few minutes later, there was no trace of the smile that was on his face just moments before. Steve reached down and scooped Robbie up into his arms and kissed him on the cheek. "I'll see you soon buddy," he said before setting Robbie back down on his feet. Karen took Robbie by the hand, nodded to Steve, and began heading down the walkway.

"Hey, what's this about you moving?" Steve called to her. Karen turned around with a momentary look of confusion. "Robbie said you might be moving," Steve said, rubbing his knuckles across the stubble on his chin. "Is that true?"

"Well, we've been talking about it, but nothing is set in stone," she said as she opened the door and slid Robbie's stuff inside.

"You're not leaving the area, are you?"

"No, God no. I wouldn't do that to him or you. No, I'd just like to get out of the area we're in, you know, a better neighborhood, some place that has a little yard for him to play in."

"Well have you checked apartments around here? It'd be nice to have Robbie close by, and the school system is pretty good here," Steve said. "They've got a great after school program, and it would be cheaper than daycare. You know, if there are days you're running late, I could pick him up and he could hang out here until you get home. Besides, Carol would get to see him a lot more, you know, with her working at the school and all."

"Oh? She's teaching there?" Karen asked Steve, and was answered with a nod. "Well, I'd like that, if I can afford it."

"I told you before, I don't have a problem pitching in my share for Robbie. I can give you something towards rent or groceries, or whatever, if it'll mean that Robbie will have a yard to play in and a safer neighborhood."

"Steve, I didn't come back here to take your money," Karen said.

"I don't give a damn about the money. I want what's best for my son, and I know the neighborhood you're living in is not known for its charm," Steve said, gesturing with his hands. "Robbie says he doesn't like it there and he keeps telling me that it's scary."

"I know it's not the best place, but it's what we can afford for right now.

If you know some place reasonable around here, I'd be happy to look into it. I'm not going to take your money, though. I can support Robbie on my own," Karen said and buckled him into his seat.

"This isn't about you or my money. It's about Robbie and what's best for him," Steve said, scuffing the toe of his sneaker against the sidewalk. "Listen, there's a place down by Dunkin's in South Ash. It's got a yard, not a lot of traffic. You ought to check it out," Steve said.

"Mommy, can we go? Can we? Can we? Please," Robbie kicked his feet up and down in excitement.

"I guess we could check it out," Karen said. Steve began jotting directions down on a piece of paper when the pager on his belt sounded, followed by the voice of the fire department dispatcher calling for battalion one to respond to a brush fire.

"Sorry, I've got to go," Steve said, handed her the paper, then jogged up the walkway and pulled his front door closed. Karen and Robbie watched him jog back down the walkway and hop into his truck. After his truck was out of sight, Karen looked down at the piece of paper she held in her hand. She couldn't help but think about his fingers in her hair, his easy laughter, his lean body brushing past hers, and then thought about how he suddenly moved away from her. She wondered if it would be a blessing or a curse to live this close to him.

# CHAPTER TWENTY

·······························

## *Name Game*

For the fourth time on the short ride home, Robbie asked if they could move to his daddy's town, and each time, Karen gave him the same non-committal answer of "We'll see." She couldn't help but think of Steve, though, and the thought of living near him made her smile. But what would Carol say? What would his family think? She already knew the answer to that. She knew the way they looked at her, knew that they held their tongues for Robbie's sake.

Karen set her phone down on the kitchen counter and plugged it in to charge. She stared at the display that showed three messages. "Why don't you go put your things away and get into your jammies," Karen asked Robbie. He nodded and dragged his duffle bag to his room. Karen waited until he was in his room before playing the message. The first one was Lillian thanking Karen for coming by and asking her to call when she got in. The second message was a hang-up, and then the third began. It was Jimmy again: "College," he said, slurring his words. "You can either pick up the phone or talk to me now or I can come on down there. What's it gonna be? Huh College? I swear I'll kick that fucking door in if I have to," he said and let out a huff of air. "Oh I see. You're so high and mighty now. Aren't you? You think you're something? Well, you're not! You're just a spoiled, stuck up college dropout. You're a whore and…"

*Tramp*—Steve had called her that once. But did she fit the definition?

She didn't sleep with five men, ten, or a hundred. She had been with only three—and only one did she love. Still, it was the label he had given her the night he found out that she had been used by another. Steve and Karen's love didn't bloom suddenly on a first date, first kiss. No, it evolved slowly, tenderly. They were a rare species, she had thought. Steve was her first. They had waited patiently for the right moment, when they knew it was love. But then he—some cowboy, some complete stranger, some bastard who kept pouring her drinks—had come between them, tearing apart all that she and Steve had built together.

Thinking back on that night, the night her world fell apart, she remembered him calling her "sweetness," but couldn't remember leaving the bar. She remembered him buying her drinks—she didn't say no. She remembered the pool hall beginning to spin. Had he offered her a ride home? She couldn't remember if she had said yes or no. But she remembered, like someone caught between sleeping and waking, slumping heavily against the passenger seat of an unfamiliar car. She remembered his nameless face, his white blonde hair, his ice blue eyes, his shadow hovering over, his weight bearing down on her pelvis. She remembered waking the next morning naked, her clothes scattered around the room as if tossed by a violent wind. But she couldn't remember getting out of the car, couldn't remember walking into the motel room, couldn't remember taking off her clothes. She just remembered awakening under his weight and wanting to vomit, remembered the stink of his cheap cologne. With a shudder, she remembered how his hard hands closed over her wrists, how he pushed himself inside of her, faster and faster, how his sweat dripped down his face. No, she couldn't remember saying yes—but couldn't remember saying no. All she remembered is falling into blackness again and waking in the morning ashamed, humiliated, and alone.

Then there was Jimmy, a man who said he loved her, yet seemed to despise so much about her. If she wanted to take a class at the local community college, he told her she was wasting money. If she stayed out late to get the laundry done or do grocery shopping, he thought the worst, accusing her of sleeping with someone else and calling her a whore—like she ever had the time or desire for another man. *Whore?* She said to the empty kitchen and shook her head, while letting out a sarcastic laugh. She must be.

"Mommy, what does whore mean?" Robbie tugged on the back of her shirt and looked up at her. Karen bit down on her lip and shook her head. "It's just a mean word, and you should never ever say it," Karen said as she massaged her forehead. "Oh," Robbie said, weighing the word in his mind. "Can we move?" Robbie asked suddenly. Karen shrugged her shoulders, wishing she could just whisk Robbie away to a better place. "I hope so, honey. I hope so," she said, pulling him into her arms.

There were no more calls from Jimmy that night, but Karen remained tense the rest of the night, waking often and double-checking the lock on the door. Robbie slept on the futon with her, refusing to be in his room all alone. When Karen awoke in the morning, she called work and told them that she would be late. After dropping Robbie off at daycare, Karen filed a restraining order against Jimmy, but didn't feel any more secure after signing a flimsy piece of paper. With no knowledge of where he was actually staying now, the officer informed her that it would be difficult to serve the restraining order to Jimmy, and he advised her to contact the police immediately if she heard from him. Karen was even more determined than ever to move from her apartment. Before heading into work, Karen spoke to the landlord of the apartment in Ashburnham about renting it out immediately. He agreed to show her the apartment that evening, but warned her that it was still being renovated and wouldn't be ready for at least another month.

Karen didn't really care what it looked like. The only thing that mattered to her was that Jimmy wouldn't know where to find them. This time she wasn't going to leave a forwarding address at the post office, and she was going to get a new phone with a new number just as soon as she could put aside a few extra dollars.

As soon as Karen finished up work at four o'clock, she picked up Robbie from daycare and drove to Ashburnham to see the apartment. They pulled over in front of the apartment, and before Karen could even take the key out of the ignition, Robbie unbuckled his seat belt and jumped out of the truck.

"Mommy, this yard is just like Irene and Hardy's!" Robbie jumped up and down and tugged on Karen's hand. Within a few minutes, the landlord pulled up in a minivan. The door opened up and three kids, varying from ages six to twelve, spilled out. The landlord, Mr. Martinez, walked over to Karen and introduced himself with a warm, friendly handshake. They made their way to the second floor and entered the apartment. It had two small bedrooms, each with a tiny closet, but both rooms were big enough to fit a twin bed and a bureau or one full size bed without the bureau. The living room had a large bay window that overlooked the small "L" shaped street and the kitchen was tiny, just big enough to fit Karen's table and chairs. It was perfect.

"I still need to paint the walls," Mr. Martinez said, pointing to the bare sheet rock in the living room. "And I am going to repaint the bedrooms, too, but I won't likely have it finished for about a month."

"I'd be happy to paint it myself," Karen answered quickly. It was a work in progress, a blank canvas just waiting for her. Mr. Martinez thought for a moment, shrugged his broad shoulders, and said he'd think about it. "You know, I work a part-time job on the weekends painting for Prime Time Painting," Karen said as she followed him around the house, Robbie hanging onto the belt loops of her jeans the entire time. Mr. Martinez turned around, paused, and then nodded. They stepped past the bucket of joint compound and rolls of masking tape that lay on the floor and went into the bathroom. Karen's smile broadened. This apartment had something her other apartment didn't have—an actual tub.

"Is it always this quiet in this neighborhood?" Karen started to ask, but was interrupted by a low rumble outside.

"Well, yes…with the exception of the train," Mr. Martinez pointed out the window towards the tracks that ran behind the apartment.

"A train? Wow!" Robbie yelled, surprising everyone with his sudden enthusiasm.

"If you look out that window, you'll see a freight train come by in just about a minute," Mr. Martinez said, jerking his thumb in that direction. Karen hoisted Robbie up against her hip, and the two of them peered out the window. Slow smiles spread across their faces as the rumble grew louder and louder, vibrating the floor beneath their feet. As the train came into view through the trees behind the apartment, Robbie whispered in his mom's ear. Karen smiled and pushed a stepladder over, then set Robbie down on it.

"How much did you say the rent is?"

"It's $600.00 a month," Mr. Martinez said. Karen nodded and walked the length of the apartment again. She looked out the bedroom window and looked at Robbie. A broad smile swept across his face as he leaned on his elbows and watched the train disappear out of view. Karen turned back to Mr. Martinez with a smile and said, "We're interested."

The next couple of days passed without a call from Mr. Martinez, and Karen began to wonder if her credit report had done her in or if he just didn't want to rent to a single mom—maybe he had found somebody with better credit, or somebody childless. A knock at the door stirred her from her thoughts. She glanced at the clock. It was five o'clock. She opened the door partway, leaving the chain in place; Lillian stood in the hall. Karen unfastened the chain and opened the door.

"Am I too early?" Lillian asked.

"No. Come on inside." Karen waved her in, and then shut and locked the door behind her. Robbie peeked at the two of them from behind a kitchen chair, and shuffled from foot to foot.

"Robbie, come over here and say hi," Karen called over to him. Robbie hesitated for a moment before stepping towards them. Robbie tugged on Karen's shirt. Karen leaned over and listened, while he whispered in her ear.

"Yes, she is the lady that owns the castle," Karen answered with a laugh and turned to Lillian. "Lillian, this is my little tiger, Robbie." Karen scooped Robbie up in her arms and turned towards Lillian. "Robbie, this is my stepmother…my mom," Karen said, finding comfort in the word.

It was the first time in a long time that Karen didn't feel the ache of loneliness. Karen couldn't remember the last time she had felt comfortable enough to have someone over to talk with, much less invite them for dinner. When she and Jimmy were together, she had never invited anyone to the house. The only people that ever came over were Jimmy's friends, not hers. Dinnertime with Jimmy was always served with extra helpings of ridicule and scorn. He had made it clear that he was all she needed and would ever have. He had ruled his house and his woman with a firm hand that left no room for questioning his authority.

Halfway through dinner, Mr. Martinez called. Karen's credit scores were weak, and because of that, he had to reconsider renting to her and apologized for any inconvenience. Karen hung up the phone and tried to mask her disappointment when she returned to the table, but Lillian wasn't fooled.

"Is something wrong?" Lillian asked.

"Well, no not really. I was just waiting to hear on an apartment," Karen answered.

"Mommy, are we going to move to Daddy's town?" Robbie looked up at her with expectant eyes. Karen shook her head and frowned. Robbie pushed his plate away and stared down at his lap.

"What was his reason for not renting to you?" Lillian asked.

"My impeccable credit," Karen said with a forced laugh.

"That man is a big dummy and I hate him!" Robbie hopped out of his chair and ran to his room. Karen let out a sigh and excused herself from the table to check on Robbie. A few minutes later, Lillian walked into Robbie's room and sat on the edge of the bed next to Karen.

"What if I were to co-sign the rental agreement?" Lillian offered.

"Absolutely not. I can take care of my bills and my son on my own," Karen answered quickly.

"I never said you couldn't, but wouldn't you two be better off in a little bit bigger place, maybe something not right in the city?"

"I didn't come back here to leach off you."

"I know you didn't. I'm not saying I'll pay your rent. I'm simply saying that I'd co-sign. I'm just offering to put my signature on a piece of paper for you. That's all," Lillian said. Karen turned the offer over and over in her head. "Can you afford it?" Lillian asked and looked around the apartment. Karen hesitated, and began running the numbers in her head again. "Steve is paying child support, isn't he?" Lillian asked.

"He's offered, but I told him I didn't want his money. I don't want everyone to think that is the only reason I came back here, so Steve can bail me out."

"Karen, Steve is a proud man, and a responsible one at that. Let him do his part for Robbie."

Karen shrugged and then nodded. "Okay. Anyway, Robbie will be starting kindergarten in just a couple weeks, so I won't have to pay out so much in daycare and I'm due for a raise in two months. Even without Steve's help, I can swing it," Karen answered with more confidence than she felt.

"Well, then how about it? Shall we give him a call back?" Lillian patted Karen on the back and gestured to the phone. Karen's gaze moved about the apartment. Robbie sat on the bed picking at his fingers. She looked at the walls, yellowed with years of smoke, at the stove with its missing knob, and listened to the blare of horns in the street, of voices shouting back and forth on the floor above. She turned to Lillian and nodded.

Karen couldn't thank Lillian enough for her help. With so much planning to do, Karen requested a personal day from work and took Friday off. She was lucky enough to get an appointment for Robbie to visit Briggs Elementary on Friday afternoon, explaining to the administration that she didn't want to start him in one school, just to have him transfer in another month. With a copy of her signed lease as proof of residency, the school gave her the okay and Karen set off to gather Robbie's paperwork. In one month's time, they would be able to leave the noise of the apartment behind and Robbie would have a yard to play in.

The following Sunday when Karen arrived at Steve's to pick up Robbie, Carol's car was parked on the side of the road. Karen jogged up the driveway, humming to herself. Carol met her in the doorway and shook her head.

"What are you up to this time?" Carol asked, pushing open the screen door and stepping outside.

"What are you talking about?" Karen asked.

"Your sudden move to town, that's what I'm talking about," Carol said and folded her arms across her chest. Karen looked at her, wishing time and circumstance hadn't destroyed their friendship and replaced it with bitterness. She drew in a breath and said "That was Steve's idea. He's the one that told us about the apartment." Karen looked at the empty driveway. "Where is he anyway?"

"The fire department went out for a big brush fire about an hour ago," Carol answered. Karen nodded, her thoughts drifting back to last week when he ran his fingers through her hair. "You're still in love with him," Carol said without trying to suppress her contempt. Karen looked at Carol and then looked away, shaking her head.

"I'm not here for Steve, just Robbie," Karen said gazing out to the street. Carol let out a sarcastic laugh and shook her head at Karen. "You never were very good at lying," Carol said as she stepped back inside the house and called Robbie. When Robbie came to the door with his duffle bag in hand, Karen grasped his hand and turned towards her truck without another word.

The following week, Robbie started kindergarten at his new school and Karen was given the okay from her landlord to do the painting herself if she still wanted to move in early. Every day after school, Robbie went to Carol's house for a few hours, long enough for Karen to get a start on painting a race track and race cars on the wall of Robbie's room. When she went to Carol's to pick up Robbie, more often than not, Karen ran into Steve over there, and each time Carol gave Karen a look that seemed part pleading, part threatening. "Steve's been through enough," Carol would quietly remind Karen when she opened the door to let her in.

Even though Robbie still got anxious and clung to Karen when it was time for him to be dropped off for the extended day program in the morning, he always came home happy and told Karen about his day and how cool it was to have his Auntie Carol working at the school. At the end of the school day, auntie would even bring him to the fourth grade wing where he would get to wait with her until school was dismissed. Sometimes, Karen wished that Robbie wouldn't love being over her house so much. It seemed that lately he'd rather be at his daddy's or auntie's house, instead of with her. But then she would chide herself, how much fun is it for him to go with her to do laundry and watch her make dinner and just sit in the stuffy little apartment?

Friday night after dropping Robbie off at Steve's, Karen didn't want to go home and face an empty apartment, so she drove to a little hilltop and parked her truck. Staring up at a dark, cloudy sky, she sat in her truck and let the warm air blow in through her open window. At the tapping of raindrops on her hood, Karen rolled up her window and watched as a streak of lightning lit up the sky. Like a faucet opening up, rain began pouring heavily from the sky. In the field in front of her, she could see small flickering lights. Fireflies flashed and glittered in the night. Karen leaned closer to the window and watched them dance in the dark. Drops of rain fell from the sky, equal to their size, yet still the fireflies continued to flicker through the night. She couldn't remember the last time she had seen them—but here, right now, there they were—passing in front of her window. Perhaps they had been there all along? Alone in her truck, she watched their flight in the dark of night, and wished she could somehow take flight with them and persist against the rain.

When the rain subsided and the fireflies had flown off, Karen started her truck and drove back home. In her empty apartment, she sat down at the kitchen table feeling exhausted and lost. Lillian was away for a couple weeks, vacationing with her fiancé, and Karen didn't realize just how much she had come to depend on her comfort. Lillian was the only one who made her feel human, who didn't look at her with scorn and resentment. As if misery was seeking company, Karen's phone rang. Without checking the caller ID, Karen answered the phone.

An unfamiliar voice came over the phone. Karen pressed the phone to her ear and closed her eyes while listening. A moment later, she hung up the phone and left the apartment.

She parked her truck in the hospital parking lot and then sat silently in the waiting room, staring down at her hands folded in her lap. After a few minutes, the nurse called her over and led her through the emergency room. She stood on the other side of the curtain for a moment, uncertain as to whether or not she should go in. Taking a breath and standing up straight, she pulled the curtain back and stepped in.

Jimmy lay motionless, except for the rhythmic rise and fall of his chest. His right cheek was marked with a deep purple bruise and a two by two bandage. Another thick bandage covered his forehead just above his left eye. Karen stepped closer to him. A large bandage was wrapped around his left arm and his right hand was in a cast from the elbow to his finger tips. Both of his legs were in casts, and a pillow was propped against his bandaged ribs on his right side.

"You must be Karen," a doctor said, entering the room. "I'm sorry we weren't able to contact you sooner, but when he was brought in he was pretty intoxicated and didn't have any ID on him."

"What happened?" Karen asked.

"Well, it seems like he had a death wish. A witness told the police that he drove his car straight into a bridge abutment," the doctor said, turning from his chart to Karen. "Ma'am, your husband is lucky to be alive."

"He's not my husband," Karen said absently, her eyes fixed on Jimmy as he lay broken and helpless.

"Oh. I'm sorry. My mistake. Well, your...ah...friend will likely make a full recovery, but he's got a long road in front of him before he'll be able to walk again." The doctor jotted something on his pad and looked over at Jimmy, and then turned to Karen. "Well, I'll just leave you two be," he said and slipped out of the room. Jimmy stirred and his eyes fluttered open.

"Baby..." Jimmy said, reaching out his hand to her. His eyes watered and he grimaced in pain, his hand still outstretched to her. Karen looked at his hand, then tentatively took it in hers. A surge of pity coursed through her coupled with the guilty feeling that he got what he deserved. Bruised and beaten, Jimmy no longer looked threatening, yet Karen still felt her breath catching in her throat at his mere touch. He looked up at her from his hospital bed, his hand still in hers. "You came...baby, I didn't think you would, but you did. I ain't got nobody, baby, nobody but you," he said, his voice weak and raspy.

Still holding his hand and sitting on a chair by his bedside, fighting back tears, Karen looked away and stared out the window. Traffic moved up and down Route Twelve past Leominster Hospital, cars probably piled with happy families out for an evening dinner or trip to the mall. No, Jimmy didn't have anyone, at least not anyone worth running home to as far as Karen knew. He had told her one night long ago, as he traced his fingers over her swollen belly, how his father used to beat him, while his mother would sit idly by and pretend not to notice. He never had a chance, Karen thought to herself. She closed her eyes, squeezing back tears without success, and wished she could erase his past. Maybe then he would have had a chance at a better future. But she couldn't change the past; all she could do was accept it. As she held his hand in hers, she knew how painfully alone he felt.

Karen walked with the nurses as they moved him from the ER to a room on an upper floor. She sat by his bedside until the end of visiting hours was announced over the intercom. When she got up to go, Jimmy reached for her hand again.

"Baby, please don't leave me. Give me another chance." Jimmy looked at her, his eyes red and watery. Karen closed her eyes and remembered the frightened look on Robbie's face the night Jimmy beat her so severely. She opened her eyes and drew a deep breath in. Leaning over him, she brushed his hair away from his eyes, and kissed him lightly on his forehead before slowly shaking her head and walking out.

# CHAPTER TWENTY-ONE

......................................

## *Letting Go*

All night long, Karen lay awake in bed. Thoughts of Jimmy clouded her head. She had abandoned him, just left him there alone. She rolled onto her side and cried into her pillow. She knew she didn't love him, not the way a man and a woman are supposed to love each other, and she knew he didn't really love her. Did he even know what love was? As she lay there staring into the black void of her apartment, she could only imagine what his life had been like, and then she thought about Robbie, his frightened face, the way the world had become such an uncertain and violent place for him. It was then that she wondered if that is what Jimmy's childhood had been like.

Karen forced herself out of bed the next morning and got ready to go to work. She had another ten hour day of painting in front of her, and her boss was eager to get in as much work as possible while the weather was good. Under a beautiful blue sky, Karen stood on the scaffolding and worked her paint brush back and forth; all the while she wondered if Jimmy had really been trying to take his own life. When it was time to break for lunch, the twins began teasing Karen and flirting with her like they always did every weekend. Karen wasn't in the mood for their antics today, unable to laugh at their jokes.

"Hey, what's eating you today?" Nate asked while taking a bite of his sandwich.

"Nothing! Don't you guys have anything better to do with your time?" Karen threw down her empty coffee cup, hopped out of the back of her truck, and climbed back up the scaffolding. She picked up her brush and set back to work. Ryan climbed up the scaffolding and sat down beside her.

"Are you okay?" All the humor was gone from his voice. He looked down at Nate and waved him away. "Karen, you know we're just joking around with you, right?"

"Yah. I'm sorry. I'm just having a really bad day, and I just have too much running around in my head," Karen said, wishing she hadn't snapped at them. Ryan patted her on the back and told her not to worry about it, then picked up his brush and went back to work. For the rest of the day, Karen worked silently, trying to keep her focus on the work in front of her. Somehow, though, Jimmy kept creeping into her mind. His father had beaten him. His mother had turned a deaf ear to his cries. And she had left him, bruised and broken, all alone.

When the work day ended for them, Karen drove to her new apartment. She climbed the stairs and looked around at the bare walls in the living room. One room down, she said to herself as she appraised the work she had done in Robbie's room. She set down a can of paint in the living room, opened it, and dipped her brush into it. She worked her brush back and forth, until her arms grew tired. She dropped the brush onto the newspaper and flipped open her phone. No one had called.

Karen drove back to Fitchburg, slowing down as she passed a liquor store. One, just one drink, she said to herself, but then punched her steering wheel and pushed down on the pedal. She pulled into the parking lot of her old apartment, jogged down the stairs, and began loading up her truck. All the while, she longed for a drink, just a taste. Keep busy, keep busy, keep busy, she told herself over and over as she yanked Robbie's mattress out of the apartment and up the stairs one stair at a time. Cursing and sweating, she pushed it into the back of her truck and then went down the stairs to take apart his bed frame. Her body told her to stop, to rest, just sleep, but she couldn't. Stopping meant thinking, when all she wanted to do was forget—forget about Jimmy, about Steve, about Carol, about all of them and their guilt, their scorn. She flipped open her phone and stared at Lillian's cell phone number, but then flipped it shut. Lillian didn't need to be burdened with her problems right now, especially while she was on vacation with her fiancé.

"Son of a bitch!" Karen shoved the bed frame into the truck, scraping her knuckles against a rusty piece of her tailgate. She shook her hand and climbed into the back of her truck. After tying down the mattress and bed frame, Karen hopped out of the back and started up her truck and headed back to Ashburnham.

She pulled up in front of the apartment and backed her truck onto the lawn, stopping short of the back stairs. Tugging and cursing, Karen pulled at the knotted rope until she finally untied it. She jumped out of the truck and felt the muscles pinch around her knee a little, but tried to ignore it. Huffing and puffing, she tugged on the mattress and began pulling it up the stairs. Stopping to catch her breath, Karen let out a sarcastic laugh. At her old apartment there were always too many people around, but at her new apartment, there wasn't a soul around. At her old apartment, the parties happened upstairs, but here in this little town with its one stop light, everyone left town for a good time. Doesn't that figure? Maybe they all went to her old apartment complex, she thought to herself and let out a laugh.

As Karen backed the mattress through the door, she tripped over the can of paint she left on the floor earlier. "What the hell!" She yelled and dropped the mattress. Karen flipped open her phone, but then shut it. Who the hell would she call anyway? She kicked a roll of masking tape and walked out the door. Nothing mattered. Everything she had done to try and make things better just blew up in her face. Robbie seemed to be spending more and more time with Steve and his family, and was never really thrilled about going home with her. Steve's parents hardly even acknowledged her, let alone said hello whenever she ran into them at Steve's or Carol's. When it came to Carol, no matter what Karen tried, she always greeted her with contempt and suspicion. And Steve, well regardless how hard she tried to show him that she changed, he just couldn't see it. To hell with them all, she yelled and got into her truck. She stopped at the convenience store down the street and went straight to the aisle in back. Waiting and ready for her, there it was—a bottle of Captain Morgan's. She picked it up off the shelf and went to the register. She could taste it already. All she needed was one, just one drink.

Karen pulled back up to her new apartment. It was empty and quiet in the neighborhood. Everyone had somewhere to be, someone else to hang out with. Well now, so did she. Karen held the bottle up in the air and flipped the world off. She climbed up the stairs to her new apartment and twisted off the top to the bottle. "Here's to you, Jimmy, you son of a bitch!" Inside her darkened apartment, she raised the bottle in a toast and took a swig. The sweet burn took her by surprise at first, but she threw her head back and swallowed another mouthful. "Fuck the world! Fuck them all!" Karen's hands shook as she took another swallow. "So this is what you want? Is it?" She screamed to the ceiling. "What else? Huh! What else do you want to take away from me? Shit!" Leaning her head into her hands, she sobbed. "Why me? Why?" Other than Lillian, there didn't seem to be anybody that gave a damn about her. Robbie didn't even miss her lately. He had his beloved daddy, his fabulous auntie and uncle, his doting grandparents. What the hell could she offer him anyway? She thought about Jimmy lying in the hospital. Why is it the only person who wanted her was a man with a fucked up idea of love?

Karen drank some more, her head beginning to spin. She waited for the pain in her heart to go away, but it still nagged at her. She took another swig and wandered around the apartment, the only light coming from the pale fluorescent that hung above the sink. Stopping inside Robbie's room, she ran her hand along the wall and looked at the race cars she had painted there. "I can't do this anymore, Tiger. I can't," she said and leaned against the wall. She held the nearly empty bottle up and regarded it a moment before throwing it across the kitchen floor where it smashed into pieces.

She flipped open her phone and stared at it. She dialed Lillian's number, and when her voicemail click on, she remembered that Lillian was still on vacation with her fiancé. Soon, she thought, Lillian wouldn't even have any space left in her life for a stepdaughter. Karen stumbled to the kitchen and sank down against the wall, shattered glass scattered across the floor. She slapped her hand against the floor, wishing she could escape and start over. "Help," she whispered to the empty kitchen. Karen picked up her phone and flipped it open. Scrolling through the numbers in her address book, she paused when she reached Carol's. She drew in a deep breath and hit the call button.

"Hello?" Carol's voice came over the phone.

"Carol," Karen said and heard her audible sigh in response.

"What do you want Karen? It's getting late," Carol answered, her voice sounding tired and irritated.

"Please, I'm sorry…I just didn't know who else to call." Karen leaned her head back against the wall and closed her eyes.

"Are you okay?" Carol asked, the edge in her voice subsiding a little.

"Can you help me, please?" Karen waited and listened to the silence, afraid for a moment that Carol had hung up.

"Have you been drinking?" Carol asked, but Karen only cried and stared up at the ceiling.

"Where you are?" Carol asked, her voice cautious and tentative.

"I'm in Ashburnham…in my apartment."

"Just stay where you are. Okay?" Karen heard Carol say into the receiver, followed by a click. After five or ten minutes passed, Karen couldn't really tell, she heard a car pull up and then the sound of footsteps on the stairs. Carol stopped in the doorway and looked at Karen sitting on the floor. Was it shock or disgust?

"Karen, what the hell is going on?" Carol stepped over bits of broken glass and around the puddle of paint on the floor. She squatted down next to her and looked around at the mess. Shaking her head, she reached for Karen's hand. "Come on. Let's go," she tugged on her arm.

"I can't do this anymore…oh God, please…I can't. I've tried and I've tried, but it doesn't matter," Karen said, still sitting on the floor. Carol stood up, reached over, and flipped on the kitchen light, its bright yellow hue filling the room. Karen blinked her eyes against the light and looked up at Carol.

"Karen, you're drunk. Get up." Carol squatted down again and put her arm around Karen, pulling her to her feet. Karen leaned heavily against the counter and began to cry.

"I messed up. I was doing so good, and then I just…oh God." Karen held her hands out to Carol and said, "Can you help me, please?"

Carol nodded her head slowly, and placing an arm around her, walked her out the door. "Easy, easy," Carol said as she steadied Karen on the stairs. When they got to the car, Carol reached over and buckled her in.

"Don't even think about puking in my car," Carol said, shooting her a warning look.

"Where are we going?" Karen asked, closing her eyes and trying to fight the dizzy feeling in her head.

"Well, I sure as shit can't leave you home alone, so you're coming to my house to sleep it off. But you can bet your ass we're talking about this first thing tomorrow," Carol said as she slid in the driver's seat. When the car came to a stop in front of Carol's house, her husband Mike met them in the driveway.

"She's wasted," Carol said matter-of-factly as she reached over and unbuckled Karen's seatbelt. When Mike opened Karen's door and grabbed her arm to help her out, Karen pushed him away.

"No! I'm not going anywhere with you," she said, swatting his hand away. Carol rolled her eyes and shook her head. She leaned in the car and called over to Karen, "Jesus, Karen, he's just trying to help you."

Karen looked at the man standing by the door of the car. She heard Carol swear under her breath and the sound of her heels clicking on the pavement as she walked around the car to the passenger side. She tugged on Karen's arm and put her arm around her. Karen walked unsteadily towards the house and looked at Carol. "You can't trust them when they say they're gonna give you a ride home," Karen said, stumbling up the steps. "That's when you find yourself somewhere you should never be," she slurred on. Carol steadied her, casting her a curious look, and walked her inside the house.

As Carol walked Karen towards the couch and sat her down, her husband looked at her, cocked his eyebrows, and set a bucket and towel on the floor by Karen. "Are you going to be all set with her?" he asked. Carol nodded and kissed him goodnight, then turned back to Karen. She let out a sigh and laid her back on the couch. Karen opened her eyes, looked Carol, and closed them again. Carol pulled off Karen's sneakers, placed a blanket over her, and turned off the light.

When Karen awoke the next morning, she could smell coffee and hear

Carol and her husband talking. Karen pulled back the blanket and sat up, her head throbbing. She stood up and walked quietly to the kitchen and looked at Carol. She had everything Karen ever wanted—somebody to love her, to wake up to in the morning, somebody to grow old with. Noticing Karen, Carol's husband leaned over and kissed Carol and said, "Well, I think I'll go fishing and let you two girls talk." He offered Karen a little smile and headed out the door.

Carol just looked at Karen, her expression unreadable. Karen took a tentative step towards her. "I'm so sorry Carol," Karen said, shuffling from foot to foot, not quite knowing what else to do or say. Carol shrugged and waved her towards a seat at the table. Karen shook her head, saying "I really should just go."

"Go? No, I don't think so. You owe me the decency of an explanation. You owe me an explanation for last night. Hell, you owe me an explanation for the last five friggin' years," Carol said, her hand on her hip. Karen looked away, but then nodded and stepped into the kitchen.

"You're right. I do, and I'm sorry for everything I've put you through," Karen said, standing in the middle of the kitchen. Carol slid out two chairs at the kitchen table and sat down in one. Karen waited a moment, and then sat in the chair beside her. "That night...at the bar...I left with this guy," she said, drawing in a breath. "I...I'm not going to tell you that it wasn't my fault because I can't say that. I can't say that because I...I don't remember much of what happened that night," Karen said, staring down at her hands. "I don't know if...if I...," she stopped to draw in a breath. "I only remember bits and pieces." She swallowed and felt a hot tear roll down her face. "I remember," she said rubbing her wrist, "I remember his hands...they were around my wrists. I can remember him over me..." she gritted her teeth against the acrid taste of memories from that night. "And when I woke up, he was gone...and I was there...and I felt so ashamed...

so dirty, and I know it doesn't make up for anything, but I couldn't face you, couldn't face Steve, or Lillian, so I tried to just wash it away somehow, to bury any thought about that night. I just didn't know what else to do."

Carol got up from the table and stared out the window. "I wish you could have just told me, trusted me to help you," she said staring into the backyard.

"To tell you that would have meant admitting that I had a problem, and then…well, I wasn't ready to do that," Karen said, looking up at Carol. "So I left. I ran. I thought I could just forget the past and start over, but everywhere I went it followed me." Karen put her elbows on the table, and leaning her head in her hands, began massaging her head. "When I found out I was pregnant, I didn't think the baby could be Steve's. I thought he was from that night…you know, because Steve and I were usually careful," Karen let out a bitter laugh. "I guess maybe I was never sober enough to know what careful was." Karen squeezed her eyes shut against the throbbing in her head.

Carol reached in the cabinet, pulled out a glass, filled it with water, and set it down in front of Karen, along with two aspirin. She sat back down and looked at Karen.

"You were my best friend. I don't understand how you could just leave like that? You didn't say a word, leave a note, or anything. You just left."

Karen swallowed the two aspirin and looked at her. "I wanted to come back, God I wanted to. But I couldn't face any of you, so I kept running and then I met Jimmy. And well," she laughed, "he was there for me, or so I thought." Karen looked up at Carol and shook her head. "He liked to drink, so he was the perfect match for me," she said. Karen looked away, and thought about Jimmy lying in a hospital bed, alone and broken. "Did you know that I had been sober for fifteen months?" Karen turned to Carol. "And then he showed up, and Robbie got scared and…" Karen leaned her head in her hands and cried.

"Did Jimmy do that," Carol put a fingertip to her own lip. "Did he give you that scar?"

Karen looked away, habitually biting down on her lip softly, and nodded. She could see Robbie's face, the tears streaming down his cheeks, feel his little hands clinging to the back of her shirt as he followed her out of the house. Karen looked up at Carol again. "I lost him last summer. I was drunk …and I crashed my car. Robbie was in the back seat. He wasn't hurt, but…"

Carol drew a sharp breath in and looked away, folding her arms across her chest. Karen let out a sigh and stared at the kitchen floor. "I was sent to rehab for eight weeks. Robbie went to a foster home. It was the best thing that ever happened to me," Karen said, turning back to Carol. Carol looked at her in surprise, but didn't say anything. "If I hadn't tried to leave…if I hadn't gone to rehab…I don't think I would have ever been able to come home."

The two of them sat in silence, the ticking of the clock the only sound in the kitchen. Drawing in a breath, Carol reached over and squeezed Karen's hand, but then went over to the counter. She pressed her hands on the counter and stared out the window. Karen got up and stood beside Carol. "Carol, I'm sorry that I hurt you. And I'm sorry about last night. I just thought I could do this on my own, but I don't think I can anymore." Karen stood next to her a moment and then turned towards the door. Walking over to her and putting a hand on her shoulder, Carol said, "You don't have to."

# CHAPTER TWENTY-TWO

## *The Road*

Carol was right; she didn't have to do this alone. Karen called her sponsor, and after talking it over, Karen admitted that she needed some time to get herself together, that Robbie would be better off staying with Steve for a little while. Steve didn't question Karen when she came by later that afternoon and asked if Robbie could stay with him for a few weeks. Karen kissed Robbie on the top of his head and turned quickly to her truck, not wanting him to see the hot tears that spilled from her eyes.

As she opened her truck door and got in, Steve leaned in the passenger side window. "Come by anytime you want. I mean it, anytime," he said, his voice tender and calm. Karen nodded, forcing a smile, and started her truck, then pulled away from the curb.

It wasn't a dusty church basement this time, but instead it was on a large porch facing Naukeag Lake in Ashburnham. Karen sat in silence, listening to a woman talking about her addiction, and she took comfort in knowing that she wasn't alone. Looking around at the people around her, she saw some spirits that were beaten, others that were bright and hopeful. It was easy to spot the newcomers, the ones who were still hanging in the uncertain balance between denial and acceptance. They were the ones who couldn't look anyone directly in the eyes for more than a few seconds. But Karen, knowing her own past, her own ugly truths, didn't shake her head in disapproval. Instead, she breathed easy and started to feel a sense of belonging and hope. Little by little, Karen could feel herself letting go of the past.

On a crisp day in early October, Karen and Lillian hiked up to the top of Wachusett Mountain to watch the sunset. As the sun slowly made its trek south, Karen turned to Lillian and said "Did you know it's been over six years since I've really sat down to watch the sunset?"

"Really? Well, I'm glad that we're watching it together," Lillian answered and put her arm around Karen's shoulder.

"I'd forgotten just how incredible the sky looks at this time of day. Just look at that." Karen pointed to the golden band that stretched across the sky. Lillian smiled and looked up at the sky. They watched the sun dip below the horizon line and the sky turn from orange to red and to purple. "Just look at all those stars beginning to come out," Lillian waved her hand across the sky. Karen closed her eyes and drew in the evening air, letting the cool breeze caress her face. Opening her eyes, she turned to Lillian, her face serious.

"Sometimes I wonder if Jimmy is right, that I'll grow old and be all alone," Karen said and pulled her jacket more tightly around herself.

"But you're not alone now," Lillian said, giving her shoulder a squeeze. "You've got me." Karen looked at Lillian and smiled. "And you've got Robbie and lots of people who care about you, and you've got your own two feet to stand on. You've just got to remember that everybody gets knocked down at some point in their life. It's standing back up that makes all the difference in the world," Lillian said. She drew her hand across the sky in an arc, and said "Karen, you have your whole life in front of you. I know there are lots of wonderful things out there just waiting for you." Karen leaned her head on Lillian's shoulder and smiled, thankful to have such a wonderful person in her life. Yes, she said to herself, there was a whole world out there just waiting for her.

www.ingramcontent.com/pod-product-compliance
Lightning Source LLC
Chambersburg PA
CBHW031611240626
47153CB00002B/720